The Key

The Key

It was a secret worth millions,
unlocked after twenty-two years . . .
but would anyone find the money?

Peter Mars

Commonwealth Publishing
Boston, Massachusetts

Copyright © 2001 Peter Mars

All rights reserved; no part of this publication may be reproduced, stored in a retrieval system, or transmitted, in any form or by any means, electronic, mechanical, photocopying, recording, or otherwise, without the prior written permission of Peter Mars.

Library of Congress Control Number: 00-136244

ISBN: 1-9664475-2-2

Cover design: Pearl & Associates

Susan Cook, editing

Photographs by Michael Glover

Book design and production by Tabby House

The Key is a true crime book based on actual events. Some liberty has been taken with names, locations and dialogue in order to protect the identity of persons who played major roles in the story. Any other resemblance to persons living or dead is purely coincidental.

Other books by Peter Mars:

The Tunnel
Drug dealers are missing in Boston . . . It's not a bad thing, but a good thing. . . . But what is making them disappear?

A Taste for Money
A novel based on the true story of a dirty Boston cop

Commonwealth Publishing
P.O. Box 1234
Hyannis, MA 02601

For Martha M. Kluzak

My inspiration to keep going when things are not always at their best. The most wonderful daughter and my hero. Sensitive to my challenges, she gives encouragement in the things she says and through the smile on her face, which radiates the love in her heart.

Appreciation

I am grateful to the following people for all their help in bringing this book to fruition. First and foremost to Art Truitt who brought this story to light. Also, to Susan Cook who edited the story and included some of the harsh reality of the abuses some people suffer. To Gary Hauger who has always managed to inspire clever thoughts, which help to bring the story to life. To Chief Mark Lecouris for his assistance from the Tarpon Springs Police Department. To Jill Palmer whose help was invaluable on Grand Cayman Island. To Cayman Taxi driver, Roy D., who gave even greater detail to the Cayman experience. To Tim Sturges of Joliet, Illinois, for his assistance in obtaining the cover jail cell key. To Ken Roderick at the Eastham Massachusetts Police Department for material he supplied for the cover of the book. To my nephew, John Lind, also of the Eastham Police Department for all the running around he did helping to gather information. And especially to my wife, Margery, who sees me through all the frustrations of writing manuscripts.

Contents

Prologue   xi

1.	No Justice	1
2.	A Tough Life	9
3.	Union Pacific—More than a Railroad	16
4.	Getting Even	20
5.	Caught	26
6.	Incarceration	39
7.	Riot in the Prison	51
8.	A Proposal	63
9.	The Search for Clues	67
10.	A Chance Discovery	74
11.	What Does It All Mean?	82
12.	Nothing New	90
13.	Gabrielle's Gun	93
14.	Anclote Cay	98
15.	A Close Call	109
16.	The Lighthouse	120
17.	Murder	127
18.	Suspects	131
19.	A Good Attorney	135
20.	Who is He?	139

21.	Deceit	145
22.	The Missing Link	149
23.	It's Gone!	155
24.	It Begins to Make Sense	164
25.	A Minute Possibility	168
26.	The Loser	178

Epilogue *188*

About the Author *191*

Prologue

It seemed so simple . . . getting back at a broken legal system, one that worked only for the undeserving. Those who had made life miserable for him would now pay for their stupid decision. He would see to it. His idea was well thought-out and clever. Except that fate always stepped in and twisted what should have been so easy.

Two million dollars was a lot of money when it was taken back then. It still is a lot of money even today. The only thing he had to do was wait; time would take care of everything. And it should have, had there not been that riot. He was the only person who had access to the money. Now he was dead. All that planning . . . all that work . . . all that waiting . . . all for nothing. Sure, he had proven a point, but he would never enjoy the fruits of his labor. And it looked like no one else would either.

CHAPTER ONE

No Justice

It was a warm summer night in 1973. Always during the month of August most New England cities suffered from unwavering seasonal heat, and this evening was a perfect example. From Bangor to Hartford there was not so much as a breeze to provide any relief.

Patrolman Ed Fitzgerald was walking a beat in Arlington Center, a fast-growing suburb of Boston. Even though he was supposed to ring in on the hour by using one of the several police call boxes on his route, he took his time on making his rounds. After all, why work up a sweat when things were quiet; there was nothing more uncomfortable than smelling one's own perspiration working its way through a thin layer of underarm deodorant early on in the shift. He had just completed the western tour of his sector when he met Tom Coughlin, the beat officer who worked the area between Arlington Center and Arlington Heights. One usually waited for the other near the call box where their sectors converged so that they could chat for a few minutes, passing along the latest station-house rumors that were a part of the police climate. They would not remain there for too long as they knew that the newly appointed, gung-ho patrol sergeant might drive by at any time. In his new position he was concerned that some do-gooder citizen might be out and about, and it was not a good habit for two patrolmen to be seen wasting the taxpayer's money standing around in conversation. That would not only reflect on the two officers but also on the sergeant who was supposed to be in command of his men. And every night at roll call, just before the men were to go out on the road, the sergeant would remind them of this.

Ed walked back toward the center of town and began making his door checks of all the local businesses. Every once in a while, some owner or trusted employee would forget to turn the key in the lock at a business. Ed would mark it down in his book after giving the building a once-over to make sure all was okay. He would then use the proprietor's telephone to call the station for the dispatcher to make notification to the owner that an officer was standing-by in his place of business waiting for him to go down immediately and secure the door. On occasion, Ed might take the initiative to fasten the lock himself if it was one of those that he could secure without a key.

As he was checking the doors in the alley behind one of the business blocks, he discovered the rear basement window to the pharmacy was open a few inches. The pharmacy had been closed since 9:00 P.M. That was five hours ago. The window was one of those small, low-to-the-ground types, which a slender person could squeeze through. There had been two bars installed across the window, from left to right, to block any entry by anyone trying to break in, but those had been pried loose and were now angled upward in an almost mocking salute to anyone passing through the alley. It was obvious that a burglary had taken place.

As Ed crouched down to peer in, he could see a flicker of light near the stairs leading to the first floor. He decided to check it out, knowing full well what he would find. At that time, portable radios were not in use by the department. Most requests by patrolmen needing assistance came by the police call boxes located on the city's streets. Because of the time factor, and the possibility of losing his quarry, Ed opted not to try to go for help. He was not a rookie cop; he had been on the job for several years. Having made many arrests during his tenure he knew he could handle himself in any situation. Experience out on the street had been his greatest teacher. Ed had become adept in the field of crime and criminal behavior and his senses seemed honed to recognize the tiniest aspect of illicit activity. He knew what to look for, and he knew what to expect.

Ed worked his way through the window and dropped the short distance to the floor. He cursed quietly as his right pant leg snagged on a splinter protruding from the broken window frame, making a slight tear in the whipcord material. This just added to his annoyance over the fact that he knew his freshly cleaned and pressed uniform was now going to get dirty from crawling through the ground-level window. The promise that he was going to work up a sweat was now the furthest thing from his mind.

The Key

Letting his eyes adjust to the darkness, he slowly made his way past boxes of medical supplies, crutches, walkers and wheelchairs over to the stairs. To Ed's advantage the pharmacist had kept an orderly storage space, which allowed for a clear path to the steps leading to the first floor. Removing his issue .38-caliber Smith and Wesson revolver from its holster with his right hand, he began to ascend at a slow and careful pace. He was fortunate that the old stairs did not creak as he climbed. He walked one step at a time, keeping his feet close to the wall-side of the stairs so as to have the greatest support and the least chance of making any sound. When his head reached the street level, he was about four steps short of the first floor. From this vantage point, he slowly and cautiously looked around to see if he could make out any motion. It was then that he noticed two figures moving at the back of the prescription counter. No doubt, he thought, drugs were on the minds of the burglars.

He remained quiet as they knelt down, put their flashlight on the floor, and broke open the locked cabinet containing narcotics. *Why the hell didn't the pharmacy have an alarm*, he thought disgustedly. *That way help would be on the way.* Not that anyone or anything frightened him. It just felt better knowing that there was backup *en route*.

He removed his flashlight from his hip pocket using his left hand and at the same time aimed his service revolver in the direction of the two individuals. He climbed the last few stairs but remained bent over as close to the floor as possible until he was finally steady on the solid landing. Raising himself up and turning on the flashlight, Ed called out to the two individuals.

"Stay right where you are!" he commanded. "Get up slowly and put your hands on top of your head!"

The two men flinched, startled at the surprise of being caught in their act. They stopped what they were doing and started to stand. The man closest to Ed slowly put his hands on top of his head as he stood upright. He was more than six feet tall.

"Okay, man," the burglar spoke out slowly. "I ain't got no gun. Don't shoot, okay?"

Ed's concentration was centered on this man as the second one, being shorter and hidden by the first, as he was still somewhat out of sight behind him, reached out, grasped something in his hand and threw it at Ed. Ed could not make out the movement in the dark until it was too late. An open bottle caught him at the temple and a liquid spilled onto his left eye. Ed let out a piercing scream as the burning pain was immediate and intense. It was followed by a smell not unlike something he once encountered at a house fire where an old man, trying to escape from inside, jumped from a second floor window onto a pile of trash. The debris nearly filled the alley adjacent to the building. The old man's body had been engulfed almost totally by the flames.

Ed had been standing with some firefighters who were trying to set a ladder up against the building just as the man took his leap. The firemen quickly covered the man with a blanket to extinguish the flames. As they prepared to lift him onto a stretcher from the ambulance that had arrived at the scene, the blanket opened and Ed got a whiff of the smoke emanating from the old man's torso. He now recognized that smell of burning flesh—except this time it was his own.

Ed could not focus on anything. The searing pain was intense. His heart began to beat wildly and his inhalations of breath became staccato in their rhythm. He did not know what was happening to him and he was scared. He panicked, dropping his gun and his flashlight to the floor. The flashlight rolled down the cellar stairs behind him breaking the lens and bulb. Ed's main thought was to comfort his eye. He tried to find something to clean his eye with as the burglars grabbed this as an opportunity to kill the cop who prevented them from carrying out their task. Ed reached into his pocket groping for his handkerchief and quickly pulling it out he covered his eye with both hands. The men raced across to where he was standing and one of them kicked him in the groin causing him to let out a loud groan and to double over. The man then kicked him in the stomach whereupon Ed, moaning in agony, collapsed to the floor, falling on top of his revolver. One of the men reached down in an attempt to find the gun, but was unable to locate it in the darkness and under the weight of Ed's body.

"What're you doin'?" the other one asked.

"Tryin' ta find his gun, man."

"Forget it. Let's just get outta here."

The men then ran toward the front door. As they did so, Ed regained some sense of what was happening. The left side of his face had gone numb. A dozen things flashed through his mind in nanoseconds. Over and over he tried to think back to what his stepdad had told him when *he* had been confronted with life-threatening situations. *What would Jerry have done? What was it that Jerry had said about criminals—no criminal is any good—has the right to live? If it were not for him and other police no one would be safe. Accidents will happen. Some cops will get killed.*

The peripheral pain was excruciating even with the numbness to his eye and cheek. *What would Jerry say now? It's no job to take if bitterness will set in and eat you up like the acid in your eye. What would Jerry do?*

Ed reached beneath himself and recovered his gun with his right hand. Holding the left side of his face with his left hand, Ed raised the gun and took aim at the men as best he could while they struggled with the large dead bolt lock on the door. Their primary objective had been to escape. The front door was nearby and appeared to offer little resistance. They were not prepared for the dead bolt lock. Had they retreated to the cellar, they would have made their exit with little effort. Now what looked easy was proving to be almost inexorable. Suddenly there was a loud cracking sound as the door splintered and began to give way. Ed fired one shot just as the men pushed their way through the door. With help from the outside street light, he observed one of the men lurch forward and then reach with his hand toward his back. He stumbled out of the door as Ed fired another shot in his direction. Immediately after that Ed fell again to the floor, his strength sapped. He lost consciousness.

When Ed awoke he was at Symmes Hospital in the emergency room. He could see out of his right eye and could feel the bandage covering the left side of his face. He tried to reach up but discovered his hands were tied by gauze strips to the railing of the bed. He knew right away that it was to keep him from touching his face. As he looked around to get his bearings, he recognized some of the people in the room. There were two nurses attending to him; young women he knew from the times he had been at the hospital to cover incidents that required medical attention. A doctor he had never seen before was just leaving his bedside. The chief of police, two detectives and some of the guys he worked with were standing in close proximity to where he lay. The chief, now aware of Ed's consciousness, approached Ed and patted him on the shoulder.

"You did a fine job, lad. I want you to know that," the chief said.

"Did I get either of them?" came the raspy response from Ed.

"Save your strength, lad. It'll keep until you've had some rest," the chief replied.

"No. I've got to know now," Ed insisted.

"Well, we don't have anyone in custody yet. There was blood on the sidewalk outside of the drugstore, so someone got injured. When you're up to it, Jerry O'Shea will need some information from you. But we don't want to rush you; the doctor already jumped on us about even speaking with you."

Jerry O'Shea was one of the detectives. It was obvious that he was eager to interrogate Ed as he often said to the officers he worked with, "You've got to take care of your own." He wanted to find the perpetrators and make them pay for what they did to Ed.

"I appreciate what you're saying, Chief, but I'd just as soon tell what I remember now," Ed answered.

The chief turned toward Detective O'Shea. "Jerry! You heard the lad. Take over, will ya?"

Three days later an arrest was made following a BOLO—be on the lookout—sent to all area police departments and hospitals. It included the details of the attempted burglary and the fact that one of two men was believed to be wounded by the responding officer. A young man was brought to Boston City Hospital with a bullet wound in his back. Giving several conflicting stories to police investigators as to what had happened, it was soon discovered that the bullet that was removed from the victim matched the weapon carried by Ed Fitzgerald. In further investigation, the man admitted to being in the area of the drugstore with a friend. However, both claimed to be walking past the store when the victim was shot. When asked by the police why they did not call for help after being shot, if that was their story, both stated they had a fear of the police and that they did not think the police would believe them. Instead, they would take a chance on going to the hospital for treatment. They did not know that all bullet wounds need to be investigated by law enforcement people.

Both men must have expected to be found as they had rehearsed their story so that, even when they were sequestered from one another, the words came out exactly the same.

Ed was elated to hear that the men were caught. This would look good on his record. Everyone congratulated each other on a job well done. The trial was set within ninety days, enough time to prepare the case and present the evidence.

Within that three months Ed had been relieved of his duty as a patrolman. This had been a crushing blow to him but it was not the worst to have happened. Even the loss of seventy percent of his sight in his left eye and the terrible facial disfigurement and scar that remained from the acid that had burned his flesh could not compare to the final blow. The man whom Ed had shot was seventeen years old. He lost some ability to walk in a normal fashion because the bullet had splintered a part of his spine. His mother, encouraged by members of a civil rights group, decided to sue Ed as well as the police department for the injuries the teenager suffered. The civil rights people supplied the attorney and filled the courtroom with sympathizers for the injured boy.

The boy's claim to have been shot while walking past the drugstore raised some questions as to the validity of the situation that took place inside the pharmacy. These were not in Ed's favor, however. There were no fingerprints to be found. Ed had not noticed whether or not the burglars were wearing gloves. It would have been difficult to determine that, given the light conditions at the time of the break-in. There was no other physical evidence available—only Ed's word. Even the flashlight and the tools the boys used to make their illegal entry were clean of any fingerprints. They had to have been experienced to have considered all the ways in which to cover themselves. And what seemed to placate the judge and to make the boys' story more palatable to the jury, which was made up mostly of the same race of people as the defendants, per a demand by the civil rights people for a jury of the boys' peers, was the fact that the seventeen-year-old had no prior criminal record. That is not to say that he had not been involved in any criminal acts previously, only that he had never been caught.

The attorneys representing the boys were good at what they did. They conceded that there was no doubt a burglary had taken place, but was there not the possibility that the real perpetrators got away and that these boys just happened to be passing by the pharmacy at the wrong time? Poor lighting, convenient alibis, the condition of the police officer, and the lack of solid evidence, all played into the favor of these young criminals. In good conscience, how could anyone on the jury be absolutely confident that these boys were guilty? The lawyers, highly paid by the civil rights group, overwhelmed the state's prosecuting attorney. It was obvious to Ed that money talked. What had seemed so right was turning out so wrong. The boys' case was thrown out of court. But that was just the half of it.

As ridiculous as it sounds, the boy won his civil rights case to the tune of $100,000. Ed, after his obvious testimony by virtue of his facial damage, could not believe what he was hearing. *What the hell was the matter with these people? Are they nuts? I'm the one who is suffering, not that thieving young snot. Is the whole world crazy?* He slowly walked out of the courtroom in a frame of mind totally opposite his normal character. His hurt had turned to complete bitterness. What little he owned was about to be taken from him. He could not afford the cost of an appeal and he would get no financial backing from the city. *This is no different from what my wife did to me. This is no different than my father never going to prison for beating my mother. This is no different than the guy who robbed and killed Mr. Danielson at his market and then got away scot-free. Mr. Danielson, the only person who would give my family food when my father had spent his entire paycheck on booze. There was not a nicer man than Mr. Danielson. Who says that crime doesn't pay? What a fool I've been all these years to believe that.* Ed vowed that some day he would get even with the system.

CHAPTER TWO

A Tough Life

Ed lived alone in a four-family apartment house at 148 Massachusetts Avenue in East Arlington. The huge gray building, which had been erected prior to the 1930s, sat back a short distance from the avenue and was one of the first homes in what had been designated as a residential neighborhood. However, with the passing of time, and with political pressure, the area had gradually taken on a more commercial look. Now the left side of the house was abutted by a small block of shops reaching to the corner where the Milton Spa, a variety store, was situated. To the right of the apartment house, a tiny building belonging to E.R. Stagg Plumbing and Heating was located.

The house was conveniently situated as the Metropolitan Transit Authority streetcars passed directly in front of it nearly every twenty minutes. Ed had no need of personal transportation of his own, but he did choose to buy a van for those occasions when he went camping or fishing, his only hobbies in life, actually his only interest in life now that he lived by himself. The van had previously been used by a parcel delivery company and had no windows other than the front windshield and the two front doors. This was convenient as Ed outfitted the cargo space for sleeping, for carrying his expensive fishing gear and for changing his clothes without being exposed to the public.

Ed had not had an easy life. Growing up, his family was poor. At first, he did not realize that as he did not seem different from most of the other kids in his neighborhood. Of course, going to a parochial school where all the students were outfitted with the same uniforms, one would not be aware of any variance in social standing. The only times he saw a difference was during afternoon play with his friends. First of all, Ed's clothes were old, well-worn, and some had nonrepairable rips in them. Secondly, when other kids went away for a week of vacation with their parents, he never went anywhere. The only comment his father made when Ed asked why they did not go places was, "Whattaya think we are . . . made of money?" This was usually followed by a slap across Ed's face. Ed would run to his mother who tried to shield him but she was no match for her husband.

Ed's father had retired from the Navy and married a woman twenty years his junior. His handsome, rugged build and easy demeanor were a natural attraction to women but those were merely a covering for a more adverse temperament. At first, he was decent to her but in time his true colors began to show. He was an alcoholic who beat his wife, Ed's mother. Ed always got the fallout after his mother was knocked unconscious. Ed's only escape was to the protection of his friend, Jerry Mahoney, a policeman who, on more than one occasion, was the officer to respond to their home when the neighbors called in a family fight at the house. Jerry lived close by and befriended young Ed, often stopping at the house even when there was no call for assistance. His concern was for the eight-year-old's safety and welfare as well as for that of Ed's mother.

When Ed's father died from an untreated liver ailment, his police friend married his mother, giving Ed a stable home life.

Ed wanted to be a cop, just like Jerry, his new dad. He would watch his dad come home from work, dog-tired, yet always making time to spend with him. Jerry would recount for Ed the day's events, many times embellishing them to his son's delight.

"Yup," Ed thought out loud to himself, "I want to be just like him." Jerry was the best thing to ever come into Ed's life.

Ed's new dad was so different from the man his mother first married. Family meant something to him. Almost every Saturday, Jerry would grab a few hours sleep after working all night and would take Ed to the Capitol Theater to go to the latest Roy Rogers cowboy movie. And on special occasions, when there was a new horror movie on the silver screen, Jerry and Ed's mom would take Ed to the Fresh Pond Drive-In Theater in Cambridge. Here Ed could squeeze between his folks and feel their comfort all through the scary scenes.

During the summer on Sunday afternoons, Jerry and Ed could be seen going down Lake Street in East Arlington, Jerry's arm around Ed's shoulder, to the railroad tracks where they would turn off and walk the tracks to Spy Pond where the closest playground was located. Jerry would push Ed on the swings or climb with him on the jungle gym monkey bars seemingly expending energy tirelessly. They would then feed the ducks bread crumbs that Jerry had saved in a paper bag over the past week. The ducks must have been used to getting their special treat as they would come waddling up to shore the minute Jerry rattled the paper bag with the crumbs. It was at Spy Pond that Ed learned how to fish one spring when the ice was out. Jerry had bought them both fishing rods and reels from the Jordan Marsh Company in Boston. This interaction between the two of them would bond them together for life.

Vacations were now a reality for Ed. More than once Jerry had taken his new family to Florida, a treat for Ed who had never been out of state before. These became a highlight in Ed's life and he would remember forever the southern coastal town he visited.

After graduation from high school, Ed was drafted into the Army. He was shipped overseas to the base in Stuttgart, Germany, where he was to serve for three years. His high school sweetheart, Arlene, wrote to him every day, expressing not only her love for him but her anxiety over the escalating war in Vietnam. What she feared most was that he would be sent there as the United States was just becoming involved in the battle. Fortunately for Ed, his stint was up and he returned home.

As luck would have it, there was an opening in the Arlington Police Department. The city was beginning to grow and with it was the crime, which was a natural parasite. Ed applied and, having passed the civil service exam, was hired. He attended municipal police training at the Massachusetts State Police Academy in Framingham and his proudest moment was when his dad was allowed to pin on his badge at graduation. It was the last event his folks would participate in with him. What had plagued his mother in her first marriage came back to haunt her as fate once more stepped in. Ed's mom and dad had been coming home from a drive to Carlisle where they had bought apples and a farm fresh turkey for Thanksgiving when a man, drunk, three times over the legal limit, swerved into their lane of travel from the opposite direction and hit them head-on. Ed's mother and dad were killed instantly.

If not for Arlene, who remained his strength, his world would have crumbled. She and Ed married soon after the accident and moved into the apartment on Massachusetts Avenue. After the few ups and the many downs in Ed's life, it appeared that things were now going to level out.

Arlene took a job as a teller at the East Arlington Branch of the Arlington Five Cents Savings Bank. She had a great outgoing personality and the bank's customers seemed to line up at her window even when the other tellers had shorter lines or were empty. Her manager recognized her charisma and her ability. Having been employed there for better than two years, she was soon promoted to an assistant manager's position. Working so closely as bank officers, they formed a bond which was to influence decisions she was to make in months to come.

Ed loved Arlene with all his heart. She had waited for him when he was in the service, and she was there for him when tragedy struck. And she supported his becoming a policeman. Why, then, did his life take another unexpected twist? Perhaps it was the long hours at work. Ed would see her for only a few minutes in the morning as she prepared to leave for work and he prepared for his eight hours of sleep. Then at night, she would arrive home close to nine o'clock as she put in extra hours in an attempt to move up the ladder in the bank. He would only see her for two hours before he had to head into work at the police station as she made ready for bed. Perhaps it was that he became affected by some of the things he saw people do to one another, although he should have been used to that; he had seen enough in his own household as a youngster. Perhaps it was the pressure of a failing court system. Or, perhaps it was the lack of attention he could give to Arlene, even as he tried to keep his weekends free for the two of them, because all of these things were wearing him down. Whatever it was, it caused problems at home. Bickering turned to arguing and arguing turned to fighting.

Arlene would often talk out her problems with the bank manager who was very sympathetic to her situation. Sympathy became empathy and empathy became an affair. It was not long before another change was to take place in Ed's life.

When Ed found out that his wife was going to leave him for someone else, it was more than he could bear. He had a flashback to the days when his father would beat his mother. He had vowed never to become the same kind of person his father was. Now he struggled with the temptation to lash out at his wife in the same way his father had done years before when Ed was a little boy.

Ed never really wanted to marry in the first place, fearing that he would turn out like his biological father. But the love he felt in his heart for Arlene had changed his perspective. Up until now, the thought never entered into his mind that he would ever beat his wife. He was a genuinely caring man, due largely in part to Jerry, his stepdad, but when Arlene told him she intended to file for a divorce, Ed went berserk and saw his father's fists in his mother's face triggering a pent-up rage that Ed nearly let loose on his own wife.

A few months after Arlene left, taking off with the bank manager for new positions that man was able to arrange at the National Shawmut Bank in Boston, Ed received counseling for his rage and he joined a gym to have a release for his anger. He vowed he would never hit a woman as long as he lived.

Ed was friendly with his neighbors in the apartment building. As the rent was reasonable and the location was convenient, his neighbors had remained tenants in the building for a long time. There had only been one other change in all the years he had lived there. Mrs. Garrett, the woman who occupied the apartment farthest from his, had inherited a large sum of money from a cousin whom she hardly knew.

Her cousin had not been wealthy. He had struggled with an idea that he thought was feasible, but he could not get anyone interested in backing him financially. Working days in an automobile garage, he invented an oil filter for airplanes that gave a better purity to the oil being passed through the engine and yet left little sediment as a by-product, by modifying those used for automobiles. He applied for and received a patent for his invention. Within weeks, a large manufacturer of airplane components who carefully watched for new patent ideas contacted him and made him an offer that allowed him to set up his own manufacturing plant. He had fallen into a business that gave him money the likes of which he had never in his life known before and which promised even greater rewards. A short time later, his untimely death due to a heart attack left him with no family or relatives other than his cousin and her two children who had been living in somewhat desperate means following many years of being a one-parent family. So his entire wealth and business went to her. Fortunately, he had hired good people to work for him and his business continued to thrive. The man who took over the management of the company was good for another reason—he did not attempt to take the company for himself and cheat the inheritors, but abided by the wishes of his former employer.

Mrs. Garrett moved with her children out to Framingham to be near her newly acquired office. She proved to be very adept in the world of business and transformed the company from a fledgling entity into a thriving corporation.

When Ed's wife left him for that other man, Ed could have become extremely hostile except for the fact that his neighbors gave him some much needed support. They took him in as sort of a part of their collective family. Ed always had a place to go for dinner. Some of the women even ironed his clothes; and before she moved, once a week Mrs. Garrett had come in and cleaned his apartment. For Ed, there was no time to be bitter. He seemed to deal with the separation well, or at least it appeared as well as anyone would in his situation. No one in the apartment complex had really known Arlene as she had not lived there for long. She left early every morning for work at the bank and did not return until late at night. So, while she had been living there, she was never around much. In recent months it had become obvious to most of the residents that she had another interest, but no one knew what it was until the word of a pending divorce was spoken.

Ed worked the midnight-to-eight shift at the police station. He would leave his house at eleven o'clock every work night and walk the forty-five minute hike to the department up on Central Street in Arlington Center. Some nights he had a walking beat; on others, he was in a two-man radio car often paired up with Harold Peterson or "Bib" O'Brien. In the morning, at the completion of his shift, he would hop on board the MTA—Metropolitan Transit Authority—streetcar heading toward Cambridge and get off at the stop in front of his house. He could have hitched a ride from the oncoming shift, but he liked being a presence among the people he served. Many came to know him as he always had a pleasant smile even after a long night. After getting off the streetcar, he might drop in at Freddie's Donuts just up the street from where he lived and grab a dozen French crullers or walk a block up to Edward's Home Made Candy and Ice Cream Shop where Jim Cokkinias would treat him to a couple of donuts and a glass of milk or a full breakfast with coffee. Jim and his brother, Steve, lived in the same housing complex as Ed, and over the years they had become the best of friends. They were there for him through his divorce and encouraged him. Jim related that he, too, had been through a tough relationship and had felt the hurt of a divorce. He would never marry again, fearing a recurrence of the same pain. Jim had also gone through counseling and it was his promotion of that aspect which convinced Ed to do the same. Jim said that it helped him cope, but the hurt, like the scar following an operation, would always be there.

Steve, on the other hand, never married because he was in love with all women and had a small, worn-out, address book crammed with the names and phone numbers of some of the loveliest girls who used to live in the area. Working at the ice cream fountain, which was so popular in those days years ago when the brothers opened the snack shop, he hit on every young lady that came through the doors. Being an Adonis in his looks and his build, he had no problem meeting women. Steve could *now* only suggest ways to meet some nice girls; after all, many years had passed since he was Ed's age.

Because the ice cream parlor was open seven days a week, it was impossible for the two brothers to get together at the same time with Ed. Steve was a bowling nut and when he had his days off, he would call Ed and convince him to go to the local alleys with him. Jim was a gambler and liked to have Ed's company over at Wonderland Dog Park in Revere. Jim was always positive that some day he was going to hit the big money when his favorite, long-shot greyhound crossed the finish line. Ed would go along for the ride, spend a few bucks and then laugh as his friend, Jim, would get all excited shouting at the dogs as they neared the end of each race; unfortunately never in the front position.

Even with his daily habit of a hefty breakfast, Ed maintained his weight in accordance with the requirements of the department. Mostly, perhaps, because of his nightly walks and the taking out of his aggressions on a set of barbells in the basement of his apartment. When his divorce was pending, he spent many hours with the set of weight-lifting apparatus. His upset over the fact that his wife had been cheating on him as he had remained faithful to her put a great deal of strain on him mentally. He found that exercise was his only way of coping with his hurt.

CHAPTER THREE

Union Pacific—More than a Railroad

As of November 1977, the Union-Pacific Armored Car Company celebrated its pride in having been in business for one hundred years and boasted of its record for never having been robbed and of never losing a single dollar in cash or valuable items from its armored service either on rail or by any other means of transportation. Up until that time, it continued its practice of remaining without notoriety as to its success in the armored transportation industry.

It had been late in the year 1877 when Union-Pacific entered the security market, diverging in a sense from their original purpose of providing quality rail transportation from New York across the country to California. Not too many years had passed since the golden spike had been driven down into the heavy wooden tie that marked the completion of the connection of the two participants—one from the east and its corresponding counterpart from the west—in the first cross-country, transcontinental railroad.

Prior to this time, only stagecoach was available as the sole means of public transportation. Without any mechanical equipment to hasten the journey along an established route, horse-drawn carriages proved to be slow moving, uncomfortable, limited in space and susceptible to interruptions which canceled a number of dangerous crossings. Broken wooden wheels, extreme and unpredictable inclement weather producing heavy snows, rain, floods, and thick mud, and attacks by Native Americans or brazen robbers often discouraged all but the most hardy or the most foolish to attempt such trips. Traversing untamed territories left the driver, and his right-hand man who sat in the "shotgun" seat, along with the coach's four to six passengers, facing negative conditions. The only means, as well, for sending gold, silver, currency, valuables, or other rarities across country was by stagecoaches. Companies such as Wells-Fargo and Pinkerton were the most notable in the years to follow.

When rail transportation was initiated, the moving of valuables across country by *this* method became more popular. Even the risk of breakage was greatly reduced by this new, modern mode of travel. Also, there were not the limitations of quantity as had been experienced in the cramped space of a wagon's roof and rear compartment, which left many items exposed to the elements.

As the rails followed the recently installed telegraph lines, another advantage was recognized. Should the operation of a train be interrupted by an unforeseen event, one of its specially trained, on-board employees could go to the nearest telegraph pole, climb to the existing wires using hooked steel gaffs which clamped to the legs of the man and dug into the sides of the pole, and intermit the signal of the telegraph by connecting two wires to the main line. Then, returning to the ground, he would make use of a portable key and tapper to send and receive messages indicating the problem and the train's location. It might take a day or so for the help to respond to the area of the train, but at least the passengers knew that help was on the way. In some locations, a telegraph wire was run partially down the side of a pole to a wooden connector box containing a receptacle for a plug. A ladder could then be placed against the pole allowing the train's officer easier access by pushing the plug from his portable key and tapper into the receptacle and, thus, automatically connect this device to the telegraph line. Eventually, a key and tapper were affixed permanently in either the engineer's cab or in the caboose and a reel of wire with special plug connectors was at the ready for a quick attachment to a telegraph pole should the occasion warrant such action.

The Union-Pacific Railroad saw a solution to a problem when they initiated the use of a specifically designated, specially designed car for the transportation of money, bullion and other valuables. The car was built much like a huge traveling safe with armored walls and multiple locks on the doors, some of which could only be opened from the inside by the men stationed there.

Of course, in those days prior to electric fans and air conditioning, the heat could become intense. To rectify this to a degree, barred windows with sliding iron plates were installed, which allowed for the passage of air. In time, a mechanical fan, operating on a chain drive connected to one of the wheels of the car, would provide cooling by some moving of the air. The only drawback was that the train had to be in motion for it to work.

During the winter months, heavy clothing and blankets were used to contain body heat for warmth. No potbelly stove, such as in use in the caboose, was allowed. The concern for the protection of currency and other combustible materials was greater than that of the comfort for the guards.

Heavy snows in the middle and western regions of the United States were a welcome natural defense against marauders who might, otherwise, attempt to hold up the train for its concealed treasures.

The men who were employed by the rail company to guard the armored car were well trained and had been chosen for their unwavering and profound honesty and unblemished character. The men were armed with Sharps military rifles, 1853 Navy model Colt handguns and the newest Winchester repeating rifles, an innovation making its debut with Union-Pacific. There were small portholes throughout the car, which allowed for the insertion of the weapons' barrels to the outside in order to protect the materials inside in the event of an attempted robbery.

Two things in the Union-Pacific's favor were the fact that it boasted of its heavily armed guards and it never advertised its cargo or the schedule for the armored car.

Even as the new century evolved, everything Union-Pacific did made them an industry leader. When Colonel Thompson invented the handheld, light submachine-gun more in compliance with the needs of the military and to provide firepower the same as the Maxim water-cooled heavy machine-gun, but without the need to set it on a tripod on the ground with a belt-fed ammunition box nearby, Union-Pacific ordered the first of the prototypes manufactured.

At the time, Union-Pacific's armored division was considered to be the state of the art. When other trains were being subjected to strong-arm robberies, the Union-Pacific was left virtually untouched.

The weekend following Thanksgiving 1977, the busiest two days before Christmas, the demand for cash by department stores during the height of the festive holiday shopping season was at its highest. Union-Pacific's office in Arlington, Massachusetts, was preparing for the incoming sixteen million dollars in cash it anticipated that it would be taking to stores and banks in the area by its armored trucks as the need arose. Once secured in its building, a standard practice over so many years of dealing with amounts of money even greater than this, it would be "business as usual" for the guards responsible for protecting the money.

Ed Fitzgerald had worked for Union-Pacific for more than four years after having been forced to take a medical retirement from the Arlington Police Department following his injury. The few dollars he would have received for disability compensation was attached by the attorney that represented the injured criminal following his winning the lawsuit against Ed. Not only would Ed have to pay the $100,000 that was levied against him, he was also responsible for reimbursing the civil rights attorney for his expenses. The small amount of savings he had managed to accumulate over the years was gone.

What his wife did not take in court as a payoff for his divorce settlement was now gone as a result of this unfair legal action. He would have suffered in poverty conditions for years had he not found work at Union-Pacific. As it was, his wages were half of what he earned as a cop, but who wanted a one-eyed, facially disfigured employee with no skills other than those he had learned for providing protection to the public? Seven years as a dedicated policeman down the drain because of a criminal justice system designed to go against the defenders of the law and to reward those who broke the law.

Ed would never forget that day and he would constantly call to mind the long-lasting results of his confrontation.

CHAPTER FOUR

Getting Even

There were four guards on duty the afternoon the money arrived at the armored car facility for the 1977 Christmas shopping rush. The canvas money bags, filled with currency, were carried into the secure holding area—a chain-link enclosure inside the confines of the building. The entire building was like a fortress—a gigantic vault—with walls of concrete and steel some eighteen inches thick. The building had no windows and entry required going through three sets of steel doors. All corners of the building had closed-circuit television cameras on the outside and twice as many on the inside. They all terminated in a central control room which had direct telephone links to the police, fire and hospital. The outside of the building was surrounded by a twelve-foot-high chain-link fence topped with three strands of barbed wire. There was only one electrically activated entrance/exit gate through that fence and that was operated by the guard in the control room.

By Friday evening only two men were left in the building.

"Hey, Chico," Ed called out to the guard in the control room. "I'm gonna bring my van inside. It's making some noise in the front end and I want ta check it out before I go home."

"Sure, Ed. Wheel it on into the yard and I'll open the garage door once I've secured the gate."

"Thanks, Chico."

During the past four years of Ed's employment at Union-Pacific, he had brought his vehicle in on several occasions for minor work, oil changes, and swapping off his summer tires for snow tires as the seasons changed. It was not unusual for employees to try and do a little auto repair work on their cars after hours or on the weekend. All the employees had to do was not get caught by the boss as this was not a sanctioned practice by management. The garage was well-equipped with every tool a mechanic could want. It even had an hydraulic lift in the back section of the building that was capable of hoisting the heavy armored vehicles high enough to be worked on. It was convenient as it was set up for minor mechanical repairs to be done on a regular basis in order to keep these specialized trucks in good running condition. One of the drivers, who had an auto mechanics background, earned extra money by doing the maintenance on the company's trucks. There was an issue of trust when it came to using any of the local gas and automobile service stations and the company did not want to take any chances leaving vehicle keys with people they did not know, especially with the turnover of personnel in those service garage facilities. In those days, before sophisticated locks came into being, even amateur locksmiths could cut keys to fit the huge money box on the back of each truck, which accommodated the large bags of cash being transported along with the guards who protected them.

Ed went outside and got into the van. He started it, drove up to the gate and pushed the intercom button and announced that he was ready to come in. He waited for Chico to look at the camera monitor and to verify that it was safe to release the lock. Then Chico hit the switch, which opened the gate. In less than a minute, Ed was inside the yard and waiting for the garage door to open.

As he pulled into the building, he paused for the outside garage door to close and the inside one to open. He could hear the loud noise of the air blowers as they exhausted the expended gasoline fumes of his van to the outside. Pulling in past the second overhead door, he drove down past the hydraulic lift and turned the van around. He then brought it up so that it was stationed sideways in front of the secured money area, the location where the armored trucks usually parked to drop off and pick up money and where repair work to the vehicles was done. In this position, the van now faced out toward the garage doors.

From his remote security room, Chico watched through the camera as Ed took out a tool box and opened it, removing a few items. Ed then lay down on a creeper—one of those low-to-the-ground flat boards with wheels that allow mechanics to get under vehicles on their backs—and crawled beneath the van until he was completely out of sight. From this position, Ed could see the chain-link enclosure protecting the stacks of money in large canvas bags. Ed knew that where he was, the camera could not focus on him as he drew the bolt cutters he had removed from his tool kit toward the fencing. The camera, also, could not see the protected bags of money as the van now blocked any view.

He stretched across and began cutting the individual links until he had an opening wide enough to bring the bags of money through. Pulling the chain links apart, he then brought what looked like a short, telescoping, car radio antenna with a hook on one end out from his pants. He extended the sections and, reaching through the hole in the enclosure, he hooked the first of the bags of money. As he drew the bag to him, he reached up under the van and slid back a panel in its floor, which gave him access to the van's interior. He placed the bag up inside the van and then sent the retrieving hook for the next bag. As he extended the retrieving hook to grab onto the third bag, he heard the familiar click of the outer door from the control room as the electric latch was being released from inside.

Ed tried to pull back the hook, but it had already snagged the handle on the money bag. There was no time to try to shake it loose as the door to the garage opened. Ed put down the hook slowly so that its metal shank would not resound on the cement floor. Then he froze.

"Ed! What's goin' on?" the voice of the shift supervisor boomed sharply causing Ed nearly to lose control of his bladder.

What was he doing here? Ed thought to himself. He knew that Zeke Cavanaugh never put in any overtime. He worked until six o'clock in the evening and was known as a clock-watcher. At first, he watched the clock to make sure that no one left work before the appointed hour. Then he became like the rest of the employees, waiting for the minute hand to stop on the designated departure time and he would be history.

Ed was short of breath as he tried to respond without the fear of guilt coming through his voice.

"Hey, Zeke, what're you doin' here at this hour?" Ed said as he rolled the creeper out from under the van in the direction of Zeke's feet, sweat now forming on his forehead, a redness covering his face, and a shakiness in his hands, which he hoped was not reflected in his voice.

Zeke had just lowered himself on his haunches to peek in at Ed to see what he was doing.

"I forgot my wife's birthday present," Zeke said. "I picked it up at lunch time and didn't remember to bring it home until she reminded me what day it was. Amazing how you can forget things after you've been thinking about them all day, huh? Anyway, for her to know that I didn't forget her birthday and was not going out now to buy something for her, I drove here with her to pick up what I already had bought. She's out in the car. What're you doin' anyway?"

Coming up in front of Zeke so as to block his view, Ed said, "I, uh, had some trouble with the front end. It was vibratin' so I wanted ta check it out."

"Oh? Let me take a look. I had a problem a while ago with my car. It turned out to be nothin' more than a needed realignment, but I'm pretty familiar with the car's undercarriage now." He leaned down to peer under the van.

"Aw, don't bother, Zeke. I think I've found it. You'd just get all dirty and your wife's waitin' ta celebrate her birthday. All you'd need is ta go outside covered with oil and grease. Your wife 'ud blame me," Ed said as he maneuvered his way back in front of Zeke preventing him from looking beneath the van.

Zeke stopped, and with a quizzical look on his face remained in place for a moment saying nothing, only staring at Ed.

Ed's mind raced. *What was Zeke thinking? Maybe I shouldn't have been so obvious about my challenging him.* Ed conjured up the worst possible scenario as he now looked into Zeke's eyes.

"Ahhh, you're prob'ly right," Zeke finally said. "Well, I've got what I came for so, I'm gone." With that he stood up and headed toward the door.

"See ya later, Zeke," Ed said although he knew that was a lie. "Wish your wife a happy birthday for me."

"Hey, take care," Zeke replied, "I'll tell her. Oh, and don't let the boss catch you working in here."

"I know. With any luck I'll be safe."

Ed waited until he was sure Zeke had left the building before he climbed back onto the creeper and pushed himself back underneath the van.

"Whew!" he said quietly to himself. "That was close."

He pulled on the hook and dragged in the money bag. After unhooking it, he sent it back for the next one.

He took only enough bags not to be noticed by the camera, those that were near the bottom of the pallets, some two million dollars.

When he was finished, he pushed the retrieval hook and bolt cutters in through the hole in the van's floor. He then replaced the panel in the van's floor, slid out from under the van and brought the creeper around to the side where the hole in the fencing was. He leaned the creeper upright against the hole, covering it completely from view. He then went to pick up his tool box, which he set on the passenger seat.

He stepped into the control room to pass some time in conversation with Chico whose shift went until six o'clock in the morning. Ed himself only had to work until ten that evening. The men took turns doing inspections of the armored vehicles and this had been his Friday to work late. He knew that no one would discover the theft until some time Monday morning. This would give him adequate time to accomplish what he had planned for several years. Ed would miss Chico. He liked this little guy who stood no more than five feet tall and had always wanted to become a cop. Had it not been for his height, he would have passed the physical requirements. But Chico seemed to take it in stride. He was even-tempered all the time. He continually kept a smile on his face and that was a positive to some of the men who worked there because it was like magic the way he could change their attitudes when they came in grumbling about some thing that happened at home or on the job.

Ed had been to the christening of Chico's newest baby. Chico now had six kids to feed and that was not easy on what he earned at the armored car company. But Chico was deeply religious and he believed that God would take care of him no matter what. As bitter as Ed had become over the events in his life, he still had a heart. Ed slipped two hundred dollars into a christening card with no signature, only the words, *from a friend*. Ed fully believed that Chico would never know who gave him the money, but somehow Chico knew.

When Ed finally left the garage, he turned onto Route 3 and made his way out through Winchester to Route 128. He then drove down to the Massachusetts Turnpike, struggling with one hand at a time to put on a sweater to cover his security uniform shirt as he steered the wheel with the opposite hand. Once on the 'pike he headed to Worcester where he parked his van in a parking lot adjacent to Route 290 not too far from the Posner Square turnoff next to a new van he rented from Avis just a day before. He had rented the van in Boston and had driven to Worcester that evening after taking off half a personal day from work. Finding a busy lot with several cars evidently parked for the night, he did likewise with the rental van, setting it in a back corner of the lot between a pick-up truck and an older model station wagon. There were several utility poles in the lot, which provided light during the night. The one nearest to this corner was not functioning. This would be a plus as the car could remain there without being readily seen. He then walked to the bus station and returned to Boston by bus where he retrieved his own van.

Ed had made only one other stop that day. During the early morning hours, he went to an army-navy surplus store in Cambridge and picked up some items he knew he would eventually need. He had spent the remainder of the morning drilling and cutting out a section of the floor of his van and affixing metal brackets to the piece he had removed so that it formed a loose cover that would rest over the hole.

Ed transferred the money bags, his newly acquired military items, his sleeping gear, and a large duffel bag from his van into the rental van under the cover of darkness, changed his clothes leaving his uniform in his old van and started out once again for the turnpike and then points south.

CHAPTER FIVE

Caught

Avis Car Rental reported the van as stolen when three weeks had passed without any word from the renter. Up until that time, it was simply kept on their records as missing with charges accruing on Ed's VISA credit card. As the charges reached the card's limit and as the rental company's internal computer showed a significant time elapsing between the due date and the current date, Avis made the usual notification through its channels. These incidents happened on occasion so it was not something totally bizarre. However, the van would be reported as stolen.

An Ohio Highway Patrol unit had stopped the van for speeding in a construction zone. Ed had just stopped at a post office outside Dayton, made a short, collect call on the pay phone by the post office entry door, and mailed an enigmatic letter to Jim Cokkinias at his restaurant. There was no return address information on the envelope and the letter contained some specific instructions including a stipulation to keep the contents in a secure place with no mention of the writer's name to be placed anywhere on the enclosed second envelope. This was not to be opened unless the writer sent additional instructions. The letter contained just enough material so that Jim would recognize the author as there was no signature included either. The outer envelope along with the original letter were to be burned.

Leaving the post office parking lot, Ed did not notice the REDUCE SPEED–CONSTRUCTION sign posted on the highway. His mind was focused elsewhere as he daydreamed momentarily about the thoughts that would go through Jim Cokkinias's head as he read the letter. Ed flinched as he took a second look in his rear view mirror and saw the flashing blue lights of the patrol car behind him.

The police car remained behind Ed until he pulled over to the right side of the road and stopped. Ed, unaware of his speeding violation, could only think that somehow the police had finally caught up with him for the armored car company theft. He shut off the engine and rolled down his window with his left hand. He was nervous as the officer approached the van and asked for his license and registration. Ed thought that that was odd. *Why would he ask for that if he's about to arrest me for a felony?* Confused and still nervous, Ed said nothing while fumbling to get his wallet out of his back pants pocket. His hand was shaking as he tried to remove his license from the pouch inside his wallet. It had been so long since he had last taken it out that it adhered to the plastic envelope pocket. Concentrating solely on his task at hand, Ed finally freed the license from its holder and handed it to the officer. He then opened the glove compartment and reached across for his registration as the highway patrolman carefully watched his hand movements as it was not unusual for people to carry a gun in the glove box. Ed gave his registration to the officer who then told him the reason he had been stopped.

A feeling of relief washed over Ed as his mind registered what the patrolman just said. *A traffic violation*, Ed thought. *A traffic violation. Unbelievable.* Ed, who had always been alert to road conditions, activity and signs, expressed his chagrin in missing something that had to have been so obvious.

Ed was cordial to the officer remembering how he had been fair to people he had stopped when they had been respectful of him. Only the idiots—the loudmouths—were treated the way in which they acted. Had Ed retained his old police badge and identification card, he probably would have driven away with nothing more than a verbal warning. But that was a part of his former life and he had cut all ties when the decision was made by the court to reduce him to nothing.

Ed was issued a ticket and, as he was from out-of-state, the law required that he be brought before a judge to pay the fine. The highway patrolman would provide the escort. Ed followed the officer's cruiser and paid the fifty dollar fine for the ticket he received to a local magistrate and, upon leaving, continued in a westerly direction. It was common practice to enter the ticket information into station records at the completion of a patrol officer's shift, and eventually do the same onto the police teletype machine at the end of the week. In this way, any other department that might stop the operator of a vehicle for any reason can check to see if there are any previous traffic violations. In this case, had Ed aroused any suspicion in the trooper, Ed's license information would have been put onto the teletype immediately and his wanted status would have come back within minutes. Because the trooper had waited those few days, there was a delay showing a "hit" indicating the rental car was recently reported as stolen. The trooper, upon being made aware of this, notified the Massachusetts State Police who immediately sent an updated teletype to all area departments with special attention to the mid-western states. Had the national law enforcement communications network been in operation then instead of two years later, Ed would have been arrested on the spot as the computer-linked system allowed for instantaneous access to criminal records and wanted persons information. Just by chance, Ed was granted a temporary reprieve.

Ed made it all the way to Castle Rock, Colorado. His intention was to avoid the larger cities of Denver and Colorado Springs by getting off of Interstate 70 and taking Route 86 to bypass the major section of either city. He would work his way up to Route 470 and connect back to the Interstate just north of Morrison. Not only would it avoid the greater cities but it looked like it might be a shorter route. It might have been a good idea in the middle of the summer, but this was considered wintertime in the west and traveling over a mountain pass that had been closed for the season was a poor decision. The days were getting colder but the brightness of the sun each morning gave Ed the promise of a good journey ahead. A brief thaw to an unusually mild beginning to the winter had given a false impression that the road was clear and safe. Paying no heed to the warning signs, which indicated that the road was closed to all traffic, Ed swung around them and up the gradual elevated slope. His thinking, in part, was that if the road was closed, obviously no one would be using it. There would be no chance of his being caught.

His ultimate intention was to make it to California and to get lost in the busy-ness of Los Angeles. He knew that if he remained inconspicuous, working odd jobs requiring no background investigation, that as time passed by and things cooled down concerning the theft, he would have a good chance of living well for many years to come. He might even be able to locate someone, who for the right price, could provide him with enough false identification materials, such as a birth certificate and driver's license, so that he would have a new identity. He knew things like this were being done as evidenced by information that would come into the police station when he had been involved in criminal investigations just a few years ago. All he had to do was make it to the West Coast and find a place to dump the van.

The road was bare and dry as he accelerated the climb that would take him over one high mountain and two of lower elevations. The views were magnificent. For a man on the run, there were times when he seemed in no hurry to get anywhere in particular. He slowed just long enough to admire the scenery and to take one or two bites out of the Big Mac he bought in the last town he passed through. It was just about noontime and he had not bothered to stop for any breakfast.

As Ed approached the peak of the second small mountain, the sky darkened rapidly and snowflakes soon filled the air. Ed showed little concern as he continued on, slowing just a bit from some of the higher speeds he had reached on the mountain pass, knowing that no one would be on the road to hinder his progress; no traffic, no police. He was alone. There was an exhilarating feeling of freedom as he topped speeds near one hundred miles per hour and rode down the center of the asphalt keeping the nose of his rented van aimed on the yellow line.

Cresting the mountain, he failed to notice a deer crossing from his left until it was too late. He jammed on the brakes and swerved to his right. The van went off the road, over the shoulder and into a ditch. The front right fender crunched as it impacted with the rock ledge that formed a wall on the inside of the roadway.

Ed was thrown against the steering wheel with enough force to bend it slightly forward. Fortunately, he did not hit the windshield. His fastened seat belt prevented him incurring an injury from the steering column. Coming to such an abrupt stop, the van stalled.

Shaking a bit, Ed got out to assess the damage and to determine the status of his predicament. His arms were sore from holding on to the steering wheel when the van hit the ledge. He rubbed them as he surveyed the condition of the van.

It was becoming bitterly cold, a fact that Ed was somewhat unaware of in the heated cab of the van. The snow was gradually moving toward him from the direction in which he was headed. Having come sixteen miles on this road, a mild panic struck him as he saw that the van was wedged at an angle, which would prevent his escape. The front bumper had pushed the fender into the right tire. It had not caused it to burst but it did form a bubble as the air in the tire was compressed and had no where to go except to distort the tire's round shape. The right headlight now rested at an angle which would be great for watching the shoulder of the road but little use for illuminating the pavement. The ledge, of course, remained unscathed.

Getting back into the van, he turned the ignition key to the start position. The van came to life. He moved the gearshift lever into reverse and gave a slight push on the accelerator. The van shivered, but refused to budge. Ed gave it more gas, but the wheels only started to spin, kicking up dirt. The front right wheel made a screaming noise as it rubbed against the twisted metal of the fender, which started to shave off bits of rubber as the tire rotated. The van was locked in place.

Anxiety spread quickly through his mind. The road was desolate and void of any traffic or habitation. The sky promised a heavy incoming snow. Why had he not at least turned on the radio to get a weather report before taking a chance on this mountain pass? For the sake of saving some mileage and time, of which he had plenty, he was now in a desperate quandary. He thought back to a TV story on "20-20" or "60 Minutes"; he could not remember which. A man crossing a mountain pass, one that was not yet closed for the winter, had become stranded. His truck broke down and he stayed in it, waiting for help. Unknown to him, the department of public works had just posted the road as *closed* hours after his entry onto the pass. No help would arrive. Still, he waited. He waited and wrote on a pad of paper that he had with him all that he was thinking and doing as he sat there in his pick-up. It was to become his diary—more his obituary—as he remained there for days, which turned into weeks. The snows came and completely covered the truck. The man never left where he was. He started the engine in his truck only to get enough heat to keep from freezing and to conserve on his gasoline. He ate some of the snow to keep moisture in his body, the only sustenance available to him. It bought him some time, but it was not enough. He finally succumbed to the cold and starvation.

Deja vu. Now Ed felt like he had experienced this situation before, until he remembered the TV special.

"Well," he said to himself, "that's not gonna happen to me. That moron coulda started walking. And he had an advantage; there was no snow in sight when his truck broke down. He coulda been home free. Instead he waits for death. That's not gonna happen to *this* guy. I'm outta here."

Ed grabbed the flashlight out of the van's glove compartment, took the army blanket that was in one corner of the floor of the van on top of his camp mattress, zipped up his L.L. Bean winter coat, took his heavily

The Key

insulated gloves and the remainder of his McDonald's Value Meal and checked to make sure there was nothing else that he needed. His duffel bag that he had been using as his suitcase and carryall could stay in the van. He would retrieve it later, he thought, once he got a tow truck up here to haul the van out.

He knew that his best bet would be to go back to where he started on this road. There was no telling how far ahead he would have to go before he reached civilization. Besides, the dark clouds and impending snow lay in that direction. "No," he said to himself feeling the comfort of hearing his own words, "better to go where I've already been."

Ed hoisted the blanket up under his left arm, put the flashlight in his hip pocket, tucked his gloves in his right-side coat pocket and held the McDonald's bag in his left hand as he headed back down the road he only minutes before had traversed in the van.

He nibbled on french fries as he walked, keeping a quick pace, which was more motivated by the fact that he was on a downhill slope. It also helped that the road was in prime condition. As the winter weather had not yet arrived to take its toll, there were no frost heaves to impede cars or, in Ed's case now, foot traffic.

Smiling at the oxymoron—slowly eating fast food, he kept his concentration focused on accomplishing a lot in a short period of time. He did not want to be caught in any kind of snowstorm up in the mountains of Colorado.

Once he finished his now-cold lunch, he hesitated as he considered what to do with the bag of trash remaining in his left hand. It seemed a shame to toss it into the woods and spoil an otherwise pristine environment. "Hopefully," Ed said aloud to no one but himself, "it's biodegradable." He then scrunched up the bag into a kind of ball and threw it as far off the sloped side of the mountain road as he could. It disappeared beneath the wide-spreading branches of the tall fir trees down below.

In the one hour he traveled he managed to cover nearly five miles. But, like Big Ben, the clock in the Tower of London, he knew that as the heavy minute hand rapidly descended during the first half hour, it slowed on its ascent during the second half hour. Ed was now in a valley and looking at the upward grade he would have to climb to get over the mountain that separated him from the final hike to population.

Halfway up the mountain, Ed knew he had lost his gained advantage. The grade was steep and proved to be a challenge. The pressure put a strain on his bladder and he laughed to himself as he unzipped the fly on his pants and relieved himself in the middle of the road almost in defiance of anyone daring to confront him in his exposed state. He continued to laugh as he added another yellow line to the one already painted in the middle of the road.

The dark clouds silently followed him and, were it not for the few snowflakes, which began to float down in front of him, he might not have noticed. He had not yet reached the halfway point. Ed marveled at how quiet it was and he was reminded of the phrase, "the lull before the storm." The snow increased in its intensity and the winds picked up on this side of the mountain causing some squalls to form.

Ed had to keep wiping away the cold moisture, which continually attacked his one good eye. Slowly the ground and the trees, losing the benefit of the sun's rays, began to cool allowing the snowflakes to gather and not melt as they had been doing. Soon the asphalt pavement would succumb to a like fate. Ed's face began to show some concern but not to the degree of any anxiety. At least, not yet.

Reaching the peak of the mountain, the wind chill became brutally bitter. Ed unraveled the blanket from under his arm after he pulled the hood out from its zippered enclosure on his coat, covered his head and pulled the drawstring tightly so that only his face lay bare to the elements. He then wrapped the blanket around himself and kept it taut against his body as he walked into the snow, which now continually whipped his face. He snickered to himself wondering if he looked like the popular caricature of the Grim Reaper.

Almost trying to beat nature, he took large, fast-paced strides down the mountain's other side. He pictured himself as a runner in the Boston Marathon only encumbered somewhat by all his clothing and the heavy blanket he wore. At first, he thought he had made some progress compared to the slow-moving storm front. Before long, however, it was not a contest. The weather was in control. The ground was now turning white as a covering of snow enveloped every bit of the black asphalt. The snow was no longer in the flaky state but was coming down as beads or pellets, like little hard balls of Styrofoam.

At the bottom of the mountain, the road nearly leveled out. The walk here would be steady except for the accumulation of snow.

"Amazing," Ed said to himself, "how much snow can pile up in an hour's time." He knew that there was only about a three-mile stretch still ahead of him. Even though there was now better than two inches on the ground, this was an easy jaunt of less than one hour. As he walked he made an obscene gesture to the clouds and shouted out at them as though they had a human personality, "There! Take that! You thought you had me, but I showed you! I win! *I* win, not you!"

The snow had reached a depth of four inches by the time he saw the main road coming into view. A feeling of exhilaration filled him once again and he got a second wind as he forged ahead to the intersection.

Perhaps it was fate or just plain bad luck, especially after defeating this enemy of a storm, but as he approached the crossroads, a police cruiser, caked with snow, appeared and stopped next to him.

The officer rolled down his window. "Hey pal, where you going?" he shouted out to Ed over the blowing wind as he looked at this strangely attired individual with a scarred and disfigured face peering out at him through the blanket with only one operable eye.

"Uh . . . my van broke down and I walked a few miles. I'm lookin' for a garage."

"Your van up on the mountain pass?"

"Uh, yeah," Ed replied.

"Which way were you headed?"

"Oh, west."

"Didn't you pay any attention to that sign?" the officer asked as he pointed to the ROAD CLOSED warning, the sign's letters now barely visible under the crust of new-fallen snow.

"I must've missed it," Ed responded.

"Where you from?"

"East," said Ed in a one word answer.

"You better get in with me. I'll take you to the local service station. They have a tow truck."

Ed climbed into the front seat of the police car.

As they drove into the gas station parking lot, the officer asked to see some identification from Ed.

Ed took out his wallet and with a little shakiness of the hand, more as a reaction to the cold than from nervousness, produced his driver's license. The officer took it, looked at it, and then looked once again at Ed, comparing his face to the photo on the license.

"You're a long way from home," he finally said.

Regaining some composure, Ed replied, "Yuh. I'm headed to California to . . . uhhh . . . visit . . . my sister."

"Mmm . . . hmmm," was the only utterance from the officer. Then he continued, "Well, this storm came in fast but it's not supposed to last. If you look beyond the mountains you can see the sun breaking through. Only a couple more hours of daylight left. Maybe you can get back on your way with any kind of luck. But," the officer emphasized, "not on the mountain road. You'll have to come back this way and take the long route around."

"No problem. Thanks for all your help," Ed said with relief as the officer returned his driver's license and Ed got out of the car and headed into the garage.

Ed negotiated with the service station operator who agreed to tow out the van to the tune of sixty dollars cash in advance and providing it was an easy tow. Ed gave the man the money and was given a receipt. The man then told one of his employees he would be back in about an hour.

"We've been out in worse weather than this," the man said. "This won't be no problem. Get into the cab of my tow truck and you can show me where your vehicle's at."

Ed smiled as he heard the man's pronunciation of the synonym for car—"vee-hick-ul," with the emphasis on the "hick."

As they pulled out from the garage bay, Ed noticed that the police car was still in the gas station parking lot. He watched it move in a path behind the massive tow truck, with its tire chains digging into the snow. He marveled momentarily at the size of the tow truck, thinking how well-equipped these service stations needed to be in order to handle the heavy winter weather.

On the way to the van, Ed managed to glimpse twice into the convex mirror that was cemented onto the large rearview mirror on the truck's passenger side door. The police car was following them up the mountain road.

Ed tried not to show any signs of nervousness. This was different from being stopped for speeding as he had been in Ohio. As the tow truck driver did not seem concerned that the police car was behind them, Ed thought that perhaps it was not unusual for the patrolman to follow along on emergency road calls such as this. Perhaps it was the fact that Ed's car was on a closed road that the police officer showed greater interest. Or, perhaps it was that the officer thought he might have to make out an accident report if the damage warranted such an action. Several thoughts went through Ed's mind as he considered some of the things he would have been preoccupied with when he had been in that line of work. He relaxed, giving little more attention to the police car. *I must be getting paranoid*, he thought, smiling slightly.

The snow tapered off and before long a few rays of sunshine made their way through the western sky. When the men reached the van, it was blanketed with over half-a-foot of snow. The tow truck operator pulled out a broom and cleaned away the area where he would attach the tow bar and chains. He also cleaned the front of the van to see for himself what damage had been done. He then moved the tow truck into position to pull out the van by backing up to the van's rear bumper and connecting the tow bar.

It took less than twenty minutes for the van to be freed from its trap and the service station man to pull the fender and bumper away from the partly squashed tire. The tire was no worse for its predicament as it regained its normal shape. As the tow truck operator prepared to release the tow chain, the police officer got out of his cruiser and walked over to the men. In his police car, the officer looked to be about the same size as Ed, perhaps with a bit more bulk. When the officer got out, Ed was surprised to see that the man stood over a half foot taller than Ed. The officer had huge hands and what Ed thought was bulk was actually the body of a weight lifter.

"Mr. Fitzgerald, you need to come with me," the officer said.

"What's up?" Ed inquired.

"I think you already know the answer to that," the officer responded as he took a set of handcuffs out of the leather pouch on his gun belt. "You're under arrest, Mr. Fitzgerald." The officer handcuffed Ed and put him in the back seat of the police car. He then did a cursory search of the van before instructing the tow truck operator to bring the van to the police station to be impounded. It was there that the van was stripped and fully searched.

Except for a few changes of clothing, the camp mattress, the duffel bag, and fast-food wrappers, the van was empty. When Ed was searched subsequent to his being held at the local lockup, he was found to be carrying eight hundred dollars in his wallet and three thousand dollars in a money belt around his waist.

In lieu of the Arlington Police going to Colorado for the extradition, the district attorney sent two Massachusetts State Troopers to accomplish the pick-up. There was some concern that Ed might have some sympathy from the men he used to work with. The district attorney did not want to jeopardize his case against Ed.

Making only general small talk after being advised of his constitutional rights, the troopers later told their superiors that Ed replied only when spoken to, never initiating any conversation and his demeanor was such that he displayed a smugness in his attitude along with a self-complacent smile.

Once booked and brought to the interrogation room in state police headquarters at 1010 Commonwealth Avenue in Boston, all talking ceased on Ed's part. No matter what questions were asked, his only response was a noncommittal smirk. Investigators made a complete examination of the rented van and eventually located Ed's own van still sitting in the parking lot in Worcester. They stripped it clean but discovered no clue as to what his plan for the money had been. No trace of the missing two million dollars was found. They interviewed his friends, his neighbors, and his co-workers including Chico, the one who was fired from his job as control room security guard the night the money was stolen. Even Chico was considered a suspect until he was thoroughly interrogated. No one could give them a hint of Ed's scheme nor where the money might have been taken.

It was suggested that some of Ed's previous co-workers from the police department be allowed to talk with him. The intimation being that he might be more willing to open up to those people he had been close to while on the job. The investigators thought it might work and was worth a try.

Ed was not stupid. He knew that the moment the conversation turned from friendly greetings to questions couched by affable comments and insincere smiles that he was no longer on an equal par with his former compatriots. The dialogue became cold and stilted. No matter how hard the men tried to coax answers out of Ed, he would not respond. When he did speak, it was usually to change the subject or to give nonsensical answers, which only he found amusing. Over the years, since he had been out of police work, things had changed. It seemed that cops kept close contact only to cops who were still actively engaged in law enforcement. Once that connection was broken, unless the person left the job for a position that could be in some way helpful to those who remained, then the man who gave up the job became an outsider.

When Ed pulled the stunt of ripping off the armored car company he was now classified as just another criminal. In fact, having been a cop, he was considered even lower than a common thief. Sure, it did not matter what graft others had taken or what corruption infiltrated different levels of the criminal justice community, Ed would still be thought of as the scum of the earth. For anyone to think that such bribery and dishonesty never took place when the times and conditions were right, or that all police officers are so honest as to be untouchable by the criminal element, would be naive on his or her part to the degree of being absolutely ludicrous. Granted, the percentage is small, but it still happens.

Anybody Ed had as a friend, either at work or otherwise, had closed the door on any continued relationship. The trust factor had been destroyed and no matter what the circumstances may have been, Ed was deemed as nonexistent. The only exceptions were his two former apartment-house neighbors, Jim and Steve Cokkinias. They knew the real Ed Fitzgerald and they tried to give him support when he was in the trial against the drugstore burglars. They, too, were upset with the final outcome of that court case and voiced their opinions every day for months to everyone they came in contact with at the restaurant. Of course, it did no good, the damage had been done. If they had had the money, they would have financed Ed's appeal. The cost, however, was prohibitive. Ed appreciated their concern. Had the brothers not understood Ed's motive and agreed somewhat with Ed's actions at the armored car company in his latest plight, they would probably have been the only ones who could have successfully convinced Ed to admit all the information the state police were seeking. Once again, they had taken his side.

The state police investigators tore apart Ed's apartment. In a segment on a localized television news program similar to "America's Most Wanted" the host appealed for information as to anyone seeing Ed during the time he was on the run. Of course, they did not give the details or the amount of money that was taken, only that he was the prime suspect in a foiled scheme to steal a huge amount of money from his last employer. There was no response to the appeal. No one had seen him; or, if they did, they did not remember him.

Union-Pacific was not particularly concerned about the theft of the money because the bonding company would make good on the loss through insurance. What upset them most was the defilement of the company's good and honorable name and the loss of respect for America's foremost armored security enterprise.

Ed remained uncooperative even throughout his court trial. At his arraignment he refused an attorney—not so much by the fact that he would state anything audibly, but more that he would not cooperate with any of the requests, demands or suggestions of the judge or anyone else. Threats by his assigned attorney, by the prosecution and by the judge, before and during the trial, had no affect on him. He just smiled and never uttered one word as he listened to the evidence presented against him and as the jury made their decision of guilty in a record forty minutes. The only time Ed showed any emotion was when Chico was brought into court as a witness. Ed could not look his friend in the eye. He never thought that Chico would have been fired for something over which the little guy had no control. *What have I done? What's going to happen to his family without any income? What the hell have I done?* Ed thought to himself.

Chico appealed to the union and for three months they did battle in his behalf stating the fact that it would have been impossible for Chico to have seen anything that was taking place or to have had any responsibility beyond what had been a normal practice of allowing men to work on their vehicles in the company garage over the years. The union failed to get his job back or his missed wages for the three months he was out of work. Ed silently made another vow to himself that when he got free he would help Chico with some of the cash and this time Chico would never know where it came from.

Ed was sentenced to twenty years in state prison. Because of his police experience, and knowing that some of the criminals were sent to the Walpole State Prison in Massachusetts as a result of the arrests he had effected, it was decided to have Ed incarcerated in a New York facility, away from anyone who might recognize him and attempt revenge.

Ed knew that with good behavior he could be released in as early as eight years. Then it would simply be a matter of caution when he retrieved the money he had so carefully hidden. It was not as comfortable as his original idea, but he could live with it. After all, two million dollars over eight years amounted to earning a quarter million dollars a year. Not bad for doing nothing but sitting back, watching television, pumping iron, wandering around the recreation yard, trying one's skills in the woodworking shop, eating decent meals and, in general, living off of the state of New York.

CHAPTER SIX

Incarceration

Ed never imagined that his role as a model prisoner could be altered. He had portrayed himself as the perfect example of a good and upstanding character—well, as good and upstanding as one can be and still remain as an inmate. However, merely by the stroke of a pen, Ed found himself facing a cancellation of his model prisoner status and an increase in his length of stay.

The warden at the prison knew Ed's entire history. He knew where to get information even outside of what was turned over to the institution by the court upon a prisoner being incarcerated. He maintained his own private file on every inmate. Those who reported to him likened him to the founder of the FBI, J. Edgar Hoover. Hoover was an expert at digging up information on people and for several generations was acknowledged as the most powerful man in Washington. Whether the warden was aware that he mimicked Hoover is not known; the fact remained that he had detailed intelligence on those over whom he was given charge as custodian as well as those within his employ. The warden had sources beyond anything readily available to the prison personnel. He did not get where he was by following the rules. He knew how the game was played in an institution where politics was as much a major role as it is in any governmental entity. He knew who to step on to get what he wanted and he knew how to frame anyone who got in his way. Even when he had been a prison guard his sights had been set on eventually holding the highest position in administration—nothing was going to deter him from sitting in the warden's chair. When his predecessor had thought he had it made until his retirement some eight years away, he never counted on the power of this up-and-coming troublemaker who aspired to his job—this Kraut named Weiss.

There had always been some minor racial tension in the prison, this was nothing new. However, Weiss had managed to leak to the news media circumstances, which made it appear that a full scale riot was about to erupt by black prisoners claiming brutal conditions. Weiss had used his domination over the prisoners as well as the men who reported to him along with a promise of special favors, including access to illegal drugs, to get a large segment of the prison population to act under his direction. When a contingent of news people arrived at the prison and questioned the warden about the rumors of racial problems, the warden, who knew nothing about the underground plot, stated that his prison had had small skirmishes in the past but that any such rumors were absolutely ridiculous. Before the media left the prison buildings, a massive uprising commenced and the cameras were there to capture it all. The warden looked like a fool and his position was quickly terminated by the governor who announced that Captain Weiss would now be the acting warden for the facility.

Weiss had gotten what he wanted. He knew he would. He could be cruel to the point of being ruthless. In his new position, he worked the prison budget in his favor not only to get items, that he wanted in order to make the prison more to his liking, with furnishings for his office equal to that of a bank president, but also any little extras he needed at home. His feeling was that he had a tough executive job and he should be rewarded accordingly. His office was enlarged by the taking over of an adjacent office that had previously been assigned to the captain of the guards. The captain was given a new office by taking space that had been used as the guards' locker room. And space for the guards' new locker room was procured by cutting down the size of the inside recreation area for the inmates. The warden's office was then paneled with rich dark-oak walls that complemented the new furniture he had ordered. The old furniture was inherited by the captain of the guards and so it went down the line until everyone had something they had never had before. Warden Weiss had a new color television and stereo system installed in his office. These were necessities and not luxuries according to Weiss. Just because his predecessors did not have them was no reason to be ignorant of what happened outside the prison walls. Knowing what was taking place in the world was important and what better means to hear about that than by radio and television. Weiss had a reason for everything although no one ever questioned his actions.

It was not unusual for Brunkhorst, the large distributor of gourmet meats, to deliver quality Boar's Head products to the prison, nor for orders of Omaha Steaks to be brought in. Of course, these were not for the prisoners, only for the warden and his immediate staff. If one wanted to maintain control over one's staff, giving them a few of life's extras would go a long way to insure that control. Weiss used the same method of obedience training on his subordinates that most dog trainers use in teaching animals to respond to commands. That is, discipline the subjects harshly until their attention has been gained and there is no aggression toward the one in command. Then reward them with little things that are reasonable but that they might not readily get for themselves and the response will be a greater respect for the trainer.

Warden Weiss had come from a poor family. He had lived with his mother in cold-water flats, moving at intervals as new men came into her life or as the landlords pressed for back rent. There was no hot water in the bathrooms, no tubs and the toilets were generally in the hallway. Most flats were four to six-flight walk-ups. Only one ever had an elevator, but it never worked. Other nonpaying tenants were the rats and cockroaches that infested the buildings.

Weiss became familiar with the mobsters in his neighborhood who ran the prostitution, gambling and fencing of stolen goods. He saw how they operated and marveled at their strong-arm control. He learned early in life that if you wanted something, you went out and took it and no one took it away from you. In his neighborhood one had to be "rugged."

Weiss, like Ed, had been the product of a broken home. But, unlike Ed, the one who watched out for Weiss taught him life on the streets early and how to take care of himself. And take care of himself he did. He was a bully who thought nothing of inflicting enormous physical pain if it suited his needs or fulfilled his wants. He lived in a tough neighborhood. Gangs had not yet infiltrated this rough environment; in time they would come. But for now, Weiss was enough. He liked being in charge of his neighborhood, lauding it over those who lived there. He picked on the elderly as well as the youthful, the delinquents as well as those who were *connected*. He did not discriminate. He took from everyone without reservation. And no one challenged him because they feared reprisal. Going to the police was absolutely out of the question. Only once did someone even threaten to call for help. That person vanished and the only indication that Weiss was linked to his disappearance was the wristwatch Weiss now wore on his right arm to complement the one on his left—the same watch once worn by the man who disappeared.

Having such power, especially over the criminal element that permeated his city block, gave him the impetus to look for a way to make more money than could be found in this little locale. He saw some of those he knew end up in prison for their acts against society and jail was not for him. Maybe there was something he could do to legitimately make the money and gain the authority he needed to feed his ego. He thought there must be something out there where he could get paid to do what he enjoyed. His first inkling came when he saw a movie with James Cagney, where Cagney played a crooked warden in a prison. Weiss was impressed by what he saw. This type of power appealed to him and he kept this in the back of his mind. Although it had been more than a year since he watched that televised movie, opportunity would make itself available to Weiss. Perhaps it was fate or just pure luck when he spotted an ad in the newspaper for employment as a prison guard at one of New York's largest state prisons. He applied and was hired based solely upon his muscular build. It would not take long for him to move up in rank as he practiced his talent for maneuvering people to where they would best suit his needs.

Weiss never married. In fact, no woman would have dated him for very long. He was burly and unsmiling; women who came into contact with him found that his inner self was a reflection of that same unpleasant surface. He had no use for women, especially in the work place. To him they had no right being involved in jobs within penal institutions, even prisons designed to handle predominantly female residents. He was very vocal in his criticism of women anywhere in the employment field. To Weiss, they were the reason qualified men had not been hired in many positions; the women's rights advocates had forced changes in the law. As time progressed, more and more women were doing work that once was relegated solely to men. So, to Weiss, women were only good for one thing—to use as a means of satisfying a man's carnal desires. When he felt a need, he would make an arrangement with one of the call girls in the city. Through the years he had become well known among some of those who were involved in that business. Not many of them would take him on as a client because he enjoyed inflicting pain; their only consolation was that he paid well for his time. Using women in this manner, he was confident that he would never have to worry about commitments and he would never have the problem of anyone of the opposite sex milking him for his hard-earned money.

The cause for his disdain of women was an issue not too complex to those who deal with people suffering from emotional and psychological trauma. Weiss's mother had no time for him as a youngster. She had four other children, all by different men, to watch over. Her boyfriend, Weiss's father, floated in and out of her life at will—usually when his libidinous desires were at their peak. He was a gruff person, very demanding, and brutal in his treatment of her. She was weak and would submit to him without hesitation. In between his visits she took up with a number of men, first in hopes of finding one to marry her and take her away from this life, then in despair trading love for money in order to support herself and her kids. Although Weiss stayed home as a youngster with his mother, he grew to be more and more a clone of his father.

The warden had created his own little fiefdom and he was its lord and master—the king. To Weiss, the inmates had no value except to serve him. He made good on threats to those who did not follow his orders exactly. Most of the inmates feared him because in every instance he had the controlling hand. And it *was* fear, not the respect Weiss surmised. If the inmates had the opportunity they would dispose of him in an instant, but the warden was too well protected by those he intimidated in his chain of command. For a rough man, the warden was smooth and clever. He took advantage of every opportunity, especially those in which he could make money. And, in his position, he discovered over the years that there were a number of ways in which he could tap the system. But he also knew that the Internal Revenue Service would pick up on any savings bank deposits for which there were no corresponding 1099s or other tax-reporting forms. Part of his cleverness was in the fact that he hired his own auditor to examine the books kept by the staff accountant. In this way, none of the money missing from certain accounts within the prison system could ever be discovered.

When the telephone company was deregulated, private communications companies flocked to institutions knowing that they could offer legal kickbacks to those people with whom they contracted. In other words, when Commtel made arrangements for the prison to come on line with them, every time an inmate put money into the pay telephone to place a call, twenty percent of that money was returned to the Inmate Telephone Fund as a reward for doing business with Commtel. Three-quarters of that twenty percent would find its way to the warden and the remaining one-quarter would actually go into the telephone fund. Likewise, profits from the sale of items in the prison commissary were to go into the Inmate Commissary Fund. A similar percentage would be divided between the warden and the commissary fund. The profits were supposed to be used to pay for replacement of telephones, televisions and any other inmate comfort devices damaged accidentally or purposely by the inmates. But, because of the heavy hand by which the warden ran the prison, most inmates feared to a degree to incur the warden's wrath. Vandalism by the inmates was reduced to a minimum.

Having skimmed money off the top of the commissary and the telephone funds and having kept that money in cash for so many years, Weiss soon discovered that he needed a convenient place in which to hide it. The skimmed money was becoming extremely lucrative and the warden was determined to find a safe depository out of reach of the IRS. That safe haven was to come to him inadvertently. It happened one night as he was watching "20-20" on television. Barbara Walters was doing an investigative report about wealthy people hiding money in banks on the Cayman Islands. The Caymans, it seemed, are a nonreporting nation to the U.S. Department of Internal Revenue; moneys deposited in island banks remained concealed from anyone but the person or persons named on the account. As a bonus to helping people hide their money was the fact that the banks also paid interest on those funds that were placed in their trust. It was shortly thereafter that the warden began taking his annual vacations on Grand Cayman Island. Not even the warden's closest confidants would ever know his real reason for traveling to the Caribbean, although his trips to that area were not kept a secret. So self-assured was he in his covertness that he blatantly decorated his office with memorabilia and photographs of his visits to the island. His walls carried fishing trophies including a full-size carving of a very colorful parrot fish indigenous to that island area. It even boasted a certificate attesting to his prowess in operating power boats following a course he took in the Caymans during one of his vacations. Next to the framed certificate was an eight-by-ten photo of Weiss at the wheel of a forty-six-foot cabin cruiser. It did not belong to him, but the inference made by the photo was that it was his. Some of the staff secretly referred to the wall as the "me wall" as it was a constant reminder of Weiss's self-importance. It was as though he had some inner psychological need to show off his executive stature.

The state of New York has numerous penal institutions, many having been built during the middle and latter part of the nineteenth century. Its best-known modern facility is Attica, some distance from the institution under Weiss's command both in miles and in mode of operation. Like Attica, it has four major cell blocks identified alphabetically, all surrounded by high, concrete walls. Unlike Attica, it has one warden in charge of all phases of the facility. Attica has changed their staff nomenclature to be more in line with current thinking. No longer are they considered a prison but a correctional facility. The man who heads the administration is now known as the superintendent rather than the warden. He has deputy superintendents who report to him and who, each, have their own assigned duties. The men who direct or interact with the general inmate population are called corrections officers instead of prison guards. The duties remain the same but psychologically there is a difference.

Both institutions have a central station where control over the flow of inmate traffic is exercised as it is at a point where the corridors for the four cell blocks intersect. In Attica, it is known as Times Square; in Weiss's compound, it is called The Pit.

Attica has seen great progress since its construction at the beginning of the twentieth century. Cell Block D, which houses the toughest criminals, is the most up-to-date with clean, brightly painted walls and doors and appurtenances equal to those found in new apartment complexes. Conversely, Weiss's compound still has dark, dingy, barred cells, some with two buckets—one for clean water and one for waste, not too much different than Sing-Sing Prison, New York's oldest prison facility, with its outmoded dungeon environment.

By the time the warden was at the top of the administrative ladder, he still had a gnawing desire to do and to have more. Now, with Ed Fitzgerald in his prison, he had the chance to be set for life because he also knew Ed had access to an enormous sum of cold, hard cash. In only a few more years, the warden could retire. What would make a retirement more palatable than to have a significant amount of tax-free cash to accompany it? If he played his cards right, maybe, just maybe, he could find out where Ed put the money. If not, there was always the extending of his existing sentence due to Ed's aggressive and noncompliant behavior as purported by the warden and made credible by entries added to the daily activity log and entered into Ed's file. However, it did not take long for the warden to learn that Ed had a very strong and stubborn will. No matter what ploy Weiss used, Ed knew what the man was after. Soon Ed put Weiss in the same category as those who tried to investigate him so many years ago. Ed became silent once again. Needless to say, the warden was infuriated and initiated another change in Ed's life. Not only did Ed serve the twenty years, he was rewarded by being lost in the system as a nonentity. The warden managed to accomplish this just prior to his retirement. Knowing that he would never get the money he had coveted these past many years, he vowed to continue to keep pressure on Ed by informing the new warden, whose position came as a result of Warden Weiss's recommendation, of the "problems" he encountered with the prisoner and the fact that there was a substantial amount of money hidden somewhere on the outside.

Time passed slowly in prison, but Ed kept his resolve knowing that someday his real reward waited; after all, even without compound interest, two million dollars was still a lot of money.

The only visitors Ed ever received were his two former neighbors, Jim and Steve Cokkinias. The brothers had aged over the last few years and Jim, the oldest, had suffered a heart attack just after their last visit to the prison.

Early one October, they again came the long journey to the prison, having made the necessary arrangements to visit as required by prison protocol. Jim looked in fairly good shape for having such a challenge to his health. He had never really been overweight, but it was obvious that he had slimmed down since the last time Ed had seen him.

The brothers had sold their store as it had become too much of a burden for them to operate. They feared the strain on Jim's heart even though he objected at first to giving up what had been their livelihood since the end of the second World War when both had been in their twenties and aggressive enough to try going into business on their own.

The visits had been few and far between. After all, it was a long ride from Arlington to western New York State especially now that the men were growing older. But these were the only times Ed really looked forward to, and the brothers never complained about making the trek.

They used up their two-hour limit in mostly a one-way conversation, updating Ed on news from home. They joked with him, encouraged him, and never let their smiles leave their face. They had really been his best friends; in fact, his only friends. Ed's life offered very little in the way of change from visit to visit even with the long periods of time in between. After all, what could really change very much in prison? Same old, same old, as the saying goes.

The Key

With the advent of another new year, Ed resigned himself to his fate of institutionalized existence. The only positive in his life was the communication he received telling of an upcoming visit by the Cokkinias brothers.

Just a week before their arrival, he learned that Jim had suffered a fatal heart attack and the time he so looked forward to was now not to be. Even though Steve had prepared him for this eventuality, it still struck him hard as Jim was truly one of the only two people he cared about in life.

He was surprised when, a month later, Steve arranged to come out alone. In the few months that had passed since their last time together, Steve looked as though he, too, were a candidate for the funeral home. He was now very slow moving and kept asking Ed to repeat himself as they spoke through the telephone intercom on either side of the thick, plate glass which separated them physically from one another in the prison visitors' area. Steve's face was thin and drawn. Lines coursed like a road map in every direction and when he spoke it was like detours being formed on secondary roads. It might have been comical except for the pathetic seriousness of the situation.

"Steve," Ed called through the telephone handset as their visit together came to a close. "How are you doing?" He asked the question more out of courtesy than anything else. The answer was so evidently obvious.

"Okay," Steve replied, nodding his head slightly as he spoke.

"Are you gonna be all right? On your own, I mean."

"Yeah. Sure. Actually in some ways it's a little easier now. What I mean is I'll miss my brother, but it was . . . difficult for me lately . . . having to take care of him and all. Y'unnerstand?"

"I understand."

"Did I tell you, we moved? I mean, I moved."

"No. Really? Where?" Ed inquired.

"What?" Steve shook his head as if he had just realized someone was talking to him.

"I asked you where you moved."

"Oh, to Watertown . . . 25 Adams Street."

"Nice place?"

"I guess so. It's okay. It's not like Arlington though." Steve had a slight smile on his face as his eyes lifted and he went into a momentary daydream, thinking back to where he had lived for so many years. "All those years there, but I just couldn't afford the rent on my own. With my brother and me on Social Security, we had no problem, especially before his illness. But now . . . now being alone . . . I just can't swing it."

Then all of a sudden, as though he had been reenergized, Steve added quickly, "Aw, geez, what am I tellin' ya this for?"

"Hey, Steve, it's okay. Don't be embarrassed if that's what's botherin' ya."

"I guess I'd better be goin'. It's a long ride back and I find I get so I need to rest as I travel any distance."

"I want you to do me a favor, Steve."

"What is it?"

"Steve, I need your help. If anything should happen to me I need you to check on something for me."

The wrinkles on Steve's forehead contracted until they resembled a bas-relief map of the Rocky Mountains. "What is it you need me to do?"

"I want you to look up a friend of mine. I haven't seen her in years but she's holding some of my belongings."

"Okay. What and where?"

"Steve, you're gonna think I'm nuts, I know, but I want you ta look through your brother's things. I mailed him a letter years ago before I came to this place. In it I instructed him to open a second envelope, which was enclosed inside, only if something happened to me. I told him not to open it otherwise. And I told him to put the letter in a safe place. My name's not on it anywhere so no one would know it was from me. But Jim knew because I called him at the restaurant just before I mailed it and, besides that, he would recognize my writing. Anyhow, you've gotta find that letter. There's some information in it that can help you. I can't tell you everything right now but, believe me, it will give you everything you need right now and then some."

"What're you talking about?" Steve asked, a confused look on his face.

"Steve, just find the letter and open it. You'll understand once you've done that."

"Well, why don't you just tell me now?" Steve was all of a sudden more lucid than he had been the entire visit.

"Steve, please, I can't. Just trust me." The pleading was obvious in his eyes as he whispered these words over the intercom.

The announcement that visiting hours were over came just as Steve was about to make one last petition. He chose not to say anything more except, "See you when I see you." He stood up, gave a slight wave, and walked out of the cubicle.

It was three weeks later when Ed heard the news of Steve's death. The story was carried in the local newspapers, a copy of which came daily to the prison library. Steve had never made it home the night that he left the prison. His car was just discovered upside-down over the embankment on one of the descending roads from the rolling terrain which crisscrosses this part of New York State. The car, hidden from view because of the heavy growth and the deep precipice in which it had fallen, was discovered by some hikers. They were walking along the roadside and saw the reflection of the sun coming up from the base of the hill. The car's side mirror had caught the rays and was shooting them back toward the sky. The medical examiner determined that death had occurred nearly three weeks earlier and may have been the result of Steve's falling asleep at the wheel. From the amount of damage done to the car, there was no way anyone would have seen the deep indentation on the driver's side made just prior to the car going off the steep precipice. Another strange part of the denouement to the story was that Steve's apartment was broken into just one day after his death, although at that time no one knew he was dead. His only living relatives were residents of Silver Spring, Maryland, and they had not kept in close contact with the brothers over the years; it was not known what, if anything, might have been stolen.

The new warden—new being a relative term after so many years—was more belligerent and innovative than was his predecessor, Weiss. Realizing that Ed had no family and had had no visitors over the last several years, he treated him harshly knowing that there was no one to whom he could complain, especially being lost in the penal system records as one who did not exist.

The warden ruled with an iron hand and his staff did not dare to confront him on any issue. Ed could rely on no one to be his witness. Other inmates, as well, did not want to do anything to provoke the warden after seeing the suffering Ed had to endure. Few of the prisoners would even associate with Ed for fear of repercussions by the warden or his staff. Very unusual for a prison whose population included many hardened criminals who would think nothing of killing another inmate or who would force lewd, lascivious and vicious sex acts to be performed on or by other inmates as their physical needs required or desired.

Ed discovered only one friend during his prison tenure. Oddly enough it was one of the corrections officers. Arthur Booker was a tall, rugged black man whose physical being connoted a tough, no-nonsense demeanor but who, in fact, was a person of guarded compassion. He treated people according to the biblical commandment, "Do unto others as you would have them do unto you." If an inmate was a jerk, his entire stay would result in like response by the CO. If he was decent, he would receive a fair shake. The majority of prisoners lived up to their reason for being incarcerated, however. This *was* a dangerous place. The worst criminals in all of New York were locked up here—Mafia chieftains, cop killers, child murderers, serial killers, exploiters of children through pornography and prostitution, and torturers of children were among the population. Most would not have second thoughts in disposing of the guards or anyone else assigned to work there; they were just another cop as far as the inmates were concerned. The guards had to continually watch out for one another as well as keep one eye on their own backs.

CHAPTER SEVEN

Riot in the Prison

Arthur Booker began his career on Riker's Island in New York City. The prison which housed inmates serving up to three years for criminal acts was an island not far from LaGuardia Airport. It could only be reached by crossing a bridge from the mainland. Upon arrival, all visitors as well as employees had to park in a lot some distance from the high-walled, barbed-wire-topped facility. Access to the prison itself was by buses provided for just that purpose. Once inside the heavily guarded compound, the buses would stop at the various buildings, whether the men's division, women's, adolescent, or hospital, and leave off the people destined to go to each specific area.

Art had been working here for several years. His one goal was to complete twenty years and take advantage of a decent retirement. Sometimes, working in a city prison was less desirable than a state-run facility. Inmates would often act in a manner far more aggressive and hostile knowing that their stay could not be extended short of some significant or outrageous felony.

While there, several times Art had been subjected to having urine and feces thrown at him by disgruntled inmates. He had been spit upon and cursed at continually. When an inmate did not like his food, it might make its way as a decoration on Art's uniform. Art, like all other corrections officers, was a target.

Things had changed over the years. There had been a time not too long ago, when such actions were met with a swift and oftentimes harsh reprisal. An officer who had been violated might corral two or three other

COs and visit the offender's cell during the middle of the night. Taking with them their riot batons, they would taunt and poke at the inmate until he would retaliate even though he was outnumbered. Then the guards would take turns loosening teeth, smashing testicles or forcing one of the riot batons up the anal orifice. On occasion, especially if the incident involved the throwing of human waste by the inmate, the guards might stand in a circle around the beaten inmate and urinate on him as he lay in the center of his cell. He would be left to contemplate his action without benefit of shower, doctor or food for forty-eight hours—just long enough to learn a lesson. Corrections officers were proud of their uniforms and they bonded with one another like a family. It was all right if they found fault with each other, but never let an inmate put them to the test. The inmate would come out on the short end of the stick.

When the state opened applications for employment in the state prison in Western New York, especially with a higher rate of pay than that being offered by the city, Art gave it careful consideration. The greatest advantage other than a pay raise being the fact that they allowed for a lateral transfer without any loss of accrued time, and life in suburbia had to be better than in the Big Apple. Of course, real estate taxes were also substantially lower. With the exception that only in New York City could one find just about anything instantly available, all else about this possible relocation appeared to be a plus.

Art's wife, Lavina, encouraged him to apply for one of the positions. Her greatest fears in the city were its level of crime and its overwhelming traffic. She had seen enough of both. Art and his wife had grown up in one of the toughest sections of Harlem, between 136th Street and 148th Street. Drug dealing and gang wars were a way of life for many of the area residents. But not all agreed with that lifestyle. It seemed that the only way to combat it was to avoid it and the only way to avoid it was to escape—to move out of the neighborhood. Of course, that was not an easy undertaking. Moving cost money and those who wanted to leave lived there for only one reason—the lack of money to go anywhere else.

Had Art not been such a big man physically he might not have been able to beat the odds against his environment. And had he not been fortunate enough to meet the woman who was to become his wife, he might not have sustained that fortitude. Lavina had been brought up by parents who instilled in her the morals, ethics and values of a Christian culture. The family walked a great distance every Sunday just to attend church— the only one still in operation close by to their tenement. Gang activity, arson, and fear of walking the streets had closed down other houses of worship in the area. If fate had not taken a swipe at her family early on, they would still be living in the Bronx in more moderate conditions. However, an attack of spinal meningitis, which eventually took the life of her younger sister, caused her folks to lose all their savings as they did not have adequate insurance to pay the doctors and hospital bills. The only advantage to their current living conditions was the fact that she was able to meet Art. Both attended the same church and discovered, while walking to their respective homes one Sunday, that they lived within a block of one another. Before long they were dating. They found that they had much in common and it was not unusual for them to get into serious discussions on topics that led them into conversations that did not end until the wee hours of the morning. Her folks recognized the obvious signs of two people falling in love and were not surprised when their daughter announced through tears of joy that she and Art were engaged.

Getting out of the ghetto became the number one priority for Art and his fiancee. Working together they soon married and made their first significant step up the ladder of improvement. They moved to an apartment in Morningside Park, a section of the city just outside of Harlem. Art worked a variety of odd jobs until the opening at Riker's Island came about. His wife took a secretarial position with a stock brokerage firm and by pooling their money, they were able to move once again—this time to a home of their own in the Bronx. The home was fairly spacious and because they did not have any kids, Art suggested to Lavina that her folks move in with them and away from the neighborhood in which they just barely survived. Her parents readily accepted Art's offer and were thrilled at the prospect of moving to a much better location which, for the most part, was out of harm's way. They were settled in within a very short time. Both families established their own individual space and by not encroaching upon each other managed to live in harmony.

Art was also concerned about his own mother and had hoped to do something to get her away from the harshness of this part of Harlem. However, this would prove to be too great a challenge.

Art's mother had fought numerous bouts of pneumonia over the years but she was a stubborn woman and although not well, would not leave the tenement she called home. This was the only home she had known for most of her life and she remembered back to a time when this neighborhood was not such a bad place. Change, for her, was difficult so she refused to leave. Change came, however, as the pneumonia progressed to a point where she had to be hospitalized and it was not long before the final change came when she passed away. Although change was not something she had been willing to do, she did support her son in his decisions in life.

In all her years of living in this area of Harlem, Art's mother had been mugged only once. Surprisingly, the incident did not scare her but it infuriated her son. She had provided the police with a description of the man but it fit so many of the characters that lived in the city, the detective she spoke to gave her little hope in finding him and getting back the jewelry she had in her purse, let alone any of the money.

The mugging had taken place just after Art moved into the house in the Bronx. For a while Art felt guilty that he was not closer to her so that he could have run her errand and saved her from being a victim. It was only a couple of weeks later that she went into the hospital and died one evening as Art and his wife sat by her bedside. Art held his mother's hand as she slipped in and out of consciousness. He was such a giant of a man and she was so small and frail that her hand was lost in his. At one point, while she lay on the verge of death and was not responding to the small talk made by Art and Lavina, Art simply said, "I love you, Mama." Her subconscious must have heard him for she squeezed his hand with all the strength left in her body. It was the last thing she ever did.

Moving out of the city itself and finding a place near the state prison would be a big transformation for Art and his wife. It was made easier by the fact that his in-laws regarded Art as a hero for he found a way for them to collect Social Security, a benefit they had been sure was lost because of some confusion in employment records. However, due to Art's persistence, the problem was found and corrected. The second thing that influenced their decision was that her folks did not want to be a burden and hinder their move. In truth, they liked where they were now living and Art was very willing to work a deal so that they could remain in the house. With their Social Security, her folks could afford to help make the mortgage payments. This gave her parents a feeling of contributing and not so much like they were receiving charity—even though Art and Lavina never looked at what they were doing for her mother and father as charity. Art also thought how wonderful it would be on those occasions when he and his wife wanted to visit the city that they would have a place to stay and not be at the mercy and expense of a hotel. Anything decent in the downtown area was exorbitant; anything reasonably priced was miles outside of the city. With all this in his favor, it was only a matter of time before Art found himself having to look for a new home. He had received notice almost immediately of his acceptance as a state corrections officer. The transition would be made easier as there were two short indoctrination courses he was scheduled to attend in order to familiarize him with the operation of a state prison. He had no problem making the adjustment. Before long he was assigned to the men's section and worked the shift from one to nine p.m.

Art watched as numerous men were added to the prison population. And he watched as very few were ever released. Most of them were there for a long term. Some were there for the rest of their life. And, as anywhere in life, people become frustrated when their living conditions are negatively impacted by those who surround them. When that environment is amplified by a total loss of freedom, the adverse reactions become forcefully obvious. Such was the catalyst which brought about the occasion leading up to a bond between Ed and Art.

Ed continued in his behavior as a model prisoner even though he knew it would not help him gain his release. His twenty years had passed and he was still in the same cell. The wardon had puposely lost his records in the system. Every day was like every other day and no one seemed to notice and no one really cared. Any of his requests to the prison administration for intervention by the parole board or any outside agency were denied. He would be kept out of sight and out of mind and God help anyone on the staff or any inmate who might feel some compassion toward him. Ed would die of old age in prison unless he shared his secret with the warden. He was convinced that he would die there anyway as telling where he had hidden the money would not guarantee his freedom. His only hope was for a change in administrative personnel.

Ed often spent hours in the prison library poring over maps, reading the classics—which were hardly ever touched by other inmates—examining numerous reference materials and always paying close attention to the daily newspapers. On occasion he would visit the law library and read new court decisions and the latest updates in the legal system. He helped organize the library, would keep the library areas picked up and spotless and would deliver books to inmates. He also spent many hours in the woodworking shop during the year making toys to go to orphanages, group homes, shelters and the children in homes of other prisoners for Christmas.

Keeping busy in this way and remaining nonconfrontational, silent, and out of sight of others, he was left alone by the warden who had other more pressing jail issues to attend to. Ed's positive efforts were only recognized by the corrections officers who dealt with him daily. No one else took any interest in him. Even that shown by the COs was superficial, ending with the completion of each shift. All most wanted to do was to get through their eight hours without any problems.

Ed, having no one else to speak to, to confide in, or to discuss situations with, found Art, the newly arrived CO, to be a ready sounding board. Many times the current events he read in the library he would use to provoke discussions or arguments with Art. And, as Art was a recent hire in the prison, he took the time to get to know the men he was employed to watch. He knew the ones who were troublemakers and he knew the ones who stayed mostly to themselves. He accorded everyone a degree of respect and he expected the same in return. Some of the inmates responded in kind; others were wary of his attitude; and a few took advantage of his good nature. Art did not let a lot of things bother him and he was seemingly the only guard who did not partake in the bizarre revenge against unruly prisoners by other COs in their late-night escapades, many of which were witnessed by Ed over the years. Ed passed many hours in animated discourses with Art, often arguing points that were unimportant in their scope, but which honed his mind and kept it sharp as a razor's blade. Never was the subject of the armored company's money brought up by either man. Because of that, Ed placed his entire trust in Art, feeling that there was no ulterior motive in his friendship.

Two brothers, who had been incarcerated for their part in an armed robbery, which resulted in the deaths of a bank employee and a customer were serving equal time—life sentences—at the prison. Their criminal involvement records were lengthy and included a variety of felonious acts. They had been arrested previously for rape, assault and battery, burglary, theft, robbery, escape, and attempted murder. While in the state prison they were the cause of a reign of terror resulting in the injuries to several inmates as well as guards. After all, they had nothing more to lose and with so much time on their hands, they used it to concoct schemes against their caretakers.

The word was out through the inmate pipeline that the brothers were going to be separated. One would remain in their present cell while the other was to be transferred to a different section of the prison complex. Here is where the administration made a mistake. Instead of moving one of the brothers during a time when all the inmates were locked down, they chose to make the move when the prisoners were out of their cells and on their way to the recreation yard or gym. The response by the inmates was fast and direct, as if they had known what was about to take place. More than likely they had been tipped off by a guard who was on the take from one or more of the prisoners. Because some of the inmates had connections outside the prison with access to money, drugs and women, they could make deals with a few of the guards in exchange for cash, narcotics or sexual favors. Once this took place, a convict owned a guard for as long as the guard remained at the prison.

Just before the transfer was to take place, some of the prisoners moved with military-like precision as numerous other inmates went to various appointed posts within the block of cells to undertake their strategy.

The guards were overpowered by more than two dozen inmates armed with handmade knives and shivs, fashioned from scraps which would not be missed from the metalworking shop and concealed within their shoes—the only place not vulnerable to the metal detector. One of the brothers grabbed the keys from a CO and the men took over one of the sections of the men's division. Had the prison undergone some modernization, the use of keys, except during a power failure, would have been replaced by an electronic locking system. Better control over the inmates would have been the result and there would have been less exposure to a potentially hazardous situation. Although there were more than three hundred men in this section, no one outrightly opposed what was happening. All of them feared the brothers and their followers. There were eight leaders, just enough to control the rest of the men.

A captain and four corrections officers were tied up with strips of bed sheets and blindfolded. All were brought into one of the cells where two of the inmates guarded them. They were kicked and punched and struck with wooden clubs smuggled into the cells from the carpentry shop.

Moments before this, at the beginning of the takeover, one of the COs had tried to wrestle a blade out of the hands of one of the inmates but instead the knife was thrust by accident into the lower chest of Ed Fitzgerald who had tried to remain out of the conflict but just happened to be in the wrong place at the wrong time. Ed was pushed into his cell where he collapsed onto the floor, doubled over. When Ed's cell mate, Tom Fowler, tried to escape the battle by running to their cell, he was hit over the head by one of the nightstick-wielding prison guards and knocked unconscious. Both men now lay in their cell.

In making demands of the administration, the brothers yanked three of the COs up to the third floor of cells and tied lengths of bed sheeting around their necks. The opposite ends they tied to the railing on the third-level tier, which was there to prevent anyone from falling to the concrete floor below. Unless their demands were met, the COs would be thrown from the railing where they would die hanging by their necks.

The only CO who was not abused was Art Booker, the one guard to have gained the respect of both the guards and the prisoners. He was tossed into the cell with Ed Fitzgerald and Tom Fowler where he would be away from the battle taking place.

The captain was cut several times by the inmates as he had been cruel to many of them over the years. The prisoners remembered the occasion when an inmate complained about the food he was given not having enough variety, he was put on a special diet for a week as punishment. He was served squash for breakfast, lunch and dinner. When the inmate protested and went on a hunger strike demanding a change, the captain offered him a *change* and brought a full meal of chicken, potatoes and peas to the inmate's cell. He then shackled the inmate to his bunk. The captain then urinated on the meal and pinching closed the inmate's nose so that he had to open his mouth to breathe, the captain shoveled spoonfuls of the soggy, tainted food down the inmate's throat. When the inmate began to vomit, the captain scooped up spoonfuls of the regurgitated food and again forced it into the inmate's mouth.

Similar punishments were cast upon other inmates in various situations. They did not forget. Now it was time for some retribution. The prisoners tied the captain's feet with a length of sheeting and attached the other end to the rail. They tossed him over the side so that he hung up-side-down, facing the concrete floor, three stories below. He would be the first to die when they cut the sheet that held him in place if they did not receive satisfaction to the demands of the two brothers. Most of the inmates volunteered to cut the tether as they wanted the pleasure of watching the captain's head explode like a pumpkin or watermelon as it hit the ground floor.

The prisoners were prepared for a standoff, not a long siege however as evidenced by the actions they had taken. During the midst of the takeover, toilet bowls were ripped from their stands and thrown down from the balcony at the guards below, forcing them out of the block. Along with those half-dozen guards who were injured when they tried to enter the block to quell the riot, seventy-three inmates were injured at the time of the takeover.

Back inside Ed's cell, blood oozed from between his fingers as Art tried to maintain pressure on the large gaping wound just beneath the area of Ed's heart. Ed's lung had been punctured. However, the rhythmic pulsation of each beat forced the blood flow to continue.

"I know it's bad," Ed gasped with a raspy voice hardly audible between the clamor outside his cell and the result of his failing physical condition.

"Yeah, it's bad, but you gotta hang tough," Art replied. "You gotta be angry. Angry enough to fight for your life."

"I just don't have the strength," Ed responded.

"Don't give me that, man! I've seen you hold out on stupid, little things. This is a thousand times more important."

Ed replied, "Art, you've been my only friend here. I'm going to miss our conversations. I want you to know that." Ed stopped speaking for a moment in order to gain some strength and then he continued, "I really appreciate that you made time for me." Ed's face contorted in a grimace of pain and then he began to hack as though he was clearing his throat. However, small streams of blood leaked like drool from the corner of his mouth. Laying there with his head propped on Art's knee as Art continued to cover the hole in his friend's chest, Ed tried to force out more words but they became increasingly inarticulate.

"I'm going to be leaving here but not the way I wanted," Ed whispered as little bubbles formed in the blood oozing from his mouth each time he expelled a bit of air. "I want . . . you . . . to have it."

"Have what, Ed?"

"The money."

"The money? . . . What money?"

"You must know by now . . . what money . . . I'm talking about." In between every few words, Ed stopped. He needed to get a breath and the supply of air was short in his lungs. Air bubbles also began to escape between Art's fingers with every intake of breath even as he held pressure onto the wound in Ed's chest.

"You mean the money you're supposed to have taken and hid years ago? You're telling me it's never been recovered?" Art asked.

Art detected a nodding of Ed's head in response. What Art did not see were the open eyes of Tommy Fowler, Ed's cell mate, who had been unconscious on the floor of the cell after the melee. Nor could he tell how intently Fowler had been listening to their conversation.

Just two weeks before, Fowler had stood before the State of New York Board of Parole and had been granted a release, which was to take effect within the month. He had served ten years for his part in an armed robbery and he was about to get out early. Both the current warden and Weiss, who had retired just a few years before, had given Fowler a glowing report, which carried significant weight with the parole board. Fowler had become the warden's snitch. It was the primary reason he had been placed as Ed's cell mate. The warden was not a person to give up easily, especially where two million dollars was at stake. Fowler had purposely remained uninvolved in the prison standoff knowing that his freedom depended upon his apathy toward his fellow prisoners. Nothing was going to interfere with his gaining access to the outside world.

Ed labored to speak. He would open his mouth forming the words on his lips, but could emit nothing. Art drew his right ear as close as he possibly could to Ed's face trying to make some, if any, recognizable sense out of what Ed was struggling to communicate.

"Tarpon . . . ," Ed breathed.

"Tarpon?" Art asked. "You mean, like the fish?"

"Reef . . . twelve miles . . . the key. . . ."

"I don't understand. What are you saying?"

"See . . . Gabrielle. . . ."

Ed stopped trying to speak. It was as though he wanted to gather up all his strength in order to get the last bit of information out.

"She has my books," Ed managed to gasp.

"I still don't understand," Art stated. "What has all this got to do with fish?"

Using the last of his strength, Ed pushed out the following words: "No! . . . Tarpon! . . . Greeks!"

Art began to speak again when he realized the blood had stopped flowing from beneath his hand. His friend was dead.

The New York State Police were called in and an immediate lockdown was put into effect for the rest of the prison. An expert police negotiator was brought down from Rochester and within hours a truce was established. For now, the brothers who had been at the core of this riot would be allowed to return to their cell. Although some promises were made, both the inmates and the prison personnel knew such an agreement was worthless. Temporarily, though, it would serve to satisfy both sides of the opposition.

As was usual practice following any serious event at the prison, a debriefing was held in the guard room. Everyone of the guards who had been involved in the melee gave statements as to what had taken place. Each was commanded to write a report of the incident and all were advised what they could and could not say if asked questions by anyone outside of the prison chain of command. Interrogatories by the media were to be directed to the prison warden. Following the debriefing at the prison, once the status was returned to normal and the lockdown of all inmates had taken place and a thorough search was made of all cells for any types of weapons, all Art could think about were Ed's words.

When Art was asked by the warden during the debriefing if the prisoner, Fitzgerald, had uttered anything during the last few moments of his life, Art simply responded by saying, "No."

Ed's body was removed from the prison by a local funeral parlor following an autopsy, which was completed at the prison by the doctor who also served as a medical examiner.

Art was surprised at being called into the warden's office following the debriefing. What surprised him more was seeing not only the warden but the previous warden who had retired just a few years ago. Both seemed unusually interested in the circumstances surrounding the death of inmate Ed Fitzgerald. Both had a number of questions as to any conversation that may have taken place between the prisoner and the guard. Again, Art was cautious not to appear curious nor inquisitive as he gave the same one-word answer, "No."

"You mean to tell me," the previous warden queried with a look of disbelief on his face, "that in three hours time in his cell, he told you nothing?"

"That's correct, sir," Art lied.

"Not one word?"

"Look, Warden," Art began, "I tried to help inmate Fitzgerald, but his lung was punctured. He could hardly breathe, let alone speak. Several times it looked like he was trying to mouth some words but nothing came out, not even a whisper. I don't know what you expected him to say. I mean, the man was dying. . . ."

"Okay, Officer Booker. I have nothing more. You're free to leave. Thank you for your time."

Art was dismissed from his interrogation with words that sounded as though they were part of a well-rehearsed rote speech that could have fit any of several occasions.

Art did not notice as he walked from the warden's presence, Tom Fowler, his head bandaged, standing in the shadows of the anteroom outside the warden's office.

CHAPTER EIGHT

A Proposal

That evening, Art sat at his supper table telling his wife only a little of what had taken place. Situations like this—ones that involved confrontations at work with the inmates—were generally not their usual topics of conversation. And, like many people involved in law enforcement and corrections, it was not always comfortable to discuss these things with anyone except the people with whom they worked—people who understood incidents such as these. Lavina knew not to push for too much. She had learned over the years what to say and what to avoid. Instead, she just listened and when he got around to the topic of Art's conversation with Ed, she suggested he write down what he had been told. Maybe together they could make some progress in solving the puzzle.

"Hand me that note pad next to the telephone, would you please, honey?" Art asked.

Taking a ballpoint pen from his pocket, he started to write. He had no problem recalling the words: Tarpon, fish, Gabrielle, reef, Greeks, twelve miles, books, the key. He looked at the list and shook his head. He looked at the list again and crossed out the word fish, knowing that that was his word and not Ed's. When he had said "fish" the second time, Ed had said emphatically, "No!" Again saying, "Tarpon" and "Greeks."

Art told his wife what little he knew about Ed's background. His reason for being in jail was his conviction for the theft of more than a million dollars from an armored car company.

"He told me he wanted me to have the money," Art stated. "It must still be out there somewhere."

She responded with, "But how many years ago was that and, if there is any money, doesn't that belong to the armored car people?"

"More than twenty years ago, babe, and let me tell you about who owns the money. Technically, the armored car company no longer has an interest because the bonding company would have paid off the sum in its entirety." Art paused for a moment and then said, "Do you remember when you had to go into the hospital for surgery on that woman-thing you all eventually have to go through?"

"You mean my hysterectomy?"

"Yeah, whatever. Anyhow, do you remember what the hospital charged you for that operation?"

"I should think I do. We're still paying on it."

"And why are we still paying on it, babe? Because the insurance company would not pick up the charges where I had only been at work for a couple of months. That was eight thousand dollars that shoulda been covered. If it had not been an emergency and we coulda waited just two months more, the insurance company would have picked up eighty percent of the tab. The bonding company works with insurance companies so, in effect, they are the ones to whom the money belongs."

"So, you think it's okay to keep the money because of what the insurance people did *not* do for us?"

"You said that, I didn't." He again paused for a moment, letting his words sink in, and then he said, "As in everything else, you read my mind."

"Honey," she said, "you've never thought of taking something that didn't belong to you. Why would you want to change now?"

Art stayed quiet for a moment.

"I'll tell you what I'll do," he finally said. "I'll investigate, see if I can find out what armored car company and what insurance company, and then see if they will offer a reward should the money be found."

"I could live with that," she said.

8—8— —8 —8

Feeling a little guilty making phone calls on company time but wanting to satisfy his wife's qualms, Art made inquiries based upon information he found in Ed's prison records. Being somewhat sketchy in their content, Art decided to call the keeper of records at the Middlesex County Courthouse in Massachusetts where Ed's trial had taken place. It took the clerk, who sounded annoyed at having to research through the court's repository, nearly an hour to find the old case file. She was not very pleasant when she returned Art's call—collect. Had he not been a corrections officer, and working on what must have been official business so far away from where the courthouse was located, there was no doubt in Art's mind that she would not have been this helpful.

Art discovered that Union-Pacific Armored Service had been sold out to Brinks, Inc., shortly after the theft had taken place. When he contacted the current owners, Art was told that the old records had been filed in the company's archives and, after closing the Arlington office and moving to a new facility, all the out-of-date materials had been discarded.

In trying to determine the insurance carrier, those records evidently were long gone as well. The court records had listed the name of the insurance company. Art called the state bureau of insurance only to discover that the insurance company was now defunct. According to their records, there were no documents showing any takeover by another company and no references made to any bonding company. Twenty years was a long time and a number of changes had taken place. Suddenly Art was filled with a feeling of exhilaration. It was like being one of the many people who hope they may hold the winning ticket to the New York State Lottery. If the combination of numbers was right, one could be a millionaire.

After giving his wife the latest news of his discoveries, a peculiar smile formed on her lips. Even the possibility, as remote as it might be, made her tingle with excitement.

She went to the rolltop desk where she had stored away the note pad with Ed's last words. Bringing it into the living room, she sat down on the couch next to Art and she asked him once again what he remembered of his fragmented conversation with Ed.

"The only thing that makes any sense to me," Lavina said after listening to Art's words, "is the Tarpon and Greeks. It has got to be Tarpon Springs down in Florida 'cause that's a Greek community. But as far as the books and the key and the woman's name, that could be anything. And the reef . . . twelve miles from where? I don't know. I just don't know what any of that could mean."

"Would you think," Art asked, "that a little vacation to that area of Florida would give us some insight as farfetched as it seems with so little to go on?"

"Well, we have been to Disney World and MGM—which, by the way, had my favorite ride."

"I know . . . I know . . . The Tower of Terror," Art interjected. "I still can't get over the fact that you made me ride that with you seven times in one day. Do you realize how much time we spent sweating in that long line waiting over and over to get back onto that ride?"

"And you're gonna tell me that it wasn't worth it? You, who acted like a little kid laughing and screaming. . . . Don't you look at me like that! Yes . . . you . . . screaming. . . . I watched you very carefully after all your moaning and complaining of, 'Oh, not again.' You enjoyed that ride as much, if not more, than I did."

"Don't I love it when I get you stirred up," Art replied, grinning.

"Well, you must. You do it so often. Anyway, we have seen some fabulous sights, why don't we check out the other sites? I know that Busch Gardens is over in that area close to Tarpon Springs."

"Hey! Forget the professional entertainment for a minute. When did you ever pass up a chance for some time alone with me," he shyly smiled at his wife, "and have a vacation to Florida to boot?"

They both giggled like little children knowing that each of them needed the time to be intimate, away from the rat race of the city and the pressure of work.

"You know," said Lavina, "besides some relaxation, maybe this might just produce something more, even with what little information we do have."

"Somehow I thought you might agree. I'll arrange for vacation time and take care of everything."

CHAPTER NINE

The Search for Clues

Art and his wife landed at Tampa's International Airport on a steamy, hot August afternoon. Lavina's makeup began to run the minute they hit the street, and it was only a short time before Art's clothes were drenched with perspiration. The flight had seemed long only because they were in a hurry to start on their treasure hunt. The temperature was in the mid-nineties but overhead, gathering clouds promised a hint of relief. Picking up a rental car at Alamo on a package deal made through AAA, they consulted their map before heading to Tarpon Springs.

It was as they were crossing the seven-mile bridge connecting Hillsborough County to Pinellas County, nature put on the most brilliant light show that Art and his wife had ever seen. Multiple flashes of lightning illuminated the sky and reflected off of the bright, white shine of their rented Ford Taurus. Nature displayed some magnificent colors across the sky as the lightning had its affect on the atmosphere and the dark clouds that dwelled in it. Hues of lavender and blue, gold and pink, covered the sky with each flash. Even above the rushing noise of the car's air conditioning could be heard the enormous claps of thunder. The rain came down in torrents slowing their progress to the motel they had reserved.

"This might be a great night to cuddle," Lavina said as she reflected upon the wind, rain, thunder and lightning surrounding their car.

"You make me laugh," Art began with a smile on his face. "Why is it you always get so . . . ," he paused, making his shoulders kind of roll as he thought of the word he wanted to use, "sensual, when foul weather threatens?"

"You mean like the times when it snows so heavy and I insist we put a log in the fireplace and snuggle up on the couch?"

"Yeah. You always have to shut off all the lights and open the curtains to watch the snow come down. I hate to be reminded that I've got to shovel that stuff."

"How soon you forget!" she exclaimed, smirking. "You're the one who insisted we build a large bathroom with a huge window so that we could have that spa put in. And for what purpose? So that we could soak in the hot water while looking at the snow falling outside. Tell me, what's the difference? You had to shovel the snow then—or, did you not remember that?"

"Oops," Art said with the smile now overtaking his face. "Well, maybe I'm just getting older and that cuddly stuff is for the younger generation."

"*Really?*" she said sarcastically. "Well, if that's the way you truly feel, maybe I ought to sign you into a nursing home now and look for someone *much* younger."

"Wow! You really are taking me serious, aren't you?" he said.

"I just know that I'm not the only one who enjoys snuggling and cuddling. You never seem to complain when you want your back rubbed or when I wrap my arms around you, especially when the weather turns cold!"

"Why do you always have to be *right*? And how do you always manage to remember everything? But now that you mention it, that plane ride was somewhat stressful on my back, so maybe you wouldn't mind just rubbing it a little?"

"*What!* Forget it! You took the whole mood out of me. You want your back rubbed? Do it yourself."

"Aw, c'mon, babe, you know I was only kidding with you," Art said with a sheepish look.

"Don't think I'm gonna fall for that. I'm used to your tactics and that look's not gonna work this time."

"But, babe . . ."

"Don't you 'but, babe' me. You dug your way into this hole, now you can struggle to work your way out." With that she turned her head away from him and looked out the side window at the pouring rain. What Art could not see was the self-confident smirk and half-closed eyes on Lavina's face. She knew she was in control.

A few minutes elapsed and then Art spoke, "I'm sorry, honey. You know how I sometimes say the dumbest things 'cause I open my mouth without taking the time to think. I don't want you mad at me now, especially where we're here on vacation and working together on this project."

Still looking away, his wife's head began to bob, almost a nodding, as she realized once again there was no contest in this interchange between herself and Art. She won, as usual. Ever since they first dated she maintained a dominating hold over him that no one else would ever have. And she loved having that power. She would let him suffer for a while but eventually she would concede to his request, but on her terms. In the meantime she said, "We'll see what the evening brings."

They pulled into the Best Western Tahitian Resort on U.S. Highway 19 in Tarpon Springs. They discovered that in Florida the word route is not used to designate major roadways as it is in the north. Art parked in front of the lobby doors and shut off the engine. He then went in to confirm their registration at the desk while his wife wilted for those several minutes in the car in the extreme heat of the season. When they finally checked into their room and felt the coolness of the air conditioning, they both forgot the heat and humidity. It took the edge off their already anxious state and they wanted to waste no time in checking out the community. The rainstorm, however, would be a hindrance on this night as Art was almost night-blind in any kind of storm, so they decided to have supper, get some rest and start out fresh in the morning. As they lay in the king-size bed in their room, Lavina did concede to rubbing his back. With his head turned away from her, he smiled to himself before he fell asleep. He was gloating in the knowledge that he had connived his backrub out of her by letting her think she had won their playful spat.

※ ※ ※ ※

The brightness of the morning sun pouring through their window awoke them a little after seven o'clock. It promised to be a gorgeous day. They got up, showered and dressed, ate a quick breakfast of pancakes, eggs and sausage at a nearby Golden Corral, and following the directions given to them by the motel desk clerk, drove down to the sponge docks. This was the heart of Tarpon Springs.

The route they took brought them down Pinellas Avenue past St. Nicholas Greek Orthodox Church, which was just north of Tarpon Avenue at the intersection of Orange Street. It was here that a sign in front of them directed them to the sponge docks. They turned left on Dodecanese Boulevard in front of Pappas's Restaurant. It was early yet so there was still room in the private parking lots even though all the spaces on the street were full. The right side of the street had just a few gift shops and small eateries as that side bordered the waterway where the docks were located. Looking across the waterway, they were amazed at the number of boats moored on that side of the inlet. The craft ranged in size from sixteen-foot runabouts to an eighty-two-foot, three-masted schooner.

They chose to park in a lot about halfway into the old tourist and business district on the left-hand side of the street, paying two dollars for all-day parking. On this side of the street were the larger shops, restaurants and spacious parking lots. Before getting out of the car, they flipped a coin to determine which direction they would walk first.

Approaching the street they turned to their left and meandered down past the greater variety of shops and restaurants, which filled every available space. The crowds were beginning to come early.

They acted just like typical tourists as they wandered in and out of several quaint shops picking up some trinkets as memorabilia for their visit; things they could look at and reflect on years from now. At the end of the avenue, they crossed to the opposite side nearest the docks but quickly reversed their direction as they caught sight of a rather new tour boat called the *Island Princess*.

Taking advantage of a five-dollar-per-person, one-and-one-half-hour tour of the coast, they climbed on board and awaited their departure. As the boat pulled out from its berth, the first mate, whose name was Takis according to the tag on his jacket, came out onto the forward deck from the air-conditioned dining and drinking area. Art approached him and asked him if there was a reef between Tarpon Springs and the open water of the Gulf of Mexico.

In a very thick Greek accent, Takis replied that he had been working the waterway for more than ten years and was very familiar with the charts leading to and including the Gulf. There were no reefs to be found.

Art then asked him if there was the possibility of a reef somewhere twelve miles off shore.

Again, Takis answered in the negative before walking away to respond to the call of another passenger.

"Why would Ed have said there was a twelve-mile reef if one doesn't exist?" Art's wife asked.

"There has to be one," Art responded. "It wouldn't make sense for him to tell me that without there being one, especially in his condition as he was trying to get out as much information as he could before he died."

"So what do we do now?" she asked.

"I don't know. I just don't know," Art replied with a frown.

Feeling disappointed but not discouraged, Art and Lavina decided to find someone more intimate with the coastline. For some people, this would have been a point to give up the quest. However, in Art's line of work, stamina and perseverance are a must, especially when one realized that it is always a challenge to deal with lots of angry inmates.

Returning to the docks following their voyage, they crossed over to the Hellas Restaurant and sampled some of the local Greek fare. Their breakfast had worn off and they were getting hungry. Looking at the number of people in line waiting to be seated in the restaurant, there was no doubt this would be a two-meals-only day. It was now mid-afternoon and their casual dining seemed to extend toward the early evening. When they finished their desserts of baklava with its honey and crushed walnuts, and galactombouriko—a custard and honey mixture in a light fillo shell—they left the restaurant and continued toward that part of Tarpon Springs they had not yet explored.

They crossed the street once again to where the sponge boats take tourists out on a deep sea adventure, watching as the divers collect their rubbery prizes. They stood and waited as the divers for the older and more popular of these ventures brought their boat toward the mooring.

As the dock workers lowered the narrow gangplank for the tourists to depart the sponge-diving boat, aptly named the St. Nicholas, Art saw someone who looked vaguely familiar to him. A cold shiver ran up Art's spine, the same kind he would get in those times when there was going to be trouble at the prison. The man glanced furtively in his direction and then quickly walked away so as not to confront him. For a moment Art puzzled over where he might have seen the man before and his eyebrows furrowed as he tried to concentrate on the man's identity. There was something about him that Art recognized, but he could not put his finger on exactly what it was.

Their attention being drawn to some of the crew now leaving the boat, Art and Lavina climbed on board. They were greeted by the captain who said that there would not be any more tours until morning as the day was now late.

Art again posed his question concerning the reef. The captain looked at him curiously without responding. Art thought that perhaps the Greek captain did not comprehend his question so he asked him the same thing once more, speaking slowly and gesturing with his hands in the form of a description as he spoke.

The captain said, "I understand you. I am just wondering why there is such a great interest in a reef, which does not exist."

"What . . . do you mean, 'such great interest'?" Art asked.

"You are the second person to ask me that question within the last twenty minutes."

"What! Who asked you that?"

"One of the passengers who just left my boat asked me the very same question."

"Do you know who he was? Which way did he go? What did you tell him?" Art asked excitedly, with all three questions coming out in one breath.

Still looking perplexed, the captain answered slowly, "No. I do not know him, and he just passed you walking over there to my left." The captain pointed with his finger in the opposite direction from which Art and his wife had come. "And I told him the same thing I told you . . . there is no reef."

Reading each other's minds, Art and his wife stepped quickly off the ramp, waved a thank you to the captain, and walked swiftly toward the spot where they had last seen the fast-moving man. He had disappeared behind one of the many gift shops bordering the street. He had almost been at a run when he vanished from sight behind the 99-Cent Store and through the alleyway, which led to the Spongeorama with its museum and twenty-plus little shops. They tried splitting up to cover the front and back of the stores but it was fruitless; the man was simply gone.

Art stopped into the sponge museum and walked quickly up and down the short corridors, which divided each of the displays. Here was a depiction of the sponge industry from its earliest days in the Mediterranean waters off the coast of Greece to the most modern diving techniques—methods that were really not too different today from those used many years ago. Art then opened the door to the free movie being shown on sponging in Tarpon Springs, disrupting the people who were fascinated by this bit of knowledge they would never have before known. Still nothing. He asked the very corpulent proprietor of the museum's sponge shop—Angelo, according to the name tag on his shirt—if he had seen anyone fitting the description of the man being sought but he said that no one like that had come into his place of business.

Art and Lavina walked back and forth through the alleyway several times and then back along the street but it was getting dark and they still were having no luck in locating him.

"Whoever he is," said Art to his wife, "he knows less than we do." Then he said, "And believe it or not, I think I know *who* he is."

"Who?" she asked.

"Other than his missing beard and mustache and his somewhat longer hair, and the fact that he's wearing sunglasses, I believe that is inmate Fowler, Ed Fitzgerald's cell mate."

"His cell mate? What is he doing out of prison?" she queried, anxiety showing in her voice.

"He was released on parole. The interesting thing is that if it is him, he is here in Florida. Parolees are not allowed to travel out of the state where they were imprisoned. That's why, at first, I wasn't sure if it was him."

"How would *he* know to come to Tarpon Springs? Did Ed tell him something, too?"

"I don't think so but I do know he was in the cell at the time of the hostage-taking. He had been knocked unconscious."

"Could he have heard everything that Ed had to say?"

"I don't know. I don't see how he could have. I practically put my ear into Ed's mouth just to be able to make out what he was trying to tell me."

As they spoke, they failed to notice the ninety-nine-cent Tarpon Trolley, which gives tours of the area, pass by them on the avenue. On board, seated so as to not easily be seen but to watch carefully what was going on around him, was Tom Fowler. He stared at them as the wooden bus, made to look like an old-time streetcar, went down Dodecanese Boulevard.

Walking back to the parking lot and their car, Art and Lavina returned to their motel feeling that they would most likely come across Fowler again the next day.

CHAPTER TEN

A Chance Discovery

The day began as a carbon copy of the day before. Somehow, Fowler had heard just enough in that prison cell to have reached the same deduction as Art and his wife. Otherwise, there was no way he could have guessed Tarpon Springs.

Spending the entire day repeating the steps taken the day before, Art and Lavina again noticed the different smells coming from the eateries. This enticed them toward one of the more quaint Greek restaurants. Art was starved all of a sudden.

"Man, these resorts make a killing off of us dumb tourists," Art's wife said as she looked over the posted menu.

They both chuckled and Art said, "Who cares? I'm starved!"

"Since when don't you care about spending money?"

"Since I'm starved," he replied.

They entered a small restaurant adjacent to the docks. It was not just small, but tiny. There could not have been more than eight tables, yet the place was packed in the middle of the afternoon. As they looked around, they also noticed that the walls were covered with pictures, paintings and artifacts from Greece. The upper portion of one of the walls was painted a dark blue, an obvious representation of the Gulf of Mexico, with no less than a dozen characters in various stages of sponge diving from three separate boats. The drawings were so well done that Art and Lavina were captivated for several minutes as they examined the work from where they stood. A waitress approached them and said that it would be about thirty minutes before they could be seated. They reasoned that the food must be good and decided to wait the amount of time it would take for a table. Their attention, once again, was drawn to the painted wall.

In less than twenty minutes they were seated at a table overlooking the harbor. First, they ordered appetizers—a variety of items written in Greek in the menu with no explanation other than the waitress being aggressively affirmative by saying, "You like. . . .You like," and two glasses of retsina—a Greek wine made from grapes but with the addition of tree resin. The waitress tried to explain the reason that resin was added to the wine, but in her broken English, neither Art nor Lavina could understand. So they just nodded politely to her as though her explanation made sense to them and that seemed to satisfy the girl. Once sampled, they quickly agreed that the wine was something one had to acquire a taste for.

From their vantage point, they watched the boats returning to their slips along the dock. The sun was low in the western sky and shone as a full, brilliant orange ball as they looked out of the restaurant window. Being on the west coast of Florida afforded them a superb view of the sun disappearing beyond the horizon.

The food was out-of-this-world good. They enjoyed lamb shish kabobs and rice pilaf along with a salad and then ordered some ouzo as an after-dinner drink.

"Whoa!" Art exclaimed as he took his first sip of the liquor, which he watched so many other patrons drinking. "This is potent! I can't even feel my lips. They're burning!'

"Good thing you decided to sip it," Lavina responded. "I've had it before. I like it. Once you have a few tastes, your mouth will become accustomed to it. You'll see."

"When did you become such an expert on ouzo? And when did *you* have it before? We've never had it anywhere that I have been."

"Mmmm . . . hmmm. Are you getting jealous—thinking that maybe I've been out with some Greek guy and shared ouzo?" she asked as she moved her head from side to side and smirked.

Art just sat and stared at her, his face deadpan. He made no comment but waited to see what else she would say.

"You are something else," Lavina finally said. "It was at the party given by the warden a few years ago. Don't you remember? I told you I tried a drink that tasted like licorice and you kept saying it was that drink they put the coffee beans in—sambuca, I think it's called. I told you it wasn't but you wouldn't listen. It was ouzo."

"Oh, yeah. I vaguely remember that. Okay, I'm sorry to have jumped to conclusions. I really do trust you and should have known better than to think any different."

She just shook her head.

The ouzo, more than the food, seemed to have elevated Art's spirits a bit. However, his wife was more tempered in her feelings. Her thoughts were that they had tried their best, had looked everywhere and had found nothing. She was reaching the lowest point of discouragement. Three days had passed with nothing more to go on. There was no one else to ask, no more clues to make any sense of, no where else to turn or to look. She made a resolution, enhanced by the fact that even Fowler was no longer to be seen, to stop their wild-goose chase. The money was obviously never to be found.

"Well, babe, a penny for your thoughts?" Art asked as he watched Lavina obviously deep in thought.

"I hate to give up; you know that. I just don't know where to turn from here. I mean, I thought perhaps the clues we had would give us better direction. Maybe it was just wishful thinking. I guess I hoped it would be easier."

"I hear ya. I must've been thinking the same thing. I don't know why I would have expected things to just fall into our laps, but it just seemed they would. Maybe I really only wanted a vacation and this felt like a good excuse to take one. Hey! I'll give you a laugh . . . I kinda thought that where Ed Fitzgerald died giving me these clues that maybe, just maybe, he would *spirit* us to where he hid the money."

Lavina just listened.

"I know it sounds crazy," Art continued, "but stranger things have happened. I'm amazed every time I watch 'Unsolved Mysteries' on TV. Not that I believe *all* of it, but some of it's got to be true. And where Ed died in my arms I really thought, especially after we got this far, even though it's only a beginning, that *he* was guiding us." Art paused for just a few seconds and then resumed by saying, "I know, I know, it's nuts."

"I didn't *say* anything," she responded seriously. "I hate to admit it but I think I hoped the same thing. But now, it looks like we're both wrong and we're at a dead end. It just wasn't meant to be."

Their conversation continued on a downhill slope. Not wanting to end their adventure in a depressive state, they decided that they would spend the remainder of their vacation visiting Busch Gardens and the attractions in Orlando.

Pulling out of the parking lot they headed back up Dodecanese Boulevard toward Pinellas Avenue. Both remained very quiet, lost in their own thoughts. Art stared straight ahead as he drove, and his wife looked out the side window, glancing at the shops as they rode past them.

Without any warning, Lavina grabbed his right arm with her left hand and pointed toward her side of the windshield with her right index finger as she screamed out, "Art! Look! . . . How could we have been so blind?"

"What! . . . What are you talking about?"

"You just passed it. Over there in that window facing out at an angle to the street..."

"What is it?"

"A sign. It says VISIT THE TWELVE MILE REEF ANTIQUE SHOP."

Art jammed on the brakes nearly causing a four car pileup as everyone behind him slammed on their brakes screeching to a halt, and leaned on their horns.

He pulled down the next side street, found a way to circle around the block, and stopped in a loading zone on Athens Street adjacent to one of the gift shops which fronted on Dodecanese Boulevard. Lavina jumped out of the car shouting at him to wait there until she returned. She ran around the corner and up the street and read the sign with its directions to the antique shop. Rushing back within minutes to where Art was parked, she jumped into the car.

"We must have passed that place a dozen times!" she began. "I never even noticed that sign in the window. Can you believe it?"

"We were just looking too hard. We were oblivious to the obvious," Art responded.

"Oh, that's cute," she said with mock sarcasm. "Nice play on words."

Art just smiled.

She told Art to drive back up to Pinellas Avenue but to go left at the intersection rather than right, which would have taken them to their motel.

Not more than two hundred feet from the intersection of Dodecanese Boulevard and Pinellas Avenue they saw a somewhat dilapidated old house, a building with a clutter of nautical items strewn on the lawn and porch. Art drove up onto the short, semicircular dirt driveway in front of a weather-worn sign which read TWELVE MILE REEF ANTIQUES. There were no other cars parked there.

They both got out of the car, ran around an old airplane engine complete with propeller, and past a gigantic ship's air intake funnel and up the seven stairs from the sand driveway and lawn to the porch, which was even more cluttered with junk. There were a ship's wheel, a part of a mast from a sailboat and some barnacle-encrusted anchors from both small craft as well as from a fairly large ship. It was odd, but the smell of the ocean seemed to permeate these objects as Art and his wife noticed the sea odor when they ran past them. Rushing to the entrance in their excitement, they found that they could not squeeze through the door two at a time. Art stepped back to let Lavina enter first.

The shop was a cluster of thousands of trivia, many nautical and many having nothing to do with the sea. The lighting was dim and the darkness was compounded by the fact that every available space was covered with bric-a-brac, odds-and-ends, and antiques. There was nobody behind the counter, which faced the entryway and upon which sat an old cash register with a hand crank next to a dial telephone, both reminiscent of the 1930s.

To the right of the counter was a variety of early glassware, pewter, pictures in wooden or plaster frames, brass musical instruments, toys, harpoons, postcards and German Reich Marks from World War I. It was as though they stepped into another time frame, but which one? World War I Germany? Or the 1860s when whaling was a main source of income in areas well north of Florida? It was quaint, even if dilapidated. There was a musty odor to the shop as well there should be in a place so compacted with the remnants of history. Surprisingly, on such a warm day the place was rather cool without the benefit of an air conditioner.

To the left of the counter was a collection of objects from Egypt, stamps, military patches and medals, and collector's plates depicting the wedding of Prince Charles and Princess Diana.

As they looked around and made comments about the many treasures they were finding, a voice from the back room called out apologizing that she had been busy and did not hear them come in. The woman, with a very distinct German accent, appeared through a doorway and asked if she could help them. She looked to be in her sixties, but had managed to keep her natural blond hair color. She was very gaunt, but attractive, and she wore glasses which rested on the edge of her nose. Only the few wrinkles on her face and hands gave any indication as to her age.

Art took a chance and said, "I'm looking for Gabrielle."

"I'm Gabrielle," the woman answered matter-of-factly. "Do I know you?"

Trying to keep any surprise from showing on his face, Art responded by saying, "No. I am here on behalf of a friend. His name is Ed Fitzgerald . . . I should say *was* Ed Fitzgerald."

Before Art could continue, Gabrielle interrupted him. "Oh, yes," she said nodding her head. "I know him. I met him many years ago but I haff not seen him since zen. Ve hadt correspondedt for qvite some time. I alvays heardt from him at Christmas and on my birssday. Zen for some reason he shtopped writing." Gabrielle moved to the back of the counter and put down a spiral notebook and pen she had been carrying.

"I'm afraid that he has passed away and that is the reason why I am here. I was with him when he died and he mentioned your name."

"Oh, I am so sorry. You vere a close friendt of his, I assume?"

"I guess I was his only friend."

"Has he been deadt for long?" Gabrielle asked.

"No, he passed away just recently."

"I vunder vhy he hadt not written zen? It must be six or seven years since I heardt from him."

Not wanting to mention the actual circumstances, Art simply replied, "He was being cared for in a special home. Maybe that is the reason he lost contact with you."

"Ach! I understandt. Zat is really too badt." She remained silent for a moment and then said, "I have somezing zat belongs to him. He told me to keep it and he vould come for it at some point in time."

"Really?" Art replied with an excited surprise to his voice. "And what might that be?" he asked as he turned and looked at his wife.

"Oh, chust some books. An odd assortment. But zey must haff been somezing zat interested him. He spent a lot uff time looking sru zose books. Now zat he is deadt and as you are his best friendt, perhaps you should take zem."

"I would be happy to," Art replied as he recalled that books was one of the words on his list.

Gabrielle walked around the counter from where she had been standing and headed toward the back of the shop followed by Art and Lavina. She passed into the next room which was filled with German souvenirs from the Second World War. No less than twenty German soldiers' helmets were lined up on a round, two-tier table. Art noticed a rare seaman's cap from the *Graf Spee*—the German pocket battleship that was sunk during one of the major battles at sea. There were also a number of brass ship's fittings and compasses on shelves close by.

They walked past bookcases containing 1930s and '40s, seventy-eight speed, phonograph records along with several hundred novels and old newspapers individually wrapped in a protective plastic.

Gabrielle entered yet a third room and stopped in front of a number of boxes stacked from floor to ceiling. She paused and looked carefully at several smaller boxes closer to the floor. With strength that belied her stature, she wrestled to the ground several of the larger cardboard containers. She then removed a box, no bigger than a twelve-inch square, with the name FITZGERALD printed across its top in red letters. Also on the paper wrapper was the imprint of the shop in a faded black ink. The words TWELVE MILE REEF ANTIQUES with the address were barely readable. She handed the box to Art who in turn gave it to Lavina. Art then went to assist Gabrielle in restacking the heavier boxes but she assured him that her husband would put everything back in place.

Before they left the shop, Art asked Gabrielle if she knew anything about a key.

"A key?" she asked. "Vhat kindt of a key are you looking for?"

"I'm not sure. It's something Ed said to me before he died. I realize it has been a long time but can you recall anything about a key?"

"No, I don't sink he ever mentioned any key to me."

"Is it possible he might have bought one—an antique, perhaps—from you?"

"Not zat I can remember. Everysing he purchased from me is in zat box your vife is holding."

"Oh, one more thing . . . might I take a look at the cards Ed sent to you over the years. I don't mean to be nosy but I am trying to get any hint I can about this key that he mentioned."

"Ach . . . I am afraid zat I don't keep zose sings. Ven I haff read ze card I toss it into za trash bucket. Ze only sing he hass ever written is, 'Take gutt care of yourself.' Nussing more."

"Can I ask you just one more question?" Art queried.

"Uff course, you don't see a crowdt in here trying to get my attention, do you?"

Art smiled at her response and then he carefully posed his final question. "What do you recall about the first time you met him?"

"Vhat do I recall? Zat vas a long time ago," she said, tucking her chin in toward her chest as though to emphasize the near impossibility of coming up with an answer. Then, not wanting to disappoint Art or his wife, she finally said, "Vell, let me sink chust for a moment."

The Key

Gabrielle raised her eyes toward the ceiling of the old building and pursed her lips as creases formed on her brow. A far away look was evident, which reflected her concentration on a conversation held many years ago. Several moments passed in silence.

She began, "I can remember him coming into ze shop. He vas looking for some trinkets, I believe, but ven I asked him if I could help him he said he vas chust looking aroundt. Zen he saw ze great number of oldt books I had for sale and he took a long time viss zem. He finally told me zat he vas interested in any books on ziss area off Tarpon Shprinks. I showed him vhat I had and he found one zat he liked. He vas a quiet man, only asking a few qvestions."

"Ohhh?" asked Art.

"Yah. Chust vould I be villing to holdt ze books he vas buying until he couldt return for zem. It might be a vhile. I said I vould not mindt but I vould haff to put zem into a packatch vis his name on it. Und he gave to me a new, one hundredt dollar bill. Zat is about all I can remember."

"That was it? Are you sure there was nothing more?"

Gabrielle began to shake her head negatively and then stopped.

"He did say somesing vich made me laugh. He said zose books he bought vere very valuable. Und ven he came for zem, ve vouldt celebrate za beginningk of his new life. I toldt him zey vere not originals so zey vere not of any real value. He smiled and said zey could be virss millions. Zat made me laugh."

She hesitated and once again said, "Zat iss really all I can remember."

Art thought about Ed's words—the beginning of his new life. He then thanked Gabrielle and he and his wife departed.

CHAPTER ELEVEN

What Does it All Mean?

Back at the motel they opened the box, which was really nothing more than a heavy brown paper wrapped many times around the contents and taped together. Inside were five books. They removed the books and checked to see that there was nothing else stuck to the paper, but it was clear. The first was a book of poems; not a first edition, not by any means rare. The second was *A History of Tarpon Springs* showing photographs of its earlier years when the Greeks first arrived. The third was John Steinbeck's *Grapes of Wrath*. The fourth was a dictionary from the turn of the last century. The only thing notable was a piece of paper stuck into the page at the letter "S." When opened, the word *spaceship* was circled in pencil and the definition was underlined. It stated an "imaginary mode of transportation between planets." The last of the books was *Treasure Island*. Apart from these, the paper container was empty.

Page by page, Art and his wife looked for any clues, any turned down corners, any notes in the margins, check marks, asterisks, anything at all. But there was nothing. They were stumped. Most curious of all was the encircled word spaceship.

Tired after a full day and so much reading, they put everything aside and went out for supper. Before leaving the motel for a restaurant, Art picked up the history book on Tarpon Springs and took it with him. Having glanced at the pages, he found the book to his liking and wanted to read a little more. He never thought of himself as an historian, but there was something about this book which drew his attention and interest. He found that he was fascinated with the development of this town and the variety of changes, which had taken place over the years as depicted in the photos, drawings and maps that were contained among the pages.

They drove to the Outback Steak House that they had passed on U.S. Highway 19 in Palm Harbor the night they arrived in Florida. It was a short ride just south of their motel. Here they ordered their supper. They needed a change from the spicy Greek food, which had been their diet for the past few days. As they nibbled on a "blooming onion," a deep-fried, whole onion which is cut to look like a flower in bloom and which is accompanied by a horseradish sauce, Art thumbed through the pages of the book. He knew that there had to be a clue somewhere but what it was he could not determine.

When their meal arrived, Art put the book aside. *Enough for today*, he thought. They had been so consumed by this search that it was time for some conversation about anything other than Ed Fitzgerald and the missing money. Finally, they were able to relax a bit and enjoy one another's company. Their dinner was wonderful.

When they returned to their motel nearly two hours later, Art turned to Lavina as they approached the door to their room and said, "Hey, babe, didn't you shut the door when we left?"

"I thought I did. I heard it click."

Art pushed the door at its center with two fingers of his right hand. It glided open. Even in the dark he could see that the room was a mess. Everything had been turned upside down. A feeling of trepidation coursed through Art as he looked at the clutter. For a moment, and only a moment, the thought of inmate Fowler entered Art's mind. Art was suspicious but felt there was no way Fowler could have known where they were staying. Yet, there was a gnawing feeling at the back of his brain.

Not wanting to alarm his wife to the remote possibility that Fowler had been stalking them, Art said, "Looks like we've been the victims of one of those Florida burglaries we're always hearing about. We'd better call the police."

Art sent Lavina to the front desk to have them place the call while he remained outside of the room so as not to disturb anything.

Before long, Lavina, accompanied by a police officer and the motel's night manager, came down the walkway to their room.

"What've we got?" the officer asked as he spied Art standing in the walkway outside the partially opened door.

"Typical burglary I'm gonna guess. We were out for dinner and came back to this mess," Art responded.

"Have y'all touched anything inside?"

"Nope. Waited for you to arrive."

"So, y'all have no idea what's missing, that right?"

"That's correct, Officer."

"By the way, I'm Officer Poulos," the policeman said as he extended his hand to introduce himself.

"Nice ta meet ya," Art responded automatically without giving any thought to the circumstance under which they were meeting one another. "My name is Arthur Booker and this is my wife, Lavina.

"I'm gonna start a report and I've already called for a print kit so we can see if your visitor left any kind of calling card. I'll need your full names, dates of birth, home address, and phone number to begin with. Then I'll need y'all to give me some details about this evening: what time y'all went out, where y'all went, did y'all notice anyone hanging around when y'all left the motel. Okay?"

As the officer collected the information a police technician showed up at the motel room.

"This is Technician Zodiates. She's gonna hafta check out your room before y'all can go in and determine what-all is missing. Y'unnerstand?"

"Yes, sir," said Art. "No problem. I'm just glad I do most a my business with a credit card and I've got that in my pocket. My wife's costume jewelry is not valuable—that's all that would've been left in the room. She wears her gold, so if they've taken anything, it's not worth much, just pretty is all."

A half hour passed before the technician said the room was okay to enter. She asked Art and Lavina for sample fingerprints so as not to confuse theirs with any others she might find, and set up her equipment to take them. During this time, Poulos knocked at the doors of the motel rooms on either side of the Booker's room. The night manager interrupted him as the officer went to the second door and explained that those rooms had not yet been rented. The officer walked the length of the building where he did manage to find some people staying in the rooms at the extreme end of the motel, but they had not seen or heard anything. There were no witnesses to the break-in.

The night manager took a quick look around the room and, satisfied that no damage had been done to the motel property, returned to the front office to call the owner and update him. He expressed to the policeman, when he returned from speaking to the couple at the end of the building, his concern as to how the burglar entered the room without damaging the door. Technician Zodiates explained that there were obvious pick marks on the door's lock, which might have accounted for the illegal entry.

Once they washed off the fingerprint ink from their hands with a gritty substance called Fast Orange, Art and Lavina began sifting through their clothing and other belongings.

"Well," she said. "I can't see that I'm missing anything."

"They must've been disappointed not to find anything," said Art, "'cause all my stuff's here, too. Kinda messed up, but I can account for everything."

"Y'all didn't leave any money, then?" Poulos asked.

"Nope. As I said we kept everything with us," Art answered.

"And your wife had all her things in her purse?"

"I believe so. Isn't that right, honey?" Art asked as he turned toward his wife.

"I don't let anything of value out of my hands," she said as Art smiled at her double entendre, thinking of himself as being precious.

"Well, folks, I hope y'all don't think this is a reflection on us here in Tarpon. We have a very low crime rate unlike that y'all may read about over towards Orlando," the officer stated.

"I'm glad to hear that," Art said. "I'm just sorry we had to be your statistic."

The police officer and the technician picked up their things and turned to leave. Art walked over to the door with them. As he walked, he turned to put the book on Tarpon's history down on the lamp table near the door. He had been carrying it with him since he and his wife returned to the motel.

Suddenly it struck him. "The books!" he shouted, startling everyone in the room.

"The books," he said again. "Where are the books?"

"Omigosh," said Lavina. "I never even thought of them."

The policeman and the technician had both turned abruptly when Art had first yelled out.

"What books?" Officer Poulos asked.

Art then explained about the books he had picked up at the antique shop. He did not go into any detail as to his friend, Ed's, history, only that the books were left to him and now they were gone. All except the one he was holding in his hand.

"Why would someone want to steal four ordinary books?" the officer asked.

"I wish I had the answer to that myself," Art replied. "Even the dictionary was a hundred years out of date. It had words with meanings that had changed over time—like *gay*. It used to mean happy, frivolous, not like today's meaning. It didn't even have some of our modern language—like *parameters*, meaning guidelines or principles. None of the books, as I said, were first editions, so I am at a loss as to why they were taken."

"A real whodunnit mystery," Poulos said, smiling.

Art then continued with, "What *is* unusual is that we have been followed by a guy the past two days, but up until now I never gave much thought to it. I figured he was just some local kook."

"What did he look like? Is it someone you've seen before?" the officer asked.

"I don't think so. He was about five-foot-ten or eleven inches tall, clean-shaven with a ruddy face, somewhat pockmarked with pimples. His hair is brown and fairly short—not quite like a crew cut. He had a ring in his right ear and the last time I saw him he had on a pair of black sunglasses with a black rim. He probably weighs about a hundred and eighty pounds. I can't honestly tell you what he was wearing, though. As near as I can remember it was some sort of dark, maybe navy blue, pullover and blue jeans. I last saw him by the gift shops near the sponge docks. In fact, when I tried to get a better look, he somehow disappeared."

"Good description," Poulos remarked, making notes on his pad. "I've added it to my report. I'll get the word out to look for him." Then, without missing a beat, he added a question, "D'yall know of any reason why y'all are being followed by this guy?"

"No," responded Art somewhat quickly, "we have no idea."

Officer Poulos, expressionless, stared at Art and said nothing, but simply nodded his head. But Art could tell by the look on his face that the policeman did not totally believe him.

"How long are y'all expecting to stay in Tarpon Springs?" the officer asked.

"I've got to get back to work next week so we're scheduled for a flight on Sunday," Art replied.

"If we come up with anything by then, I'll let y'all know. Okay?" Poulos stated. "Oh, one more thing. Y'all might want to change rooms; maybe get something closer to the office where there's more activity and light."

"Good suggestion. Thank you. We'll certainly do that," Art said, and with that, both people left and Art closed the door.

"Why did you tell them about Fowler?" Lavina inquired.

"Because if he gets picked up he's not gonna say anything about the money—he wants that for himself. Besides, if they find him and they run his name for a criminal records check, they'll find he's in violation of his parole. That'll eliminate him from the competition."

"Yeah, you're probably right. I mean . . . *y'all* are prob'ly right," she laughed as she imitated the southern-accented officer.

Then she added, "Did you notice? He also took the paper that the books were wrapped in. Remember, it had Fitzgerald's name on it as well as the antique shop's stamp? If he's clever, he'll discover that there is a book missing based on the creases in the paper."

"Good. I hope he comes back for the other book thinking that it holds what he's looking for. I would welcome a face-to-face with him."

"I wouldn't," she said matter-of-factly.

"Get out your list of words," Art said to Lavina. "Let's add a few more things."

"Like what?" she asked as she reached into her purse and took out the memo pad.

"Like '*Treasure Island*' and 'spaceship' and 'poems' and '*Grapes of Wrath*' and '*A History of Tarpon Springs*.' There has got to be meaning in all of these things."

"Okay. I gotcha."

"Can you remember anything out of any of those books besides the spaceship in the dictionary?" Art asked.

"I've racked my brain trying to recall anything that would stand out as a clue, but I'm clueless. How about you with your history book?"

"It's a great history. I will say that. Did you know that the Greeks did not arrive here until the middle of the year in 1905? I would've thought that they were the ones to establish this place."

"Why would you think that?"

"Because there are so many of them here. Did you notice that even the high school is designed like some of the temples to the gods in ancient history—you know, like the Parthenon in Athens to the queen of the goddesses, Athena?"

"My, aren't you the expert," she chided, but to Art it came across almost as sarcasm. "I never would have thought that you'd have paid any attention to European history when you were in elementary school."

Art held the book down and looked at her with an element of annoyance on his face. It was obvious he did not like being challenged or put down in any way. Finally, he said, "Do you want to hear any of this or not?"

"Yes. Go ahead. I didn't mean to get you so touchy. I was just ribbing you a bit."

"I know you were. I'm just a little moody, I guess, with all that's been happening here."

"What else have you discovered?" she asked.

"Well, it also says that the sponge industry was active for many years here and that fishermen would use long poles with hooks on them to scoop the sponges off of the shallow Gulf floor not far from the shore. They used glass-bottom buckets to peer into the water and look below the waves in order to see where the sponges were to be found."

"Well, we are learning something, aren't we?" she said sincerely. "I will say that I have never given much thought to sponges before, except the ones we buy in packages of four to clean the bathroom."

"Yeah, but what we buy are cellulose. I bet we've never even had a real ocean sponge. Listen . . . the first Greek to dive for sponges here came from the Mediterranean where he used to make his living there doing the same thing. Somehow, word got to him that there was a fortune to be made here with the vast harvest that was discovered. His name was De-mos-then-es Ka-va-si-las," he pronounced each syllable so as not to make any errors.

"You certainly do have his name down pat. Now try and say it fast."

"Don't get wise," Art remarked. "Do you mind if I continue?"

"I'm just having fun with you. We've been so serious about everything we really need to take a break."

"I suppose you're right. But let me finish this little bit so that we're both sponge-smart. They found thousands of these creatures—did you know they were alive?—down on the sandbars among the corals and wild grape vines. I would never have imagined grape vines below the ocean surface. Maybe that's just a figure of speech. The book says that a tremendous garden of sponges was found just off Anclote Cay, whatever and wherever that is."

"I think that's a part of Tarpon Springs. I saw the name Anclote somewhere in our travels here. It could be a section of the city near the water," Lavina interjected.

"The Greeks first arrived in St. Augustine, Florida, before Tarpon Springs. In fact, the oldest Greek Orthodox church is in that city. They discovered sponging in the Atlantic and it was not until some years later that word was brought to them that there were greater, more fertile sponging resources in the Gulf of Mexico on the west coast of Florida. It did not take long for the Greeks to ply their trade there.

"There was one drawback to the move to Tarpon Springs. For some reason after the Greeks left St. Augustine, seagulls began to die off. The people of the city wanted to know why so they initiated an investigation. What they discovered was that when the Greeks were coming in from a sponging dive, they would often fish as well. And as they traveled back toward shore, they would clean the fish and throw the guts to the seagulls who were following their boats. They were so used to being hand-fed by these fishermen that their young never had to learn to dive for fish in the ocean. When the Greeks left St. Augustine, there was no one left to feed the seagulls and they began to die from starvation.

"It says that by the end of 1905, there were more than five hundred spongers who arrived in Tarpon Springs from Greece. The first Greek to actually start a business here was a guy named John Co-co-ris," Art again pronounced the last name with care.

"Wow! You had no problem pronouncing that guy's *first* name. You're becoming adept in Greek already," she said chuckling to herself.

Once again lowering the book and looking this time with mock disdain at his wife, Art said, "And you're becoming adept at being a pain in the rear. All right, if you don't want to hear any more, I'll quit. I just happened to find it interesting, that's all."

"So did I, *Mister Sensitive*, all kidding aside."

Before they went to bed, they made arrangements with the motel night clerk to have their room changed in the morning to another location near the office. Not wanting any problems, the clerk complied without any hesitation and advised the motel manager by telephone. He was in complete agreement.

CHAPTER TWELVE

Nothing New

The rest of the week passed without anything new materializing. They read and reread the book until their eyes were sore and bloodshot. They took long breaks in between chapters in order to set their minds free from the frustration of finding nothing.

"What are we going to do?" Lavina asked.

"Whattaya mean?"

"I mean, we're supposed to fly back to New York in the morning. Are we just going to go, or what? You can't afford to take off any more time from work; your vacation time is up. So, what's the plan?"

"I don't know. I hate to leave here just yet. But you're right. If we had the money, we wouldn't have a worry. But the fact of the matter is, we don't."

"How about this?" she suggested. "Let me stay down here awhile. If nothing shows up, I'll fly back. If something clicks, then I'll call you and we can decide what to do from there."

"Have you got something going on with that other guy—Fowler?" Art said with a twinkle in his eye and a half-smile.

"Kiss my butt!"

"Okay, honey. I hate to leave you, especially alone, but you're our only hope with that other guy down here. I'm really not comfortable with you being here by yourself, though."

"You don't have to worry about me. I can take care of myself. I'm very cautious when I'm on my own. Oh . . . and take that history book with you. Maybe something will strike you."

"Before I go, I'm going to call Officer Poulos and let him know that you're staying here a few more days. I want him to be able to keep an eye on you just in case anything else should come up."

"I'm really going to be fine, honey," she said. But Art went to the phone and placed the call to the police station. Officer Poulos was not on duty, but the dispatcher assured Art that he would get the message.

Late that afternoon, Art and his wife drove to a local locksmith shop where they asked the owner what he might suggest for extra protection for their motel room door. They explained that they had already been through one break-in. The man showed them an item called a New York Security Bar. Art snickered to himself at the name as he thought, *Of course, where else but New York*. It was a heavy, long, adjustable pole designed to be placed under the door handle inside the room. The other end rested at an angle on the floor. It would be impossible to open a door when this was in place. Art liked the device and bought it. That night, they tried it out and found that it was exactly as the man had described it. They slept very soundly, comforted by this added defense.

The next morning, Lavina drove him to the airport where they changed her departure date and where she waited as he boarded the plane for his trip back north. She held back tears as he walked down the ramp and into the Delta flight that would take him home.

Returning to the motel, she took out the list and began to study it once again, playing a game with it trying to fit the words together and then adding some, which might make sense to what it held secret.

The next day, Lavina again went to the center of Tarpon Springs and decided to visit the sponge museum and its free movie. She did not have an opportunity to see it the day they were chasing around trying to find Fowler.

Much of what she saw and heard seemed familiar to her and then she realized it was similar to what Art had read to her out of the history book. Now she felt more knowledgeable as she nodded in the affirmative as each new fact was being released by the narrator. She saw the few people who were in the room with her glance over in her direction, probably thinking, she thought, that she was a savant student of sponge history. She smiled to herself at the thought of this boost to her ego.

She watched intently as the speaker mentioned the Anclote Islands where so many sponges were harvested. "So," she said to herself quietly, "that's what it is. The Anclotes are islands. I'll have to tell that to Art when he calls."

She spent the next few days wandering in and out of the same shops she and Art had visited when they first arrived. There really was not much else she could do besides that and think about the books, which became a source of great frustration. Some of the shopkeepers recognized her as she had been in several times. They were very pleasant to her, sometimes engaging her in bland conversation, even though she did not buy much of anything, but merely picked items up and looked them over carefully.

She heard nothing more from Officer Poulos other than seeing him on occasion as he passed by her in his police car or as he stopped every couple of hours out in front of her room at the motel to check on her welfare. She would wave at him through the window, if she happened to be sitting watching the traffic and saw him pull in, and he would return the wave before going on his way.

The worst part of the three days she spent alone was the fact that she was alone. She was not afraid, just lonely. She wished Art could be there with her. She loved him very much and she missed him greatly.

One more day and she would be returning home. She felt disappointment because this whole venture was a waste; a waste of time and a waste of money. The only good part was that she and Art had spent some time together and it was, for a while, a bit exciting as they thought about the possibility of discovering a missing fortune. "One thing is for sure," she said to herself, "the fact that we haven't found anything means that Fowler hasn't found anything, either." She smiled as she pondered what Fowler might be thinking. *I bet he's been watching me and questioning what we're doing. Well, wait until he discovers that we've gone. I wonder what he'll think then?* she thought to herself. That one thought alone uplifted her spirits.

CHAPTER THIRTEEN

Gabrielle's Gun

It was late Wednesday morning when the phone rang in the motel room. Lavina was just packing her things, making ready for the return trip to New York. Nothing had panned out and she was trying not to let the disappointment overcome her. She had called the airline and had agreed to pay the extra fifty dollars for a change of flight from the previous Sunday to today. Her flight was scheduled to leave at two-forty in the afternoon.

"Hello?" she said as she picked up the receiver.

"Mrs. Booker? This is Officer Poulos."

"Yes, what's up?"

"Mrs. Booker, it looks like we've got a lead on your man."

"What do you mean?"

"A man fitting the description that your husband gave us paid a visit to the woman who owns the antique store where y'all bought your books."

"Really?" she said before the officer had a chance to continue.

"Evidently, there must be something more to this story than we're aware of. The man beat the proprietor pretty badly. When her husband found her, she was bleeding on the floor underneath a pile of junk that she said was pulled over on her in a rage when she could not tell the man what he wanted to know."

"What! What happened? Oh God, is she all right?" she asked.

"She was hurt pretty badly. I could only see her for a short time as they were taking her in for X-rays. They told me to come back today and she should be in a more stable condition."

"That man . . . what did he want to know? Did she say?"

"I've only been able to speak with her for a few minutes. She's over at the Helen Ellis Hospital on U.S Highway 19A. I was hoping that y'all might meet me there. She asked for your husband but I told her that he had already returned to New York. I did tell her you were still here."

"Are you there now?"

"No. I'm at the station, but I can meet y'all there whenever y'all are ready."

"I all are ready. I mean, I'm all ready. I'll meet you there as soon as I can. By the way, how do I get there?"

"Y'all will be coming down through the center of town. The Greek church is up on your right by the stop lights. Take a left on Pinellas Avenue and you'll see it on the left just a ways down the road. She's in room three-nineteen."

"I'm on my way."

Taking only enough time to call Delta Airlines, she advised them of another change in plans, canceling her flight for that afternoon. She then headed out of the motel and over to the hospital.

Officer Poulos was standing in the waiting room when Lavina arrived. Before she had a chance to say anything, he explained, "Sometime around closing last night, a man walked into Miss Gabrielle's shop, locked the door, and tried to beat some information out of her. When her husband called on the phone and no one answered and she had not come home, he went to see where she was. He found the door to the shop open. The lights were off. When he flipped the switch to turn them on, he found Miss Gabrielle on the floor. She was conscious, but just barely. He then called 911 and told them he needed an ambulance. The shop was a mess when the responding officers arrived. I got the call around nine p.m. The detectives knew I was working on a case with y'all involving this same guy. Now, y'all know just about as much as I do."

Lavina just listened. She was floored by what Poulos had told her.

"If y'all will follow me, I'll take y'all up to Miss Gabrielle's room." He then started walking down the corridor away from the lobby. Lavina fell into step beside him.

As she entered the hospital room and saw the woman's bandaged face, Lavina involuntarily drew her right hand up to her mouth and gasped as she realized how savagely Gabrielle had been attacked. "Gabrielle, oh my gosh, I am so sorry that this has happened to you. I don't know what to say."

"*Sank* you for your *concern*," Gabrielle replied somewhat sarcastically. "Chust who are you? Und, chust who iss your husbandt?" she demanded icily. "Look vhat ziss man hass done to me!" The hurt came out in her voice and she began to cry. With that, a man who had been seated in a corner of the room came over and took hold of Gabrielle's hand. He gave a quick glance toward Lavina, but it was not a pleasant look.

"Oh, please, Gabrielle. I don't understand all of this myself. Believe me, I don't know what is so important about these books and I don't know why that man would do this to you. You must believe me," Lavina implored. "Do you think I would have come here to see you if I was not concerned for you? I never thought anything like this would take place." Tears began to stream down Lavina's face.

Gabrielle lowered her head. A moment passed in silence before she looked up.

"You must excuse me," Gabrielle responded, her emotions now under control. "It is chust that I am not myself. I do belief you, of course. I chust do not understand vhy ziss hass happenedt to me. Vhat did ziss man expect me to tell him? I know nussing of zese books."

"You know as much as we do, Gabrielle. That is the truth. We have looked through each one of the books and cannot understand why they seemed so important either to Ed Fitzgerald or to this other man."

Gabrielle apologized feeling empathy toward the tearful woman, "I am sorry to have said vhat I said to you." She paused momentarily. "Oh, und zis is my husband," she then said as she indicated by motioning her left hand toward the man who had previously been seated next to the bed. As acknowledgment, he nodded in her direction, this time a more cordial look on his face.

"Officer Poulos told me zat your room vas broken into by a man who looked like zah one zat beat me. He said zat zah man took zah books you picked up from me. I toldt Officer Poulos zat zah man asked me qvestions about vhat I hadt said to you and vhat you hadt said to me. Zere must be somezing about zese books zat makes zem very important. Vhy vould he haff done zis to me, ozervise?"

"I wish I knew what he was after. What did he do to your shop?" Lavina asked as the officer listened to their conversation.

"He wrecked everysing he could get his hands on. He vas so madt zat I could not tell him anysing."

"What did he say to you?"

"He vas very demanding. He came in und asked vhat you and your husbandt vere doing here. I toldt him zat you came in to pick up some sings zat belongedt to a friendt and he asked vhat zey vere. I vass afraidt of him from za moment he valked into my store, so I toldt him zat it vass chust some oldt books. Zen he got mad und slapped my face. I could not believe it. He asked me vhat vere zese books und I toldt him I did not know. He kept hitting me vis his fist but I could not tell him anysing."

"I feel so badly for you."

"I am vorried for you," Gabrielle said.

"I'm all right."

"Yes. But I vorry because I don't know vhat he might do to you if he did zis to me."

"Well, I don't want you to worry. I'll be okay."

"Did Officer Poulos tell you zat he took somezing from my shop?"

"No. What was that?" she asked with a concerned look on her face.

Poulos, who had remained quiet as the women talked, then spoke, "I was going to tell y'all once I had the opportunity to speak with y'all alone. The guy took a German Luger, which Miss Gabrielle kept under her counter for protection."

"A *gun*? He has a *gun*?"

"Yes, ma'm. But I don't want y'all to fret none 'cause we're looking for this guy and chances are he's gonna stay away after what he's done. He knows we're looking for him."

Now visibly shaken, Lavina sat down in the seat opposite the hospital bed and Gabrielle's husband.

"I don't want y'all to worry now," Officer Poulos said. "I've told my supervisor what's happening and we're gonna be watching over y'all very carefully. I do have something I've got to ask y'all though."

"What? . . . What's that?"

"There must be something y'all aren't telling me about this guy. He's going to an awful lot of trouble and taking some big chances over a few books. Is there something I'm missing here?"

"Nn . . . no. I don't know. I don't understand what's going on. After that break into our motel room, my husband and I tried to remember anything in those books that might have been important. But there was nothing. No underlined words, no drawings, no notes, not even any bent-down page corners. Nothing. I don't know what the man could be looking for. I just don't know."

"Maybe y'all better get a hold of your husband and tell him what's taken place here. I have a feeling he might want to come back if y'all aren't going up to New York now."

"You . . . you know I canceled my flight?"

"Yes, ma'm. I wasn't sure if y'all were returning north just yet so I called the airport and they said y'all were scheduled to leave on a flight this afternoon. I told them that I needed to detain y'all for police business. I called them again just before I came here so I could be sure y'all'd be around, and they told me y'all'd changed plans."

"I guess I'd better get back to the motel and call Art."

"Yes, ma'm. I'll have some plainclothes officers in an unmarked police car watching the motel and I'll be in touch with y'all later. And, I wouldn't go out of the room if I were y'all without calling me at the station."

Lavina took a hold of Gabrielle's hand and again told her how sorry she was for what this terrible man had done.

"I know the police will find the man. He will pay for hurting you."

"Sank you. I vill be all right. It iss you zat I am vorried aboudt. Please be careful."

"I will," Lavina replied. She then excused herself and returned to her car and then to the Best Western where she placed a call to her husband at work.

CHAPTER FOURTEEN

Anclote Key

"I'm coming down!" Art said without any hesitation after hearing his wife's latest news.

"But what about your job?" she asked.

"I'll take my three personal days and call in sick if I need more. This just confirms that things have to be brought to a conclusion. I spoke with one of the inmates yesterday who was friendly with Fowler. I think you'll find his comments kind of interesting."

"What did he say?"

"First off, Fowler bragged that he'll never have to work a day in his life because his pot of gold is waiting for him at the end of his rainbow. Obviously, he was talking about Ed's pot of gold. I asked him if he ever overheard conversations between Tom and Ed. I really never expected him as an inmate to respond to me. But for some reason he was tired of listening to Fowler's cockiness. He said, 'Yeah, on several occasions.'"

"Did he tell you what was said?"

"Not exactly. What he did say was that Fowler tried to gain Ed's trust but Ed remained wary of him. The one big factor was that Ed talked in his sleep and Fowler would sit for hours trying to decipher the mumblings that Ed blabbed out during the night. Fowler tried to converse with Ed when he found him in these sleep-talking conditions. He said that Fowler was most emphatic in probing Ed about his hidden money."

"Do you think he learned anything?"

"That I don't know. If he did, I don't think he would be so dogged in his determination to discover what we know."

"When will you leave?"

"As soon as I can get a flight. We'd better get something out of this; these on-the-spot flights are very expensive."

"Well, call me from the airport when you pick up your ticket so I'll know when to get you. I'll wait at the motel until I hear from you."

"Okay, honey," he said and hung up the phone.

Art called Delta Air Lines and was lucky to get a flight with only one stopover. Being off-season and midweek helped. He feigned sickness in order to leave work early. He was glad his wife remembered to call him on the unrecorded line at work. He would have had to use quick thinking to cover his conversation otherwise.

Lavina picked him up at the airport at 8:36 p.m.

"I was worried about you," he said to her when he got into the rental car. "Ever since you told me what happened to Gabrielle and the fact that Fowler took her gun, I've been a wreck. What if he had come after you? For myself, if I was the one remaining behind, I would not have any concerns. In fact, I would have welcomed his visit."

"Oh, Mr. Macho speaking," she said in response to his last comment.

"No. I mean it. And now I mean it even more."

They drove in silence to the Best Western.

Once settled in their room, Lavina said, "Officer Poulos wants to talk to you."

"Oh? What about?"

"He wants to know what you haven't told him about the books."

"What's there to tell? Exactly what did he say?"

"It's not so much what he said but what he *didn't* say."

"What do you mean by that?"

"I guess it's just his manner of inquiry. He knows there has to be a reason why Gabrielle was questioned and beaten by this man, especially where it concerned *our* books."

"What did you tell him?"

"I just played dumb, but I don't really think he bought it."

"Boy, could I have fun with that statement."

"Just try it and see where you sleep tonight."

"Hey! Not fair!" he said and then quickly got back onto the topic at hand. "I'm just gonna do the same thing. We don't know anything except that we picked up some books for a friend who passed away."

"Officer Poulos thinks we bought the books, remember?"
"I never told him that, did you?"
"No."
"Well then, if he asks we'll just say that they belonged to a friend. Even if he gets Ed Fitzgerald's name from Gabrielle he won't be able to trace his background 'cause he won't have a date of birth or a previous address to go by. He will know only what we allow him to know—which will be nothing."
"Okay. I must have known you would want it that way because that's the way I handled it."
"Good girl. Man, but you are talented."
"Sure. You say that just because I act like you."
"You got it," Art said.

In the morning Art called Poulos only to discover it was his day off. He left a message that he was back in town if he needed to speak with him. Art and his wife drove to the hospital and spent the day with Gabrielle. Art was shocked by what had been done to her. He had seen men badly beaten before, but not women. This bothered him greatly. When the nurse came in to give Gabrielle a sponge bath and to bring in her lunch, Art and Lavina went out for a sandwich. They stopped at a florist and bought a beautiful bouquet of flowers. Then they went to the hospital gift shop and picked up a small, stuffed dog. Gabrielle was surprised by the unexpected presents they had bought for her. This small act would endear them to her from then on. Art and Lavina remained with Gabrielle until her husband showed up about four o'clock. In order to give Gabrielle and her husband some time alone, the Bookers returned to the motel.

On Friday Poulos called.
"Mr. Booker? Officer Poulos. I think we've found your man."
"What?" Art said. "Where?"
"I sent out a description of the man to all the local motels and businesses. The clerk at the Marco Hotel on 19A called and says it fit one of their guests. He gave the name George Weekly. Does that name ring a bell with y'all?"
"No. I can't say that it does," Art responded while thinking, *They've got the wrong guy.*

Poulos then continued, "He wasn't in his room but I took advantage of the door being opened when the maid was doing her cleaning. Guess what I found in there without even having to do a search?" Before waiting for an answer, he said, "Your books."

"Really?" Art said in surprise. He then thought, *Fowler must be using an alias; I wonder whose credit card he's got to pay for his room?*

Art then said, "Do you have the books with you?"

"Yes, sir, I do. I'd like to have y'all come to the station and sign for them so I can release them to you. Besides that, I do have some questions to ask y'all."

"Okay. What about the suspect—Mr. Weekly?" Art asked.

"As I said, we haven't found him yet, only where he's been staying. We've got his room under surveillance at this time so, hopefully, he'll return and we can question him."

Before Art completed the call he asked the officer for directions to the police station. Once satisfied that he could find his way, he hung up the receiver.

"Who's Mr. Weekly?" Art's wife asked having eavesdropped to the one-sided conversation. "Has he got our books?"

"Let me tell you the whole story so that we aren't playing twenty questions." With that, Art explained his telephone conversation with Poulos.

When they arrived at the police station on North Ring Avenue, Officer Poulos invited them into an interview room, empty except for a table and some chairs. The retrieved books were on the table along with a release form. As he gave them the release form to sign, the officer asked Art what he knew about *why* the antique store proprietor would have been assaulted over the conversation he and his wife had with her concerning these books.

Although Art claimed ignorance, Poulos instinctively knew that the truth, for some reason, was being avoided. He had no alternative, no way to force an answer out of these people, so he had to go along with their act.

"By the way," Art asked, "did you locate the stolen gun?"

"No. That's still among the missing," he answered while wondering if that, too, had a connection to the mysterious books. Then he added, "Legally, I had no right to search the room without a warrant. So I technically broke the law when I went into the room and would not have been able to take it even if I had found it." And, although the books were in plain sight, the only way he could get away with removing them would be to skirt around the restrictions imposed by law. Should he be challenged for this at some point in the future, he could possibly have some problems. For now, he was willing to take a chance because his curiosity over this entire matter was eating away at him. He had hoped that his turning the books over to their rightful owners would result in some cooperation on their part. Being professional in his duties as a police officer, even with a little bending of the law, he expected a better response to his inquiry. Perhaps, he had thought, with just a bit more time and some slight additional, nonconfrontational pressure, he would get the answers he was looking for. But, not being able to accomplish anything further, Poulos handed over the books, thanked them for their time, and escorted them from the building.

Returning to the motel, Art turned to Lavina and said, "I think we had better find a different motel. I don't like the idea that Fowler not only knows where we are but that he has that gun."

"There aren't a lot of places to choose from in Tarpon," she responded. "There were some smaller motels on 19A but then that's where he's been staying."

"No. We're not going to make it that easy for him to locate us. I did see a place when we were driving around near those beautiful big homes by one of the inlets."

"I remember. It was even closer to the center of town. Can you recall how to get there?"

"I think so. Let's take a ride."

They put the books in the trunk of the car and drove the streets of Tarpon Springs until they located the Scottish Inn on Spring Boulevard. It was just off of Tarpon Avenue. Feeling secure that no one had followed them, they pulled into the parking space by the lobby and arranged for a room not readily seen from the street. It was not as plush as the Tahitian Resort but they were here for business and not for a true vacation. Besides it was safer than where they had been. At least Fowler would not find them easily as before; Art would see to that.

They returned to the Best Western and packed up their things. When they felt comfortable in making the move, they transported their bags to the car and started driving in an erratic pattern around Tarpon Springs and the surrounding area. If they were being followed, it would be evident and they could govern themselves accordingly.

They rode for over an hour before they were confident that no one had pursued them. Finally reaching their destination, they unloaded their belongings and settled into the room. Once again they immersed themselves in the books they had retrieved from the police station, determined to discover something—a hidden message, a hidden clue, anything. They were getting tired, discouraged, and their money and Art's personal days were all used up. They had to find something out quickly or scrap the whole idea.

They spent the entire day reading in silence, putting their intuitions down on paper as each read parts from the books. They skipped lunch, still, nothing jumped off the pages at them; nothing illuminating came to their minds. This was going to be a one-meal-only day.

"It must be so obvious that we can't see it," Lavina finally said. "You know, like the old saying about not seeing the forest for the trees."

"I wish I could just get some idea," Art replied.

Both eventually had to put down the books. They had reached a point wherein they needed a break.

"How about going for a walk?" Lavina suggested.

"Where?"

"Well, if you look around this place you'll notice that there is a sidewalk which follows the inlet. It'll be getting dark soon and we're away from where Fowler will be looking for us, if he hasn't discovered that we've gone by now. Besides, it's a beautiful area—so calm and peaceful."

"Okay. Whatever you want. I just know that I need to get away from these books for awhile. My eyes are starting to cross and nothing is making any sense."

They locked the books once more in the trunk of the rented car and then sauntered down to Whitcomb Bayou just across the street from the motel. They went down the fourteen steps of the elegant entrance that led to the sidewalk, which bordered the waterway. Turning to their right they walked in the cool night air past the very few boats that had been moored to the slips along the bayou. They were impressed, as they looked across to the other side of the bayou, by the yachts that were tied up to private docks in front of the houses belonging to the wealthy homeowners. The sidewalk ended after several hundred feet where a wall-barricade prevented them from going further. They then reversed their direction and went around to the other side of the bayou.

"It sure is pleasant out here," Art said.

"Just beautiful," his wife responded.

"You were right once again."

"How's that?" she asked.

"This was a good interruption to our reading."

Lavina just smiled and put her arm through his as they walked along.

They continued past the war memorial monument, which was erected for all those who had served and died in battle from the Tarpon Springs area. Then they passed by a section where a gigantic shell was constructed and used for concerts during the summer. Obviously a smaller version of the well-known one situated along the Charles River in Boston. They then found a memorial dedicated to a former police chief in Tarpon Springs. *Odd*, Art thought to himself, *I would have expected it to be a Greek name and not Bergstrom.* They completed their walk at the end of the tennis courts by the town landing where boats could be put into the water. Here the road picked up where the bayou walkway ended. They proceeded down the street itself, admiring the magnificent homes bordering the water.

"These places are palatial," Lavina commented.

"You're right, babe, but you know what? Even if I had the money I would not feel at home in one of those."

"What?" she exclaimed. "How could you not feel at home? I could be very comfortable in any one of these places."

"You say that now but once you've cleaned it a couple of times you'd think differently."

"Arthur Booker, if we had the money to own one of these mansions, you can bet your sweet butt we'd have a cleaning lady to do the work."

"Yeah, I should have known you'd have an answer like that. You don't care how you spend my money." Art turned aside his head so that his wife could not see the smile on his face.

"Your money? What's this 'your money'?" his wife retorted.

"Well, I am the one who is working, not you."

"And just whose idea was that? You said my job was in the home and that you didn't want me working outside. You're the one who said that with your job we could afford to have me stay at home. And besides, what was there available for me to do around there? Just answer me that," his wife countered as she thought back to when they first moved to the small western New York city. She had interviewed with two financial firms located just a half-hour's travel from her home. She told Art at that time, "You knew you were outside of the Big Apple when you found out the salaries being offered elsewhere. It's a good thing the cost of living here is lower." The salary would not have been a real problem; it was the lack of an available position. As a result, Art convinced his wife to stay at home. A few extra overtime hours on his part would compensate for her deficiency of income.

"I love the way you get so defensive when I give you a little jab," Art said, smiling.

"Yeah, and I love the way you try to back down gracefully when you know you're in the wrong."

Art put his arm around his wife and pulled her close to him. He flashed a huge smile and said, "C'mon, baby."

"You're such a jerk sometimes," she replied as she returned his smile and leaned her head against his shoulder.

"I know. But what would you do without me?"

"Don't ever give me the opportunity or you'll find out," she said giving him an evil smile.

Walking back to the motel, both found that they had worked up an appetite. As they approached their car, Art's stomach growled loudly enough for his wife and a passerby to hear. Lavina looked at him, poked his belly and said laughingly, "My, how loud you protest when you've missed a few meals."

He grinned and said, "I'm starved! What do you think of something quick to eat instead of going some place fancy?"

"Oh, I really don't care. I feel like I've been on that game show 'Wheel of Fortune.' I get all excited when I think we're onto something, like I've spun the board and the pointer stops at five thousand dollars and then I get so depressed when everything falls apart as my second spin goes right to BANKRUPT."

"I know. I feel the same way. Hey, how about taking one of those gambling ships out? We can eat on board and throw away some more of the money we haven't found?"

"I'm really not into gambling. We've done enough of that just coming down here and trying to answer the riddle of the books."

"Well, why don't we go out on that other boat—the one we first took a ride on. They serve meals and it might be nice just to watch the sunset."

"All right!" she replied excitedly, smiling and clapping her hands, "I'm game."

"Let's go now before I find something to complain about there," Art whined as his stomach groaned again.

They drove back to the center of town in silence. Fortunately, a car was just pulling out of a space on the street not too far from the loading platform for the *Island Princess*. They bought their dinner tickets and climbed on board. The music system on the boat was playing some upbeat Greek songs, which lifted Lavina's spirits. "I almost feel like dancing," she said.

"Go ahead. No one knows us so who cares?"

"No way! Do you know how embarrassed I'd be even though I don't know anyone?"

"Yup. That's why you'd never catch me doing anything like that."

They went inside the enclosed deck where some two dozen tables were set up for dinner. A white linen tablecloth and napkins graced each one. Most were already taken by people who had boarded the boat before them.

A table near the bow was still available so they moved rapidly to claim it. Where they now sat afforded them a panoramic view of the inner waterway. With the sun almost out of sight, the harbor took on a different quality. The lights on the boats and outside of the businesses located along the dock gave everything a romantic appeal.

"This was really a good idea, Art," Lavina said.

"Beautiful, isn't it. Yeah, I guess every once in a while I come up with something cool."

A waitress approached them and asked for their drink order.

"Give me something that'll make me feel good," Lavina said to her.

"And give me something that'll knock me out tonight. I need a good night's sleep," Art said.

"Wow!" said the waitress. "*You're* both gonna have a great night; I can tell." Walking away, she then disappeared up the steps to the upper deck where the bar was located.

As they waited for their drinks, the deckhand pulled up the gangplank and released the mooring lines. Within minutes, the boat was turning around and heading toward the Gulf.

The waitress returned with a tray from which she placed each glass along with a small paper napkin, embossed with a border in the Greek key design, and a menu on their table. She excused herself and said she would be back shortly to take their orders for dinner.

The boat began to pick up its pace and the captain's voice came over the sound system welcoming everyone and telling them what the tour consisted of and where they were going.

The waitress was in the middle of writing down their dinner requests when the captain again spoke over the speaker system announcing that they were passing into the area known as Anclote Key.

"What did he say?" Art asked the waitress. The captain's Greek accent made him difficult to understand.

"This is called Anclote Key. It's a string of islands just off of Tarpon and it's known for the many sponges grown here," she responded.

"I thought it was called Anclote Cay?" he said, remembering the term he had read in the Tarpon history book.

"Hmmm . . . I never heard it called that before," she said.

"The other thing," Art interjected, "I thought The Keys were off the tip of Florida."

"Oh, you mean Key West. That's not the only keys we have. There are quite a few along the coast. I'll ask the captain about the 'cay' though."

"You learn something new every day," Art said to his wife as the waitress departed.

Lavina sat staring at him, a somber look on her face.

"What?" he asked, raising his hands palms upward and shrugging his shoulders; a quizzical look on his face as though he missed something.

"Art!" said Lavina. "Are you listening to what you're saying?"

"Whattaya mean by that?"

"The islands—they're called Anclote Key."

"Yeah, so she said. So what?"

"Art! Key! . . . The key . . . maybe it's not a *lock* key but an *island* key."

Looking stupefied and not saying anything for a minute, Art finally responded, "I haven't even taken my drink yet and look how fuzzy my mind is. It never even struck me. Of course, that has to be it. The money has to be out on one of the islands. I wonder which one of the islands, though?"

At that point the waitress came back. "Key is cay," she said. "The captain says the old word cay has been changed over the years. It's the same as key."

"Thank you. Thank you very much," Art said all smiles and looking like he just got a new lease on life as the saying goes. "How many islands in this Anclote Key?" he asked the waitress.

"All of them," she said in return, obviously not comprehending Art's question.

"How many's that?"

"I don't know. I think there's about six or seven."

Again he thanked her and then he turned to Lavina and said, "Tomorrow, we rent a boat and check out the key."

"You know," she said, after the waitress had gone, "the book *Treasure Island* now has a new meaning."

"You're right! It fits! Finally, something else that makes sense. He *must* have buried it out there somewhere."

CHAPTER FIFTEEN

A Close Call

Early the next morning Art and his wife put on Bermuda shorts, drove to the docks and asked where they might rent a boat for the day. One of the local fishermen said there was a marina close by and that would be their best bet.

Following the directions they were given, they drove to the marina on Roosevelt Boulevard and met with the owner out on one of the boat landings as he was assisting a customer who was contemplating the installation of a new electronic fish finder on his boat.

The marina operator left the man to make up his mind and walked Art and Lavina back into the building adjacent to the docks. The building was larger than it appeared to be from the street. It was divided into three sections: a display area for new equipment, a small office, and a large work area where installations of new devices or maintenance to watercraft can be performed in and away from the outside elements. Being well-appointed with the latest in seagoing technology, it was very obvious that the marina did a thriving business during the peak seasons of the year.

Filling out the necessary papers and offering their VISA card, the Bookers rented a small motorboat. Donning the required life vests, they motored out to the first of the islands. They circled it and discovered a spot where they could climb to shore.

Art removed his running shoes and got out in the warm water at knee level and gingerly, walking across the stones and rough sand, he pulled the boat up onto the gravel so that Lavina could get out comfortably.

They wandered around the island looking for anything that might give them a clue as to where the money might be buried, should this be the correct island.

Although the island was small, the going was rough due to the thick weeds, grass and vines, which covered the ground between the scrub pines. Art copped an attitude as he got tangled up in some of the brush.

"You know," said Art, "it's been over twenty years since the money was buried. It could have washed away, disintegrated, maybe even been found. And with the amount of growth on this place, it might never be found if it really exists here."

"Well, we won't know if we don't at least give it a try, will we?" she said somewhat disgusted by his attitude. Then she added, "It might not even be on *this* island, we've got quite a few more that are larger. In fact, it might never have been *buried*. You're just assuming that."

"I'm sorry. I get your point. *If* he buried it, what would he have put it in to keep the moisture from damaging it? I mean, Florida has a high-water table—so it couldn't be a metal container. Assuming, of course, that it is buried."

"Well, where else could it be if not buried?"

"Are you trying to test me?" Art asked.

"No. I just want you to keep open to all possibilities."

"Well, then, to answer your question, I don't know. When you think about it, nowhere, I guess."

"Then let's search each one of these islands for anything that might indicate where it could be buried. I know it's going to be like shoveling sand against the tide, but if we don't at least give it a try then we will never feel satisfied that we gave it our best shot."

"Yeah. You're right, honey. Thanks for reminding me," Art admitted.

"You know, it wouldn't be so bad if it were not for these clusters of vines. They're everywhere and they make it almost impossible not to trip."

"I know. What we need is a machete. Only problem is we'd attract attention to ourselves walking around with a big blade like that and we'd prob'ly be breaking some law."

They spent nearly two hours scouring the island before climbing back into the boat and pushing off to the next one.

The second island was much smaller. It, too, was covered with thick weeds and marsh grass like the first one. There was no place to station the boat as the shrubbery and vines grew right to the water's edge. Art decided that they would attempt this one last, although he did say it probably would make the most secure hiding place—no one would think to look here. It was too inaccessible.

They moved to the third island. This one was bigger than the other two put together. It appeared that this was a popular spot, maybe for fishermen or for swimmers wanting some seclusion. It was crisscrossed with dirt paths where the vines had been cleared out of the way.

"I would almost doubt that Ed would've buried anything here. It's obvious that these paths have been here for quite some time and he'd have taken a chance maybe gettin' caught in the act or havin' people who are usin' the island discover it," Art said.

"We're here, so let's look anyway," Lavina said.

They took their time wandering about the island, checking out every path. The growth in the areas that were not near the paths was so thick as to be almost impossible to traverse.

Walking toward a tiny clearing, Lavina got tangled in some of the vines. Losing her balance and falling in some low-lying bushes, she let out a string of curses, which surprised Art as that was out of character for her. Rather than say anything aloud, Art would remind her later on that she owed forty dollars to the charity jar—a large plastic container his wife had placed in the kitchen with a slot cut out in the top. In order to curb Art from using four-letter words, she "fined" him five dollars every time he said something foul. The money was then to be used for some charitable gift at the prison. She knew that where her husband detested many of the inmates for their crimes and their actions toward the guards, he would hate to give anything to them, which might benefit them. It worked. In no time at all, his bad habit of using bad language was almost completely eliminated. Of course, he told her that this was a two-way street. She would be, likewise, responsible, to which she immediately agreed. Now would be payback.

Art did a high step to overcome the vines and made his way to his wife. Helping to free her from her prison of branches, she asked him, "What are those things anyway?"

"I have no idea. They've got some dry berries on them but what they are I don't know."

"Let me see some," she said as she managed to move into the clearing.

Art yanked up some of the vine and pulled the berries off and handed them to Lavina. "They look a bit like raisins," he said.

She spread them out in her left hand, moving them around with her right thumb and forefinger.

"They are raisins," she said. "These must be some kind of wild grape where they grow so low to the ground."

"They appear to be on all the islands. I'm just guessing from what we've already seen. It's like what I read in that history of Tarpon. It says that the underwater sponges in some areas here are surrounded by grapevines. I just never thought of grapevines underwater, and saltwater at that. Of course, it could be that those were at one time on the surface and are now submerged."

They checked out the section of land that was without any brush or any access other than the few scrub pine trees, which blocked it from view by anyone passing by the island on the open water. The ground was hard rather than sandy and would not have supported growth of any kind.

Odd, he thought, *maybe it's this way for a reason.* He began to kick at the ground with the heel of his shoe. He could not make much of a dent.

"What are you doing?" his wife asked.

"I find it strange that out of everything we've looked at so far, there's this five-foot-wide circle with dirt that's hard as a rock."

He took out a folding pocketknife and opened the largest blade. Bending down, he began to dig in the dirt. It started to crumble as he stabbed at it.

"What are you finding?" Lavina asked.

"Nothing yet. I think I'd like to get some tools, though, and take a better look. I still can't believe he'd choose a place like this to bury that amount of money. It just doesn't feel right."

"Who knows what he was thinking. I mean, he was on the run. Maybe this was his only opportunity."

"You could be right again," Art said.

They made their way back to the boat and headed to the marina. Once there, Art arranged to rent the boat again the next day. They then drove to the shopping district of Tarpon, which was away from the harbor and close to the Greek church.

Finding an Ace Hardware store, Art purchased a small pickax and two folding shovels similar to the portable ones the military uses for digging foxholes and trenches. He also bought rope, a heavy-duty pocketknife and some commercial-grade plastic garbage bags.

Tired from traipsing all over the first of the islands, they could not wait to get some sleep. Probably not the healthiest thing to do, they stopped at a convenience store, picked up some junk food, sodas, and premade sandwiches and went back to their motel. They turned on the TV, kept the volume very low, gorged themselves on their munchies and fell asleep. The TV remained on all during the night; they were so exhausted that it never disturbed them.

They arose early the next morning and were at the marina when it opened. They made sure the gas tank on the boat was full before starting out on their journey. The water was calm and they made good time getting out to the island.

As it was yesterday, there were no people on or near the island. In fact, as they left the harbor inlet, there was no activity anywhere as the hour was still early.

Art piloted the boat onto a natural ramp that had been created by the waves pushing sand onto the low gravel, then took the boat's mooring line and tethered it to one of the scrub pines on shore.

They took their equipment from the boat along with some sandwiches and sodas they picked up at a 7-Eleven store in Tarpon just before going to the marina that morning. Lavina brought along a portable radio saying she worked better to music.

Within minutes, they were back at the clearing. Art immediately began to strike at the ground with the pickax while Lavina set the radio onto a local FM station and placed it on a rock at the edge of the work site.

As Art picked away, she would shovel the dirt off to one side, covering some of the vines she had decidedly grown to detest—they were beasts that made it impossible to travel through these islands where the money could possibly be hidden.

Although the day was bright and hot, the wind picked up sending a warm breeze across the island, keeping them somewhat dry, as sweat had previously poured off them like water dripping off a rock ledge.

Art was down about two feet below the land surface. The hole he had dug was some three feet in diameter. He was encouraged when he unearthed a half-dollar dated 1973. It could have been dropped by Ed when he was digging the hole. He also found a glass Coca-Cola bottle and some soda cans.

"Do you think he left these things here on purpose?" Lavina asked.

"Prob'ly to throw anyone off if they dug here without knowing what was buried here. They would think it was nothing more than a trash pit.

Or, he could have used them as a marker—you know, showing him that this was the right place from where he first dug the hole."

Art kept digging. The wind picked up making a rushing noise as it passed through the trees and brush. Between the music on the radio and the sound of the wind and, perhaps, as their concentration was focused on the digging and the noises made by the pick and shovel, neither of them heard anything else.

With all the boat activity in the channel, no one heard the nearly silent skiff with its engine shut off and only the quiet whirring of an electric trolling motor approach the moored boat on the island.

Tom Fowler had been prowling the sponge docks keeping his eyes open for any sign of the Booker's rental car. He was disappointed when he discovered that they had moved out of the Best Western and had no idea as to where they went. His luck was uncanny, however, as he at last caught sight of them driving down Dodecanese Boulevard early one morning. He had parked his car on the boulevard and sat slouched down where he could watch the activity on the street without being easily seen. When Art's rental car suddenly went by in the heavy morning traffic, Fowler tried to back out of the parking space he was in in order to catch up to Art, but the car had already vanished.

Fowler drove down every street and alley way for several hours until he finally spotted Art's car in the parking lot at the marina. But neither Art nor his wife were anywhere in sight. He thought for sure that they must be on foot somewhere close by. Driving around the area he would often stop and watch for any sign of his two adversaries. He spent the entire day searching but had no luck until he returned to the marina and he saw them standing next to their car as Art unlocked the doors.

When Art and his wife drove out of the parking lot, Fowler tried to follow them, but the route they took would not allow him to stay on their trail without being obvious. He tried to second-guess them by driving up parallel streets, but that proved to be futile. They managed to lose him on one of the side streets.

Pretty smart, Fowler thought to himself, *parking in the marina lot rather than on the street or in a public parking area. Well, if you thought you outwitted me, you're wrong.*

The next day, Fowler returned to the marina only to discover that Art's car was already there. This time he decided to wait for them. Late in the afternoon he thought he recognized them coming in toward the marina in a small boat but he could not be sure as it pulled up to the dock out of his view. When he saw them walking out from the opposite side of the marina building close to the water, he knew his eyes had not failed him. He was able to remain out of their sight as he carefully surveyed their movements. He was not prepared for them to have rented a boat, but when they returned to the marina that day and, after seeing their animated gestures, he knew they had found something. He also knew he had to stay close to them.

Playing a hunch, the next day Fowler returned to the marina before it opened. He stayed out of sight and waited to see if the Bookers would appear. Just after the marina opened, Art and his wife pulled into the lot, parked their car and went into the building. *Thought you put one over on me, didja?* Fowler thought. *Well, surprise.* Fowler watched them get into a boat and start out past the docks. He then rented a boat shortly after the Booker's headed out on the water. He followed them at a distance, watching them carefully through a pair of binoculars he had stolen off of one of the pleasure boats at the marina. He had thought it convenient and thoughtful that someone had left those glasses there for him.

After he tied his boat to the same pine tree on the island as had Art, he loosened the rope that held the Booker's boat fast. He gave it a shove, and the boat floated out slowly into the water. With the increased wind and water current, it would not be long before it was far away from the island.

Fowler could not believe his good fortune. The wind was in his direction and he could hear the music of the radio and the noise of the digging as each strike by the pick hit ground and each shovel full was scooped up out of the hole. Not only could he locate where the Bookers were, but any noise he might make as he made his way over to where they were working would be diminished by that same breeze.

He was careful to not get hung up in the vines; they were a trap and a pain in the butt. He was almost directly in front of them when he decided to wait before surprising them. He was impressed that they had dug so deeply so quickly and had, obviously, been convinced that the money was not much further down as Art was cautious now not to strike so hard with the pickax.

Fowler took the Luger he had stolen out of Gabrielle's store from his belt and pointed it at Art.

"Nice job you're doing!" he finally called out, startling them.

Both Art and Lavina turned abruptly. Art started up out of the hole he had dug, the shovel raised defensively.

"Uh . . . uh!" Fowler exclaimed as he slowly shook his head. "Get back down in there and don't even move a muscle. I'd have no problem pulling this trigger 'cause we're all alone out here and no one would ever hear it. All I want is the money. I don't want to hurt either of you, but understand that I will if I have to."

"It took me a few minutes to recognize you the other day, inmate Fowler."

"Don't call me that!" Fowler shouted angrily. "My *inmate* days are over. In fact, you're helping to guarantee that right now."

"You know, you didn't have ta hurt that old lady."

"I do what I have to do. Just like now. I want you to keep digging until you find my money."

"Yeah, *your* money. Once you have it, what happens to us?"

"You'll be free to go."

"Right. Like you're gonna let us go."

"By the time you get off this island, I'll be long gone."

"Whattaya mean by that?"

"Well, I'm the only one here now with a boat. What does that tell you?"

Alarmed, Lavina finally spoke, "What did you do with our boat?"

"It should be about halfway to Mexico by now, judging from the wind and the current. Now forget it and get busy digging."

Art and his wife did as they were told. As they dug, Art was slowly becoming convinced that maybe there was no treasure here. After all, they were down more than four feet and water was beginning to enter the hole from below ground.

Fowler remained at a distance where he could keep an eye on them but not see very far down into the hole.

Art continued to dig until he came across a very thick vine at the bottom of the hole. Now he knew there was no treasure here but it gave him an idea. The vine looked like heavy rope that had been buried for some time. He tested the vine with his shovel and with a bit of pressure it moved. *Perfect*, he thought to himself.

He called out, "Hey! I think I've found something."

Suddenly Fowler sprang up. "What is it?" he asked.

"It looks like the rope that was wrapped around the money container," Art said, hoping that sounded plausible.

"Give me the rope we bought," Art said to Lavina, pointing to the coil on the ground near where she had piled the dirt from the hole.

She handed him the rope.

"What're you doin'?" Fowler asked.

"I'm gonna run this through the other rope down here. It's gonna take the three of us to haul this out of the dirt, stones and the little bit of mud that's holdin' it in place." Without waiting for any response, he continued what he was doing.

Once the rope was passed beneath the vine, Art climbed out of the hole and tied one end of the rope to the nearest pine tree with a decent-sized trunk. The other end he pulled in the opposite direction. He told his wife to stand beside him.

"Are you gonna help us or what?" Art asked Fowler.

"You don't need my help. You pull it up," he replied.

"Okay, suit yourself," Art said.

As Art and Lavina yanked on the rope, nothing happened. All Art feared was that the vine would give loose and then he would have to think of another plan.

With a grimace on his face, Art acted as though he was struggling with all of his strength to free up the buried treasure. In fact, he was letting his wife do all the pulling knowing and hoping that she could not release the vine.

"There's no way we can do it alone," Art finally said. "Two million dollars is a lot of money and from what Ed whispered to me in his cell, it's in denominations from tens to fifties, so it's got to weigh quite a bit, especially in the watertight container."

"Try again," Fowler commanded.

Art put on the same act as he did before. This time he grunted as though he was pulling some great weight and he spoke between gritted teeth, "Come . . . on . . . you . . . two . . . million . . . ucchh! . . . dollars!" Art knew he sounded corny but he did not care. He wanted Fowler at a disadvantage and if it meant using a trite statement, so be it.

"Come on, pull!" shouted Fowler.

Once more Art put on a show that could have won him an Academy Award.

He released the rope and then said, "I'm in as much of a hurry as you are to see this come up. I've never seen two million dollars and I really don't care that I won't get any of it; my *life* means more to me than *that*. I just want to see what it looks like."

Playing on Fowler's greed and anxiety, Art turned away from Fowler, looked back down into the hole, picked up the rope, tugged on it, shook his head and once again suggested his help. This time, as Art pretended not to pay any attention to Fowler, Fowler came over and grabbed ahold of the rope next to Art and his wife. He could not grip the rope and the gun at the same time. Seeing that Art was focused on the treasure, Fowler slipped the Luger into his belt. Art could sense without looking what Fowler had done.

Now as they got ready to pull, Art gave the word as well as all of his strength.

Unexpectedly to Fowler, the tremendous intensification of force pulled that vine out like someone lifting a thread off a piece of clothing.

Fowler flew backwards, his feet caught up in the vines surrounding the clearing and he fell on his back with Art crashing down on top of him. Lavina fell off to the side of both men.

Although somewhat disoriented, Fowler tried to get up but not before Art plowed him in the face with a solid punch, one that he had built up in himself since Fowler's first threat with the gun.

Blood gushed out of Fowler's mouth. Art had loosened every tooth in the front of Fowler's head.

Art lifted his massive arm and, making a fist the size of a softball, slammed it into Fowler's face once again. This time he hit him just under the left eye and directly on his nose, breaking it. More blood rushed profusely out of the flattened orifice.

Art raised himself up off of Fowler, removing the gun from Fowler's belt at the same time and tossing it aside. Still angry, he gave Fowler one more hard punch to the abdomen. This winded him and caused some trauma to his internal organs.

Helping his wife to her feet, Art told her to pick up their belongings. He then went over and dragged Fowler from on top of the vines. Using the strength of his anger, he hoisted Fowler up over his head and threw him into the deepest growth of vines he could find.

"Let him work his way out of that," Art said to no one.

Turning back to Lavina he said, "Let's get outta here."

They ran back to Fowler's rented skiff, threw all their items on board and untied the tether. Art washed Fowler's blood off his hands in the warm Gulf water, pushed the skiff out off the gravel and started the engine. He circled the island in hopes that he might see the boat he had rented, but it was not to be found.

When they reached the marina, the owner came running out shouting to them, "Are you all right? What happened? Your boat was just towed in by a fisherman who found it floating in the Gulf. I was about to call the Coast Guard. And where did you get my other boat?"

Art explained that the man who had rented the skiff he was in tried to rob them and took away his boat. They got into a fight and he left the man on an island. He would notify the police now that both boats were safe.

The marina operator appeared to have bought the story. Art, however, was going to leave Fowler on the island without telling anyone. "If he makes it back," he said to Lavina, "then good for him. If he doesn't, then good for us."

They made arrangements to rent the boat again the next day.

That night Lavina looked at the books once more.

"You know," she said, "this book of Steinbeck's makes sense all of a sudden."

"How's that?" Art asked.

"I'd call those stinking vines the grapes of wrath."

Art bolted upright in bed, "You're absolutely right! What an accurate description. Again, a clue that fits. Just like you said about things being so obvious we seem to miss them. The history book gave us the cay or the key. That book, *Treasure Island,* seems to tell us that the money is on one of the key islands. The *Grapes of Wrath* are what we keep encountering. All of a sudden, these *clues* seem so sophomoric—so childish in their simplicity. I keep thinking we should be looking for something more obscure. Yet, as plain as these signs appear to be, it still has been a challenge figuring them out. I wonder what we aren't seeing in the book of poems and the dictionary?"

"We just have to keep looking now," she stated.

"We must be getting close," Art said, more positive than he had been in quite some time.

CHAPTER SIXTEEN

The Lighthouse

Art called into work sick the next morning because his personal days were all used.

The Bookers stopped at the Price Rite Food Mart on 19A before going to the marina to take out another rental boat. Art had spotted the sign that advertised Boar's Head Premium Deli and he knew from his experience with the former warden that the best sandwiches were made with that quality product. He ran in and picked up enough food to keep them nourished and strengthened throughout the day.

They piled everything into the boat and headed straight for the next island in the chain.

As they passed the island where Fowler had been abandoned, they looked, but did not see any sign of him. They continued without stopping.

They approached the fourth island. This one was small but not quite as small as the second one they had visited. They found that pathways, short ones, also led from one side to the other. The biggest difference here was that there were not many trees. It took them no time at all to examine the entire island. There was not one thing which would have given any indication that this was Treasure Island.

The fifth island was the largest in the chain. It was the farthest out and even had a lighthouse on one end.

They landed their craft on the opposite end of the island from the lighthouse. This had the only place that made for an easy approach. It was obvious that this, too, was a popular place to visit even though no one was present at this time. Beer cans littered the ground close to shore along with candy and snack wrappers, fishing sinkers and lures, and cigarette butts. *Some people are such pigs!* Art thought.

Once they secured the boat and removed all the gear they anticipated using, they started their search.

As the other islands, this one was covered, except for a few paths, with the same growth. Coming near to the end where the lighthouse was located, they noticed that the paths stopped. The lighthouse could not be easily reached. Evidently, the approach to the lighthouse was from the water.

They knew from the beginning that the exploration would be difficult—perhaps even fruitless. The island was so big and so overgrown, where to look would be their greatest problem.

There were several sites where clearings could be found. It was Art's opinion after probing their surface that these were like the other one, just places to bury trash.

Art said, "Let's go take a look over by the lighthouse."

"How are we going to get there?"

"The brush is too thick here, so let's take the boat. It'll be a challenge to find a place to moor."

By the time they got back to the boat, both were hungry. They opened their sandwiches and cooled off from the intensity of the sun's heat with some soda. As they sat on the boat's bench seats, they discovered they were ravenous. They devoured what they had brought and it gave them renewed stamina.

Art piloted the boat around to the side of the island where the lighthouse had, for years, given warning to sailors of the rugged outcroppings and shoals, which could sink any ship that ran aground. There was a tiny inlet usable only at high tide. It had a sandy bottom and led inward some twenty feet. When Art spotted it, he turned in, cut the engine, raised the motor and glided onto the sand. Again they took their tools and Art secured the boat.

They made their way to the lighthouse, passing three weather-battered signs stating NO TRESPASSING. The building was actually much larger than it had appeared at a distance.

"That certainly looks majestic, doesn't it?" Lavina commented.

"Yeah, looks like the shuttle at Cape Canaveral," Art responded.

As Art said that, both looked at one another, mouths agape. Then they started to laugh as they said in unison, "The spaceship!"

"It really could not have been this easy," she said.

"Well, we're not there yet."

"No, but what better clue. It looks like the description in the dictionary—'an imaginary mode of transportation between planets.' After all, this would be what someone would have imagined a rocket ship to look like back then."

"I wish we had brought the book of poems with us. I locked all the books in the car's trunk again."

"Well, we've come this far. At least we can look around some. Then if nothing hits us, tonight we can read love poems to one another."

"Yuh! Right!" Art mumbled.

"I can remember when you were *so* romantic. Now you're getting just like all men when they start to take their wife for granted."

"Oh, c'mon, baby. You know I love you. I've just got this whole business on my mind."

Walking up close to him, putting her face up to his as near as she could get on her tiptoes, and placing her right hand forefinger to his chin, she said, "You better remember that I'm more important than money because that's how I feel about you."

"I'm sorry, honey. Of course, you are. You're the most important thing in my life and worth much more to me than any two million dollars."

"You always know the right thing to say," she said as she walked away and over toward the lighthouse.

As they approached the lighthouse they saw how deceiving it was from a distance. The tower was much bigger than it had appeared. It was a cylindrical tube much like the booster rocket on the Challenger space shuttle, braced by steel legs that held the dome at the top and then spread out at the bottom to give it support. There was a steel door at the base of the cylinder. The entire structure was surrounded by a high, chain-link fence with a chain-link gate. At the top of the fence were three strands of barbed wire. There was a large sign on the gate with the words RESTRICTED AREA followed by a warning to keep out.

"Looks like the fence was put up fairly recently," Art said. "They must have had some problems with local kids getting into the tower for parties or mischief."

"That thing doesn't look very safe," Lavina responded. "Look at the rust!"

"Yeah. Well, it's old. There's no doubt about that."

"So, where do we start?" she asked.

"I'd like to get a look-see from the top of that tower, but I guess that's out of the question judging from the size of that padlock on the gate. Let's check the ground around the fence."

Unlike the other islands, this one was large enough to sustain the growth of a greater variety of vegetation along with the vines and low-to-the-ground brush. Palm trees were plentiful along with other leafy hardwoods. Marsh grass grew to three-foot lengths.

Working their way outward from the fence, they searched the ground for any area that appeared to have been disturbed over the years. The few bare spots yielded nothing encouraging. The rest of the earth was covered with plants having deep roots.

"I'd like to check the inside of the fenced-in area," Art said.

"But Art, the sign says it's restricted, besides it's locked," Lavina replied.

"I know. Maybe I can get over that fence."

"Did you hear me? I said the sign says it's restricted."

"Yeah, baby. But I'm just gonna take a look. I'm not gonna disturb anything."

His wife raised her eyes toward the sky and just shook her head.

Art gripped the support pipe for the chain-link just below the barbed wire on the gate and raised his right foot to step on the lock that would act as a rung on a ladder. As he hoisted himself up, a curious thing happened. The lock opened and gave way and Art found himself kissing the restriction sign as his right foot struck the ground.

"Whoa!" was all he could say.

"Quality government equipment," he finally stated as he reached down and picked up the lock. "The insides must have rusted or . . . maybe . . ."

"I know what you're thinking," his wife interjected. "Or, maybe, Ed Fitzgerald *spirited* the lock open. We'll never know."

They swung the gate open and went inside the compound. The steel door to the tower was ajar. It gave out a screeching noise as Art pulled it open further on its rusted hinges. The noise was amplified by the hollow inside to the cylindrical tube which formed the lighthouse structure. There were circular stairs that reached all the way to the dome. They were littered with glass from broken bottles, obviously the remnants of uninvited guests over the years.

The metal stairs showed signs of decay in some places, but not enough to be dangerous. It was dark except for the light from the large square portholes cut every twenty feet upward into the side of the cylinder.

Art took out the Mini-Mag pocket flashlight he always carried when he was on the job. It had an adjustable lens that gave a piercing brightness that illuminated the section in front of them. A metal hand rail followed the curvature of the outside wall of the tower.

Art tested the stairs just to be sure they were safe enough to hold them. He went up a dozen of them and then called to his wife, "It's okay, hon, come on up."

They climbed the long flight of steps to where they ended at the base of the dome. There was another lock that held fast the trap door leading into the dome. This one was made of heavy brass and would certainly not give as did the last one. It was easy to see up here as there was an open porthole, which let in not only plenty of light but also the elements of weather. The lock was encrusted with material similar to the barnacles found on metal objects under seawater.

"Quite a view out this opening," Art said.

"Don't get too close, you could fall out!" she admonished, as she sized-up the open space that could easily have accommodated Art's large frame. "From the ground, these openings didn't seem that big."

"I'll be careful," he replied.

"Oh!" she said, looking out the opening and taking in just a cursory view. "I can't look down. It makes me dizzy."

"We did come up quite a ways," he said. "I wish Ed would spirit us into the dome. I'd like to get a full view of the island."

"I guess we can't have everything."

There was no way they could get into the lighthouse for a look from this height. They descended the stairs and decided that the next best thing was to work a pattern out from the base of the building's frame. The ground inside the compound still had to be examined.

They tied one end of the rope they had brought to a bolt protruding from the lighthouse metalwork but close to the ground. The other end they stretched out some fifteen feet and holding that end they walked in a semicircle. Had they been able to walk the circumference of the building it would have looked like a giant maypole. Moving slowly, they could examine the ground carefully in this area, which was fairly clear of brush and vines.

Trying to keep track of where they had been and where they needed to go to search the other side of the lighthouse was not working out well. They decided to cut the rope into ten-foot lengths and lay the pieces in a grid-type pattern fanning out from the base of the building.

Standing side by side, checking each grid carefully, and picking away at the ground with their axes, they covered the area in a short period of time. It produced nothing, however. They repeated this pattern until they had covered all the exposed ground.

It was getting late and they did not want to spend the night on the island. Before it got dark, they replaced the lock on the fence gate, closing it to give the appearance of being locked. They then put their things back in the boat and returned to the marina, once again making an agreement to have the rental boat yet another day.

Once in their motel room, they opened the book of poetry and started reading each one beginning with the first page. Beneath the title of each poem was the name of the author, many of which showed to be anonymous.

"This was the only book I did not enjoy," Art said.

"Why not?" she asked.

"Because I could not understand a lot of what the poets were trying to say."

"Like what?"

Flipping through the pages he said, "Like this one: 'My Galley,' by Sir Thomas Wyatt. See what you get out of this: 'My galley, charged with forgetfulness, through sharp seas in winter nights doth pass 'tween rock and rock; and eke mine enemy, alas! That is my Lord, steereth with cruelness; and every oar a thought in readiness, as though that death were light in such a case.' See what I mean?"

"Yes, I see. It's not easy especially when we don't know their thoughts at the time of their writing."

"Look at this one. I've heard it before but I don't remember a thing about it. 'It is an ancient mariner, and he stoppeth one of three. By thy long gray beard and glittering eye, now wherefore stopp'st thou me?' What's he talking about?"

"I think you'd get a better idea if you would go to the next verse. See," she said as she pointed to the words on the page, "he's speaking about a wedding and if you realize that then you can see that this ancient mariner has stopped one of three wedding guests and then that guest addresses the mariner with his long gray beard and asks him why he is being stopped."

"I'm glad you see that. I guess I just don't have the patience for poetry unless it's written in today's language. Even then, I'm not much into poetry."

"It seems to me I can remember some clever poems you once wrote to me back when we first started to date."

"I don't remember. That was a long time ago." Art then lifted the book up and continued to thumb through the pages. The conversation was, obviously, over.

CHAPTER SEVENTEEN

Murder

The motel room door shook as Officer Harry Poulos attempted to wake the sleeping occupants. Out of a sound sleep Art shot bolt upright in the bed, his heart pounding.

"Who is it?" Lavina asked him in a low, raspy voice.

"How should I know," Art said as he got out of bed and grabbed the pair of blue jeans that he had left draped over the chair next to the writing desk.

"I'm coming . . . I'm coming. . . . Who is it?" he shouted through the closed door.

"Officer Poulos, Mr. Booker. Open the door, please, I've got to talk to y'all."

Art unlocked and opened the door as he asked, "What are *you* doing here in the middle of the night?"

"I've got to ask y'all some questions."

"*Now?* About what?"

"About the man y'all left out on the island," Poulos replied.

"Oh, you found him. I knew the fellow at the marina would eventually be worried about him enough to call the police after I told him about our encounter. He must have been upset about that guy pushing his boat out into the Gulf. Had it disappeared he'd have been out some major bucks. Anyway, what did *he* have to say?"

Officer Poulos stepped through the entrance and into the motel room followed by another officer—a man wearing plain clothes but with a gun, badge and handcuffs on his belt—who, up until now, had remained out of sight. The man, surprised by Art's dimensions, slowly looked up and scrutinized the physical proportions of this man who stood more than a foot taller than himself and had arm muscles the size of the detective's thighs.

"I'm afraid there wasn't much he could say. The man is dead," Officer Poulos said.

"What!" came the incredulous reply in a loud whisper. "What do you mean . . . *dead?*"

"That's what we're here to talk to you about, Mr. Booker." This time it was the voice of the other officer.

"Hey, look . . ." Art began but was cut off abruptly when the second officer raised his hand in a halting motion.

"First, Mr. Booker," said the officer, "I have to advise you of your rights before you say anything. You have the right to remain silent. If you give up the right to remain silent, anything you say can and will be used against you in a court of law. You have the right to an attorney and to have him present with you before any questioning. If you cannot afford an attorney, one will be appointed for you by the state of Florida. Do you understand your rights, Mr. Booker?"

With his mouth hanging open and his eyes showing grave concern, Art slowly nodded his head and quietly said, "Yes."

"Are you willing to speak with me, knowing that you may stop me at any time during questioning and may refuse to further answer any questions?" the plainclothes officer asked.

Again Art said, "Yes."

"Before I begin, I want you to know that I am a detective with the Pinellas County Sheriff's Office. The reason I have been called into this case is because the Anclote Keys are divided between our county and Pasco County. Pasco handles any incidents that take place on the northern group of islands and we have jurisdiction over the southern section, which includes the island where the deceased was found. This, however, will be a shared investigation with Tarpon Springs as our original contact came through the Tarpon Springs Police Department. Now, it is my understanding that Officer Poulos has been working with you in another situation involving the deceased. Is that correct?"

Art simply nodded affirmatively.

"Why don't you tell us what happened on the island, Mr. Booker."

Art then related the unexpected meeting as it took place out in the Gulf.

"But I don't understand . . . he was unconscious," Art said, "but not dead when we left him." Art then asked, "Am I under arrest?"

As the words came out of his mouth, Lavina sobbed. She was in a state of confusion between upset and anger and slowly moving toward hysteria. Being the wife of a corrections officer and thinking of the possibility that her husband might go to jail, she could just picture him on the inside of a prison with the men he had kept locked up. She had heard the stories of what happens to cops and COs that end up in prison. She began to shake as she considered this.

"But that man was the one who had been following *us*!" she blurted out. "He's the one who beat up Gabrielle! He's the one who came after us with the gun!" She spoke so quickly, neither officer had the opportunity to reply.

"No, Mr. Booker, you're not under arrest, we're just trying to gather some information. However, you would be wise not to leave Tarpon Springs for awhile."

"Oh man, oh man," Art exclaimed. "Do you know what my job is? I work at a state prison in New York. I'm supposed to be on sick leave for a couple of days. Now how'm I gonna explain that I'm in Florida and what's going on down here?"

The officer only smiled.

Poulos then spoke up. "We do have all y'all's fingerprints on file along with your information following that break-in to your motel room, so we won't need you to come down to the station. The medical examiner will be doing an autopsy in the morning. We will be in touch with y'all once we have the results."

"An autopsy?" Art asked.

"Yes, Mr. Booker. We want to be sure of the cause of death."

The plainclothes officer then began to inquire of the Bookers details about the man who had been stalking them. Receiving evasive answers, some of which were obvious, but giving them the advantage of the lateness of the hour as a loose reason for them not being coherent, the officer stopped his questions. But he again reminded the Bookers not to leave Tarpon Springs. He would be in touch with them soon.

Art knew that after the officers left he would not be able to get any more sleep. He was wound tighter than a clock spring and there was nothing to do but wait until morning. But what would morning bring? He began to imagine the headlines, STATE PRISON CORRECTIONS OFFICER FACES MURDER CHARGES. He felt a chill come over his body and he began to get sick to his stomach. Lavina was pacing the floor and mumbling to herself, "I can't believe this is happening to us. We came here to get rich and now we're gonna lose everything. It's unreal. Is this really happening to us?"

CHAPTER EIGHTEEN

Suspects

It was about one-twenty in the afternoon when the phone rang in Art's motel room. Their desire to go treasure-hunting was just about nonexistent after learning that Fowler was dead and they were suspects in his murder. The voice on the other end asked if Art and his wife would please come down to the police station.

Without even asking why, Art simply said, "We'll be there in about ten minutes." Then he hung up the receiver.

"You know, babe," Art began, "they must feel that we are innocent."

"Why do you say that?"

"Two reasons. First, they did not haul us into the station last night and sequester us before asking us any questions. And second, they did not really interrogate us here at the motel. It was more like they wanted to see our reaction to the news of Fowler's death."

"I wish I felt as confident as you do," she replied.

Upon arrival at the police station, Lavina was asked to remain with one of the detectives in an office off of the main lobby. Art told her it would be all right, he was sure that what they were going to do is question them one at a time out of hearing of the other; they wanted to make sure their stories were closely aligned.

Seated in that same interrogation room where the Bookers had recovered their stolen books, Art was asked if he owned a gun.

"Yes, but it's in New York. I don't have a permit to carry it in Florida."

"What kind of a gun is it?"

"A Ruger Black Hawk," Art replied.

"Do you own any other guns?"

"I do have a Remington shotgun and a Weatherby Magnum rifle, but those are also in New York."

"You don't own a nine millimeter?"

"No," Art said.

"Let me ask you something . . . what did you do with the gun that belongs to Gabrielle?"

"What did *I* do with it! I never took it. It must still be where it landed in those grape vines on the island. I tossed it aside once I got the guy down on the ground. I just wanted to be away from that place and I never gave the gun a second thought. It's still got to be there."

"We scoured the entire island and found nothing. The reason we were so late in coming to see you last night was because of all the time we spent searching it. The gun is missing, Mr. Booker."

"Well, what has this got to do with anything?"

"The autopsy shows that the deceased died of a gunshot wound through the eye and into the brain."

"You never said he was killed by a gun!" Art interjected.

"The bullet was a nine millimeter. It *could* have come from the missing Luger," the detective continued. "And, yes, as you already know, the man's real name is Thomas Fowler. And, Mr. Booker, by coincidence his last known address just happened to be at the prison where you work. Now why don't you tell us the whole story?"

At first, Art hesitated. His stubborn streak was fighting to retain this information. However, he felt that by doing so would only hurt his chances of coming out of this unscathed. He knew he needed their help so he relented. Giving them as much information as possible except for some explicit details, Art told them the entire story.

"Well," said Poulos, "I can better understand why y'all were being so cagey with me. If this ever got out, those islands would be crawling with people looking for the money. I'd probably be there myself if I thought there really was any money; however, I don't want to waste my time on what y'all are probably going to discover . . . and that is, this is nothing more than a wild-goose chase. I don't want to discourage you none, but I think from the number of times treasure hunters have searched these islands over the years, if anything *was* there it has already been found."

"You see," said the second officer, "Anclote Cay was thought to have been a pirates' stash for centuries and once in a while, some lucky person will find a piece of eight or even a gold doubloon."

"Right now," said Poulos, "I'd suggest that y'all might want to find an attorney and y'all might want to suggest to him that this whole issue could have been one of self-defense."

"What!" Art exclaimed. "What do you mean 'this whole issue?' I told you I didn't kill him!"

"Easy, Mr. Booker. I'm not saying that y'all did anything wrong, but I believe in helping out a fellow law enforcement officer if he is being unfairly accused."

"Then I *am* being looked at as a suspect," Art commented.

"Without the gun and without more information from the FBI laboratory concerning the bullet that was lodged in Mr. Fowler's brain, we have nothing concrete on which to hold you. The circumstantial evidence is too weak and there are no witnesses. Basically, it comes down to the story y'all told to us. Besides that, we now know how to reach you so we will not continue to insist that you remain in Tarpon."

Art breathed a sigh of relief knowing that he could go back to work, yet he was still plagued at being considered a suspect. And he knew from having dealt with men on both sides of the law that Poulos was cutting him some slack—the young cop believed him and wanted to help out a brother law enforcement officer.

As Art walked from the interrogation room, he saw Lavina was waiting for him in the lobby.

"Is everything okay?" she asked.

"I should ask you the same question. Yeah, everything's okay—for now."

"Oh, God, I'm so scared," she began, her hands trembling nervously. "I was so uneasy without you being in there with me that when the detective started to ask me questions I just blurted out everything I knew."

"That's okay, babe. I know you were uncomfortable. Don't worry."

"But I hope I didn't say the wrong thing!" she exclaimed.

"You told the truth, right? So you have nothing to worry about."

"Of course I did. And I told the detective I would be staying in the area. It's not a matter of choice. After he told me that you would be free to go to work I suggested I remain as I am as much a suspect as you but I know we did nothing wrong."

"Ucchhhh . . . don't use that word *suspect*. I don't even want to think about it. My blood runs cold when I hear the word suspect—it hits too close to my job—if I was ever found guilty of murder, you know what they'd do to me. We've got to get cleared of this. In a way I am glad that you're willing to stay; it shows that we're not running away. But somehow I've got to get some time off and be here with you. There's too much going on for you to be here alone."

CHAPTER NINETEEN

A Good Attorney

"The real question is," Art said to his wife after they had returned to the motel, "who could have done this? Had they found the gun, it could have been a suicide."

"I don't know. I just . . . don't . . . know."

※ ※ ※ ※

Art called the airport and made arrangements for his flight home. He felt as though he was operating in a trance; nothing seemed real to him. *What could have happened on that island?* he wondered.

There was an available flight at eight o'clock the next morning. It made one stopover in Pittsburgh before reaching its final destination in Albany. He booked passage using his American Express card even though there was a premium to be paid to the airline for such short notice. The one big advantage in using American Express was the bonus airline mileage he would accumulate by charging all of his expenses to that card. And right now, any savings for air travel would be welcome.

Art and Lavina spent a sleepless night. The stress of something so unexpected worked on their minds until the early morning hours. They were exhausted but could not release the tension that enveloped them. Art hoped that the humming of the plane's engines would lull him enough to grab a few winks. Lavina was hoping that a cup of coffee would wake her fully so that she could think through what they should do from here.

Leaving the airport following the departure of Art's flight, she remembered seeing a law office near the hardware store in the center of

Tarpon's business district. Her first thought was to stop there and introduce herself and see what kind of a reading she would get from their meeting providing the attorney had time to see her.

Parking about a quarter mile from the office in the nearest unoccupied space, Lavina locked the car and walked the distance to the center of the block of two-story buildings while thinking in her mind how she would approach the attorney. She climbed the stairs leading to the second-floor offices and opened the door to the reception area as the stenciling on the frosted glass window in the door said PLEASE WALK IN.

"I'm sorry, but Mr. Apostoles is in with a client," the receptionist, a smartly dressed woman in her mid-forties wearing very ostentatious gold glasses, announced to Lavina Booker following her inquiry. "He has appointments all day today. Could I ask what this is in reference to?"

"Of course. My husband and I are suspects in a murder and we need legal counsel," Lavina said matter-of-factly.

Taken back by such an abrupt response, the receptionist uttered, "Uhhh . . . just a moment. Perhaps if I alerted Mr. Apostoles as to the nature of your request, he might want to speak to you." With that, the receptionist got up from behind her desk and walked to the closed office door to the left of the lobby entrance. She knocked twice, lightly, and entered without waiting for a reply.

Within minutes a tall man about sixty-plus years of age, somewhat portly, his gray hair in a crew cut, came out of the office followed by the receptionist. He was wearing a three-piece, pin-striped suit that to Lavina seemed oddly incongruous for someone working in an extremely warm tourist/retirement area like Tarpon Springs, notwithstanding the fact that the office was quite cool from the air conditioning system.

"Mrs. Booker? I'm George Apostoles. I understand you would like to see me about a very serious allegation. Could you give me just a thumbnail sketch as to how you and your husband managed to get into such a difficult circumstance?"

With that, Lavina explained their predicament leaving out most of the peripheral information and sticking just to the main points.

Apostoles asked her if she could remain in the office while he handled the matter his client was on hold for in his private office.

She agreed without hesitation. She liked this man and felt comfortable with him and she believed he could help them.

The attorney returned shortly, escorting the man he had been speaking with in his office—an elderly gentleman who winked and smiled at

Lavina as he entered the reception area. The two men shook hands and the client walked out into the hallway. Apostoles asked Lavina Booker to come into his now-empty office, gesturing with his hands at the same time as an indication for her to enter.

They met in his inner office for about an hour keeping yet another client waiting in the lobby. The attorney could see the distress in Mrs. Booker's demeanor and he would not let her leave until she felt more at peace. He took copious notes rarely looking up except when he asked for her to repeat something she had said so as to be accurate in writing down exactly what she was telling him.

He explained that although there was limited circumstantial evidence, there were no witnesses and no proof that could convict them; even the murder weapon was missing. On top of that, the dead man was a convicted felon who had continued his criminal behavior even after his release from prison. Compounded by the fact that he had held them at gunpoint with a weapon stolen from a person who was physically attacked during the commission of another felony, they had a defense in self-protection—it was weak, but still it was a defense.

Lavina felt a great burden removed from her as she left the attorney's office. She could not wait for Art to call so that she could relay to him the good news.

Arriving back at the motel, she lay down on the bed and promptly fell into a sound sleep.

It was seven o'clock when she heard what she thought was a doorbell ringing in a house, which looked like a temple with dark-paneled, interior walls. The doorbell was incessant in its demand to be answered. *Why isn't someone looking to see who's there?* she thought.

As she awoke from her sleep, she realized that she had been dreaming and that the telephone in her motel room was ringing and not a doorbell.

She reached across the bed for the receiver and with a very dry mouth eked out a pathetic, "Hello?"

"Hi! It's me. I'm home," Art said with a cheerful voice. "What took you so long answering the phone?" he asked.

"Oh . . . give me a minute to wake up and collect my thoughts. What time is it anyway?"

"Seven."

"Day or night?"

"Night."

"Well, at least I got a few winks. I am still beat."

"I got some rest on the plane. I'm glad you finally got some sleep. You were so wired, how did you manage to relax enough to wind down?"

"That's what I want to tell you. I had a great day after you left."

"Thanks a lot!"

"No, no, that's not what I mean. Let me tell you . . ."

With that, Lavina explained her meeting with the attorney.

"You did great, honey," Art said after she finished her story. "Now if only I have similar luck when I meet with my commanding officer in the morning. I'm gonna ask for time off without pay. I don't know what reasoning I'll use, just personal business I guess."

"That's what it is now, for sure, so it shouldn't be a problem," his wife began. "You've never abused any benefit at work so you should be okay."

"I've got my fingers crossed. I'll call you as soon as I know anything. Okay? I love you."

"I love you, too. Just come back as soon as you can. It's creepy being here alone not knowing what happened out on that island after we left."

"I've been thinking about that since we walked out of the meeting at the police station. I still don't have an answer. . . ."

Art was given a month's time to work out his personal problems. He was careful not to tell his commanding officer any details, only that he had a family situation which needed to be resolved. Art was fortunate that the warden was out of town. This way, the captain was acting in his place and it was somewhat easier dealing with him than with the man at the top. Lately, any time-off requests initiated by Art seemed to be met with resistance and a lot of not-so-subtle questions being asked by the warden, who had to approve such petitions, about where Art was going. Since the death of Ed Fitzgerald, Art became more cognizant of peculiarities concerning those who had taken an unusual interest in the inmate who had stayed relatively quiet the past few years of his incarceration. As strange as they were, these actions had not yet raised any suspicion in Art toward the prison administration.

In no time at all, Art was reserving a flight back to Florida.

CHAPTER TWENTY

Who is He?

It was coincidence that Art arrived back at the motel from the airport with his wife at the same time that Officer Poulos showed up at the door.

"I tried to call y'all on the phone but I see y'all were out," the officer said looking at Lavina Booker. Then, turning his focus to Art, he said, "Hi Mr. Booker, y'all just get back from New York?"

"Officer Poulos . . . just about the last person I see when I leave this state and about the first person to greet me when I come back. I feel like a celebrity. What's the latest?" he asked as he closed the door on the rental car.

"We received a report from the FBI laboratory this afternoon. The bullet was a nine millimeter and the rifling indicated that it was consistent with that found in Luger handguns," the officer stated matter-of-factly as he walked to the front of the Booker's car and sat down on the hood, raising his right leg and resting his foot on the bumper.

"I don't understand," said Lavina. "What's rifling?"

"Well, ma'am," Poulos began, "rifling in a gun is a series of grooves etched in the barrel. When a bullet is fired, the grooves form a circular spiral that force the bullet to spin"—the cop demonstrated with his hand as a means of visual explanation while continuing—"and that insures an accurate shot to the target. In this case, the eye of Mr. Fowler."

"That gives me the willies," she said. "Oh, by the way, we took your advice and contacted Mr. Apostoles, the lawyer."

"Well, he's about the best, so y'all made a good choice. I should know; he's my uncle."

"You know," said Lavina, "now that I take a closer glance, I can see the family resemblance. He looks a lot like you."

"Yes, ma'am. My dad and he were brothers."

"Then why don't you both have the same name?"

"We do, ma'am. The family name is Apostolopoulos. He shortened his to Apostoles; I just took Poulos. You see, my full name is Charlambos Apostolopoulos. That's the name I was given at my christening at Saint Nicholas church. Where we are in a tourist area that caters to many non-Greeks, no one could ever pronounce my name correctly, so I Americanized it to a degree. Now I am Harry Poulos."

Lavina just nodded her head as she said, "I can fully understand that. My husband would never have been able to get his tongue around that one. He's had hard enough time with a few of the names in the *History of Tarpon Springs* book he's been reading."

"Was there anything else you wanted to tell us, Officer Poulos?" Art asked, interrupting his wife.

"Just one more thing. We have divers searching the water around the island for that gun."

"Makes sense. Anything further?"

"No sir. Just wanted to let y'all know what we received and what we're doing. I'll leave now and let y'all get settled in." With that, he stood up by pushing his right foot against the bumper, raised his right hand in a wave and walked back to his car.

"Okay, honey, what's our plan?" Art asked as they went into their motel room.

"Oh, so now I'm the one calling the shots, huh?"

"Well, you've done such a great job so far; I figured why press my luck."

"I think we'd better get back to that island with the lighthouse. Everything is leading in that direction, don't you think?"

"Hey, babe, whatever you say."

"You're being awfully nice to me. What do you want?"

"Nothin', babe, honest . . . I'm just being myself."

"Oh wait a minute! Now I know you're up to something. What is it?"

"Why are you always so suspicious?"

"Because I know you, Arthur Booker."

He stayed quiet for a moment and then a smile crossed his face.

"Okay. You got me. I was hoping you'd be in a mood to rub my back tonight."

"Hah! I knew it!" she piped up but then softened her tone. "Well, you deserve one, so when we get back from dinner I'll rub your back 'til you fall asleep."

"You are so good to me."

"Don't you ever forget it . . . ever! Now tomorrow we go back to the marina, rent a boat, load up with supplies and head out."

"Sounds like a plan to me," Art said.

Both of them washed up and left the motel to get their supper.

The sun came up with a brilliant brightness. There was not a cloud to be seen in the sky. It looked to be a perfect day.

Art and his wife could not have slept if they wanted to. The entire motel room was illuminated by the sun's white intensity.

Art pulled his pillow over his head but it did no good. There was no way to feel comfortable. He was awake now whether he liked it or not.

"What time is it?" his wife asked.

"Five-fifteen," Art answered.

"Time to make the donuts," she said.

"Ucchhh! I am so tired of that old ad from Dunkin' Donuts. Can't you find a new slogan?"

"I happen to like that one."

"All right . . . all right . . . let's get up."

They arose and within an hour were ready to head out.

"Do you think any place is open yet?" Lavina asked.

"Let me tell you, the marina will be open because people go fishing early. The sandwich shops down by the docks will be open for the same reason. We can get a bite at Dunkin' Donuts because we know they were up early 'to make the donuts.' What else do we need?"

"I think that about sums it up," she said. "Okay. Let's go."

They locked the door to the motel room as they walked out. Art carried the book of poems with him—the last clue to their treasure hunt.

When they arrived at the marina, the dock man was hesitant to rent them a boat.

Art said to the man, "You don't really believe that I killed that guy, do ya? I mean, do you think I would have come back here and told you what I did tell you about leaving that guy on the island if I *had* killed him?

Does that make any sense? Don't you think I'd a made up some kind of a story and then disappeared?"

"Well, I don't know what you were thinking," the man responded. "I waited 'til the next day before I called the police. I called them because I was ticked that that guy would cast one of my boats out to sea. I didn't care about what happened to him 'til the cops said they found his body."

"I kind of figured that was the reason you called them," Art replied.

"Well, I got a little nervous when they told me that," the marina operator admitted.

"Let me ask you this . . . did anyone else rent a boat from you that day? Ya know, someone without any fishing gear?"

The man thought for a minute and then said, "I can't recall right off-hand. But let's take a look at my rental book to see how many people took boats that day. Maybe something will strike me." With that the man went inside the building while Art and Lavina followed closely behind.

The man walked over to the chest-high counter and opened a ledger-style book. He thumbed through the pages until he found the date in question. "Well," the man said, "other than my regular customers who operate their own craft, there were only five boats rented out. There was your boat, the dead man's boat, one to Dr. Schoenfeld—I know him, he rents from me every year. I've also got one to a Carmen Rinaldi; he was obviously going fishing. He had so much gear I suggested he rent a bigger boat. Oh, and I remember now, he had a fishing companion with him. Now the last one was an older gentlemen. I can't say what kind of equipment he took with him. All he seemed to have was a tackle box so he could have been carrying one of those small Pocket-Pal fishing gadgets like used to be advertised on television by that Ronco Company. Ya know which ones I mean?"

"Not really," Art said. "When you say *old*, what do you mean?"

"Well, he could have been in his sixties. In a way it would be hard to tell."

"Why's that?" Art asked.

"He had very dark hair, almost black. But the wrinkles and the sagging of his face make me think he is older than he tried to look. And he seemed to be in pretty good shape otherwise."

"Did you have any conversation with him? Can you remember anything he might have said? Have you seen him before? Is he from around here?" Art asked animatedly, noting nothing of the man's description striking any chord of recognition.

"Slow down . . . slow down. Now you've got my curiosity up. Are you thinking he might have had something to do with this murder?"

"I don't know," said Art. "What I do know is that neither my wife nor I killed that man."

"Hmmmm. . . ." said the man. "Nope. Never saw him before and nope, he really didn't have anything to talk about."

"Did he pay with cash or a credit card?"

"He paid in cash according to my ledger."

"So there's no way of knowing who he is then," Art stated, the disappointment reflected in his voice.

"Oh yes, there is," the man replied. "I don't take identification from people who pay with a credit card, but I do require a driver's license from anyone who pays cash. I lost a boat only once and learned my lesson."

Excitedly, Art said, "You have his name and address?"

"Yup," said the man, "right here. It's a fellow named George Weekly and he's got an Ithaca, New York, address."

"Weekly!" Art shouted out. "The same name that Fowler used when he signed in at the motel," Art said as he turned and looked at his wife.

"Omigosh!" she exclaimed. "Who *is* he?"

"I don't know but I think we'd better make contact with Officer Poulos. Can we borrow your phone?" Art asked the marina operator.

"Are you calling the police?" the man asked.

"Yes."

"I'll get them for you." And with that he dialed the number.

Poulos was not due in until the second shift. However, after Art explained the importance of making immediate contact with him, the dispatcher at the police station said she would page him. Art gave her the telephone number for the marina.

After hanging up, Art said to his wife, "I think we had better wait until we hear from Poulos before we go anywhere."

"I agree with you," she said.

"Hey! This is turning out to be a real whodunnit," the marina operator stated.

Now he sounds like Officer Poulos, Art thought, as he heard the marina operator's comment.

"Do you have any idea who this guy Weekly is?"

"No," responded Art, "but we are certainly going to find out."

Within twenty minutes Poulos was on the phone. Art told him what they had discovered to which the cop replied, "I guess I should have been more thorough in examining the marina's records. I am really embarrassed."

"Well, Officer Poulos," Art said, "don't take it to heart. The important thing is, this gives us something more to work on. Maybe you can find out some details about this man, Weekly, for us."

"Y'all can bet I will. I promise."

"Oh," said Art, "and if you need us, we'll be out on the island with the lighthouse."

"Okay, Mr. Booker. Y'all be careful out there."

"You know we will," Art said as he hung up the phone.

"What is it you people are searching for on these islands?" the marina operator asked, his head cocked to one side and his eyebrows scrunched together indicating his curiosity.

"Oh," said Art's wife, her mind racing a mile a minute, "we're botanists and we're intrigued by the rare form of grape vines found on Anclote Cay."

"Hmmph!" grunted the man. "I can't think of anything more boring than looking at grape vines. They must be rare, all right, where someone is willing to commit murder. That goes beyond my thinking."

He shook his head in disbelief and agreed to rent them the boat.

CHAPTER TWENTY-ONE

Deceit

Once their supplies were secured in the small motorcraft, Art pumped the rubber bulb that forced gasoline from the gas tank into the outboard engine. He then turned the key to START and pulled on the starter cord causing the engine to come to life. As he did this, Lavina released the mooring lines and pushed the boat away from the dock.

As Art put the motor in reverse and began to back out into the bay, he said to his wife, "You're getting to be quite a sailor."

"Thank you," she said, his words boosting her pride.

They set a course for the island with the lighthouse. It would take them a good forty-five minutes to reach their destination even with the help of the ebbing tide. There was some traffic on the waterway and Art initiated or returned waves to the friendly boaters who passed by him.

"I am really surprised," said Lavina, "at how congenial all of the people seem to be who own boats."

"Yeah," said Art. "Certainly a lot different from the ones driving on the highways. Their waves are mostly with one finger and never a smile."

As they reached the island they again forced the boat up onto the sand in the shallow water produced by the receding tide. Art rolled up the pant legs on his blue jeans and removed his sneakers before jumping into the water. He took hold of the boat's mooring line and brought it with him. He attached the loose end to one of the more hardy shrubs on shore. His wife tossed the supplies from the boat to Art. She then removed her sneakers, climbed out of the boat, and waded the few feet in the pleasantly warm water onto dry land.

After slipping their sneakers back on they made their way to the lighthouse. Keeping low to the ground so as not to be too obvious to any passing boaters, they made several attempts to cut into the earth in those areas that were free from the grapevines outside of the restricted compound. The ground, however, was hard like concrete; a good deal less forgiving than that which they encountered on the other islands. Once again, they entered the chain-link enclosure by pulling on the broken lock on the gate and slipping it from its hasp. They double-checked the ground they previously covered and probed even the areas that were hidden under the growth of the tormenting vines.

For nearly four hours they struggled to find any sign that might lead them to Ed Fitzgerald's buried treasure. All that their effort produced was a great appetite and weary muscles.

Stopping to eat, Lavina remarked, "I just don't understand. We seem to be at the end of the rainbow and yet where is this pot of gold?"

"I don't know," Art replied. "For something that seemed so easy we again reach a dead end. There has got to be a clue somewhere in that book of poems."

"Well, we are *not* going to give up after coming this far. Let's make sure we have thoroughly covered everything in this open area."

Art mumbled something to the affirmative as he took the last swallow of his can of Dr. Pepper. Both stood up, stretched almost in unison, and began to retrace their steps.

"I really wish we could get a look inside that lighthouse," Art commented as he gazed longingly up at the massive tower.

"But, Art, it's not as though Ed would have had access either. There's no way he could have passed through that locked trapdoor."

"Maybe it wasn't locked back then. I've got to take a look. There must be some way to get in," said Art as he opened the noisy door at the base and started up the metal stairs of the lighthouse.

Nearing the top of the structure where it meets the light enclosure, Art examined the large brass padlock which prevented the trap door from being opened. It was obvious that no maintenance inside the light's enclosure had been required for many years as the lock and the door were encrusted with sediment brought by the wind as it skimmed over the water and entered through the large open port.

Art shouted down to Lavina to bring up the multi-blade Forest Master jackknife they had purchased at the hardware store.

"What have you found?" she inquired.

"Nothing yet," he replied. "I just want to see if I can pick this lock."

"Art! You can't do that! That's a restricted area. It's *government* property. Are you crazy?"

Art simply looked down through the open porthole and said, "I'm not breaking in to steal anything or to damage anything. I simply want to see if Ed left any clue here."

"Ohhhh!" uttered his wife, obviously exasperated, "If we get into trouble for anything, I'm going to claim I don't know you."

"That will be pretty tough to prove especially where the cops know we're married."

"Well, then, I'm going to claim you forced me to come with you."

"Do you think the cops are gonna believe that after these last two weeks?"

"Well, then, I'm going to claim I didn't know what you were doing up there."

"Oh, that sounds reasonable," Art said sarcastically. "Now give me the knife."

Hesitantly, and with great care, she climbed the structure.

Picking the lock was impossible. Art was just about to say, "Let's forget this idea," when Lavina, standing just below him, spotted something from beneath the sediment surrounding the lock on the trapdoor.

"Art," she said, "can you scrape away some of that corrosion just to the left of the lock?"

"Sure."

With the sharp point of the knife's broadest blade, he pecked away at the sediment.

"Careful," Lavina called out, as several flakes loosened and fell to the floor. "Look! There's something scratched in the metal."

"What? You're right!" exclaimed Art. Spitting on his thumb, he rubbed at the engraving removing the loose particles and making it appear more clear. "It's upside down from where I'm positioned. Can you make it out from where you're standing?"

"I think so," said Lavina. "It says, 'Oh . . . what a . . . tangled . . . web we weave,' and its got the initials E. F. after it."

"Now what's that supposed to mean?" Art's shout more an exclamation than a question.

Art's wife began to laugh and she descended the tower.

"What is it? What is it, babe?" Art called out as his wife moved quickly down the stairs.

Reaching its base, she sat down on the ground, now laughing and crying at the same time, nearly an hysteria.

Art pocketed the knife and came down the metal steps to join his wife. He sat next to her and put his right arm around her and his hand on her shoulder. "I don't get it. What's the matter with you?"

"Oh, Art," she cried, "don't you see? This has all been a big hoax. No wonder we haven't been able to find the money. There is no money. This has been a joke and the joke is on us. Your *friend*, Ed, was taking his last slap at the society he detested."

"Will you explain to me what this means. What are you talking about?"

"I know what the book of poetry means. It all fits into this ruse. Those words up there are part of a poem. One of the stanzas begins with the words, 'Oh what a tangled web we weave' and ends with 'when first we practice to deceive.' Don't you see, Art, this was all a deception."

"No! I don't believe that! I won't believe that!" Art shouted. "That man was dying in my arms. There is no way that he was not telling me the truth."

"Oh, Art, you're such a gullible fool. If he had meant for us to find any treasure, he would not have used this poem. Let's just pack up and get out of here. I don't ever want to see this island again."

Art's wife stood up quickly and grabbed everything within reach that belonged to them.

Art knew there would be no arguing with her. There was nothing he could say that would change her mind. Disheartened, Art stood, took one long look around, secured the compound once again, and then followed his wife back to the boat.

The ride to the marina was the longest Art had experienced so far. Both he and Lavina sat in silence the entire way. The Gulf water was choppy; a fitting reflection to the way the day ended.

They returned to the motel and, at the lowest point of their entire journey, Lavina called for airplane reservations to return to New York. Art was quiet, not knowing anything else to do.

CHAPTER TWENTY-TWO

The Missing Link

The return to work was not an easy one. Art maintained contact with Officer Harry Poulos and with the attorney who represented them in the shooting of Tom Fowler. Art knew that he was not yet out of the woods as far as the shooting was concerned because the sparse circumstantial evidence still worked against him.

Art and his wife had no further discussions about Ed Fitzgerald or the stolen money. In time their lives returned to normal; the way it was before the riot at the prison. Although Art never voiced anything concerning this issue, he still believed Ed Fitzgerald's story.

Coming home from work one evening, Art noticed the five books from Gabrielle's shop sitting next to the bags of trash ready to be taken out to the sidewalk in front of their home. It was there that the refuse collectors would make their pick-up early the next day.

Art carried the trash outside along with the books. He struggled within himself to discard them. He still had that gnawing feeling. Taking a quick glance back toward the house, he took the books and placed them on the front seat of his car. He would keep them at work out of sight of his wife.

Every time Art opened his locker at work he would see those five books on the upper shelf. It was not until he had been back on the job for quite a while that he was asked to work a double shift because of a stomach illness that attacked several of the guards. He hated the midnight shift. That was okay for the young bucks who wanted to have a career in some segment of law enforcement. As for himself he was beyond that. Nonetheless, that was the shift he was going to pull.

Knowing that things would be quiet, he went to his locker and took out the book of poetry. He had a number of hours to kill, why not do it giving this book one final examination.

Seated at a small desk on the second tier, he began with the very first page. It was unusual when five o'clock rolled around and he was still awake. Unusual because most guards cannot keep their eyelids open at the rising of the sun. Unusual because reading something so foreign and uninteresting to him, he should have fallen asleep. Unusual, also, in that he finished the book. He felt that he was no further ahead than when he had begun. His only question came as a result of his reading a poem by Sir Walter Raleigh called "The Lie." All of the lines in the beginning of the poem had a rhythmic quality to them. The same held true of the ending lines in the poem, but the content between the first and the last half did not seem to make sense. Now Art realized that he had trouble when it came to poetry but the two halves of this poem were so divergent as to be totally confusing. The only person he could ask for clarification would be his wife. But what would her reaction be? Confrontation . . . because he had not thrown these books away with the rest of the trash?

At the supper table the following night, Art considered how he might broach the question. Lavina knew something was on his mind and, without his saying anything, she blurted out, "What is it?"

"What's what?" Art responded.

"You know perfectly well what's what. What is on your mind?"

"Nothing," he countered.

"Arthur Booker, don't you play games with me. I know you like I know the back of my hand. And if you don't want the back of my hand, you'd better tell me what's bugging you."

Art was silent for several minutes, staring at the ceiling and pursing his lips. Then he began, "Okay. But you gotta promise not to get mad."

"Uh . . . oh. What's that supposed to mean?"

"Just what I said."

"Okay. Let's have it."

"I have a question concerning poetry."

"What? Concerning poetry?"

Without waiting for any more questions from her Art continued, "How can you have a poem that starts out with one subject and ends up with a completely different subject?"

The Key

"I don't understand what you're talking about."

"Well, let me read something to you and you tell me what it means." With that, he got up from the table, went out to his car, and returned with the book of poetry.

"Oh, for gosh sakes!" Lavina began, a disgusted tone to her voice. "I thought you threw those books away."

"That's what I was afraid of. I probably should have."

"No. You've come this far. Go ahead with your example."

"Well," said Art, "I read this entire book last night. I found nothing that meant anything as far as the missing treasure. So, you were probably right."

Art's wife simply smiled an all-knowing smile and nodded her head in silence.

Art continued. "But this one thing stumped me." He opened the book to "The Lie" and read to her all five of the verses. When he finished she asked him, "Are you sure you're reading from the same poem?"

"It's got to be. Look for yourself. The first three verses are on the bottom of the left-hand page and the last two verses are on the top of the right-hand page."

"Well, something's not right. First of all, look at the number of lines in each verse. On the left-hand page there are six lines in each one. On the right-hand page there are two and then four. Even the meter is wrong."

"The what?"

"The meter. When you read the lines on the left they are written in iambic trimeter and the ones on the next page are in iambic tetrameter. So you see, they do not belong together."

"Whoa! What you say, woman?"

"Don't go talking to me in Harlemese. I'm simply telling you that there is something wrong here. The poems don't match up; the rhyming is all wrong. Let me take a look at that book."

Lavina took the book and examined all the verses. Then she looked at the page numbers, which were written in Roman numerals. On the left-hand page was the number XIV. On the right-hand page was the number XVII.

"Art!" she exclaimed. "There *is* a problem here. Two pages of the book are missing."

"What!"

"Yes! You see on the left-hand page the Roman numerals indicate page fourteen. On the right-hand page the Roman numerals indicate page seventeen. This means that pages fifteen and sixteen have been removed from the book."

Art grabbed the book from his wife and looked closely at the center of the inner binding of the two pages.

"Someone used a razor blade to cut out the page. No wonder we didn't see it. And because the pages use Roman numerals it was not easy to catch. What do we do now?" Art asked.

"Assuming that Ed Fitzgerald told the truth, we're going to have to find a copy of this book in order to determine what we are missing."

"The library!" Art called out. "The town library ought to have the book."

"Well, it's worth a try. We'll have to look it up by the title, the copyright date and the Library of Congress number."

Art handed the book back over to his wife. She turned to the first page, found the information and made the comment, "I only hope they have a copy where this is so far out of date."

Art called Lavina from work the next day. She told him that she had tried the public library, the school library, and called the libraries in the surrounding towns. No one had a copy of that book. She also told Art that she made a call to the printing company in New York City but the book was so out of date they had no record, according to their computer, other than it had been published by them.

"Oh, great!" said Art. "Ed certainly didn't make things easy."

Over the next two weeks, Lavina visited book stores and antique shops within a reasonable distance, only to be disappointed time and again.

"It looks like we're back where we started, honey," Art said. "I guess it's like the saying, 'If we didn't have bad luck, we wouldn't have any luck at all'."

The next day at work as Art got ready for his shift, he opened his locker to change into his uniform. Staring down at him were those remaining four books, a constant reminder of their failed mission. He took the books off the shelf, slammed the locker door shut, and slapped the books down on the bench next to where he would sit and lace up his boots.

One of the other officers came into the locker room, also to get ready for his shift.

The Key

"What ya got there, Art?" Officer Charlie Doane asked.

"Aw, nothing. Just some old books. Picked 'em up when I was in Florida on vacation. Read 'em. Turned out to be just some extra junk I don't need."

"So, what didja bring 'em inta work for? To add to the prison library?" Doane asked.

"Yeah. I guess that's just as good a place as any to leave them."

Art finished lacing up his boots, latched onto the books and walked over to the prison library building.

The library was a room that at one time had been used for storage. It was twenty feet square and had been furnished with shelves made in the prison carpentry shop as well as some that were resurrected after having been discarded by the local town library when it was being remodeled.

The door leading into the library was centered on one wall. To the left and right of it were shelves of reference books. The center aisle ran from the door to the opposite wall. There were shelves that ran perpendicular to the aisle that were stacked floor to ceiling with books organized by category and by author. The Dewey decimal system was not utilized. Midway down the aisle on the left was a counter behind which were a desk and a large wooden file with numerous skinny drawers designed to accommodate a multitude of three-by-five cards.

Art told the inmate in charge of the library that he had a gift for the prisoners who enjoyed reading as he plunked the books down on the counter.

"Kinda old, ain't they?" the inmate stated more as a comment than as a question as Art separated the books on the counter.

"I guess," said Art. "But if you don't want 'em for the library, you can heave 'em."

"Okay," responded the inmate. "I'll see if they're anything we can use."

Art turned away from the counter and started to walk back toward the door. As he passed by the section of reference materials he noticed several books in a compartment called Prose and Poetry. He stopped for just a minute, put his left hand up to his chin and wrinkled his brow as he began to think, *I wonder if the prison library would have that poetry book?*

He returned to the inmate at the desk behind the counter. Art asked him if he could look and see if there was a book by the title he and his wife were searching for.

153

The inmate opened the drawer in the old wooden card file and began thumbing through the hundreds of index cards. Without saying a word, he left his position at the desk, walked over to the poetry section and within seconds returned with the book Art had been seeking.

Art could hardly contain himself but somehow managed to keep his cool. He opened the book and turned to the pages that were missing from the book he had at home. He saw immediately that the book was intact. He told the inmate that he wanted to borrow the book for a couple of days to which the inmate responded, "Sure, why not."

Art made out a borrower's card, gave it to the inmate and raced back to his post, whereupon he called Lavina and related to her his amazing good fortune.

"You aren't gonna believe what I found!" he shouted excitedly into the phone.

"What is it?" she asked.

Quieting down, realizing that others might be listening, he said, "I found the poetry book. The prison library, of all places, had a copy."

"You've got to be kidding," she replied. "Right under your nose all this time. Didn't Ed Fitzgerald work in the library there?"

"Kind of makes sense when you think about it, doesn't it? It must have been coincidence, though. He could not have known when he was at Gabrielle's that this particular book would be among prison property. Heck, he didn't even know he was gonna get caught or end up in this prison."

"Yeah. I guess you're right. Is the book complete? I mean, are the missing pages in it?"

"Pages fifteen and sixteen are in the book. I'll be bringing it home with me tonight," Art told her.

She replied, "Maybe Ed Fitzgerald is still looking over your shoulder after all." That night when Art arrived home, the first thing he and Lavina did was to examine the poems that had been missing from the original book.

The only poem that made sense was written by Robert Herrick and was called "To The Willow Tree." Art remembered as he took that long look from the porthole at the top of the lighthouse tower, a dwarf willow tree not a hundred feet from the fenced-in compound. It was the only willow tree on the island.

Upon telling Lavina, she, too, remembered seeing it.

CHAPTER TWENTY-THREE

It's Gone!

One last chance—one last shot at finding the money—that's all I want, Art thought as he walked into the administration office to request his remaining leave time unused from his last visit to Florida. He had photocopied the missing pages from the book of poetry the night before and had returned the book to the prison library. Now he had been summoned to the warden's office after making his leave request known to his supervisor who had notified the warden that Art wanted time off *again*.

"What's the story, Booker?" the warden asked.

"I've got some personal business to attend to, sir," Art responded.

"What kind of personal business?"

"That's personal, sir. I don't mean to sound curt but I'm afraid I can't tell you anything further."

"Is it a health issue, Booker?" the warden queried.

"No, sir." Art knew the warden would be a jerk. He had dealt with him in the past and each time Art played the political game—no confrontation, just "yes, sir; no, sir." But he was reaching his limit.

"Very well, Booker. You don't have any time left so I'm afraid this will have to be denied," the warden replied.

"Sir, several weeks ago I was granted a leave without pay. I did not use all my time. I'm simply asking for the remainder of those days to take care of this particular problem. I really don't want to go to my union steward with this, but if I have no choice then that is what I'll do."

"Are you threatening me, Booker?" the warden demanded sharply, his eyes now glaring.

"No, sir. The time was granted to me previously so I'm simply asking for what should be rightfully mine."

"Get out of my office!" Seething, the warden spoke through clenched teeth.

"Does that mean I have authorization?"

Scowling, the warden looked directly into Art's eyes and with all the nastiness he could muster in his voice, said, "Just get out . . . and when you get back, mister, you better make sure everything you do is by the book!"

After Art left the warden's office, he went to the nearest telephone and called his wife.

"We're all set. The warden had no choice but to allow me my time off. We better find what we're looking for because I have a feeling that my time here as a CO is about to come to an end. Call Triple A and arrange our flight for as soon as we can go. Oh, and make sure to get us a rental car. We'll probably stay at the same place we stayed at last time. Most important, make sure that we bring those photocopies of the poems with us. I know you've most likely got them memorized but let's not take a chance forgetting anything." With that, he hung up.

The earliest flight was at 7:52 the next morning. Luckily, there were seats available. Upon his returning home from work, Art and his wife scurried to gather the things they would need for the trip. Then, with less than three hours sleep, they dashed to the airport.

They arrived late after making two stopovers at airports; one in Cincinnati and the other in Charlotte. It seemed like a long day for such a relatively short distance. The fact that they were tired from so little sleep the night before did not strike them. However, they made up for it on this night. The minute they were settled into their room, they fell asleep. They could not even stay awake for the evening news.

In the morning, they awoke to the wake-up call that they had requested just before hitting the pillows. The day appeared overcast but as they listened to the early news and weather on the TV, another glorious Florida day was promised. They hurried through their morning rituals and quickly dressed. Not taking any time to grab a bite for breakfast, it was just seven o'clock when they pulled into the parking lot at the marina. Within a few minutes they greeted the marina owner.

"Well, we're back," Art said as he approached the man.

"So I see," replied the man. "Still after those unusual grapes?" he asked. His words were neither in jest nor sarcastic; he still believed their story.

"Yeah. Well, we thought we'd give it another try. After what we went through the last time we were here, it kind of dampened our spirits. I still don't know what that guy wanted from us. That was so scary," said Lavina.

"I must say things have been fairly quiet since you left," the man responded.

"Hopefully, they'll stay that way," she said.

"We need a boat," Art interjected.

"Sure, small skiff like you had last time?" the man asked.

"That'll do just fine," Art answered.

They went into the marina and made out the paperwork for the rental. The man walked with them out to the dock and over to where the rental boats usually were tethered. Only one boat remained.

"I've got a boat right over here," the man began. "It was the last one to come in last night so I didn't get a chance to fill the tank. I try to keep them full of fuel overnight so that condensation doesn't form but last night I was just too tired. This is the only one I have available today. You're right in the middle of our busiest season so you lucked-out by getting here when you did."

He untied the rope lashing the boat to the dock and pulled it alongside to the gas pump where he attempted to fill up the tank. But, nothing happened. The pump motor did not operate.

"That's funny," the man said. "I filled up two boats that pulled in this morning just before sunup. It worked fine then. Let me check to see if the level is low; maybe the holding tank is close to empty. I know I have a delivery coming the end of the week but there should have been enough gas until then . . . even as busy as we have been."

The man then went into the marina and returned with a twelve-foot long, wooden dipstick. He opened a round metal cover in the asphalt and plunged the stick down into the hole. When he brought it up, it registered one-third tank.

"Now what?" the man exclaimed as he refitted the cover back onto the holding tank access. "I know the pump is getting power because the lamp is lit in the windows that show gallons and price. I'll be right back."

He returned to the marina and came out with a toolbox. Going to the pump, he released the cover from the front of it and was about to start checking the mechanisms inside. It was as his eyes adjusted to the dark enclosure that he discovered two wires had been yanked from the motor housing. There was no power going to the motor. He cursed and threw down the screwdriver he had used to open the cover. "Who the heck would have *done* that!" the man spit out the words as he shook his head in disgust.

"What is it?" asked Art.

"Take a look for yourself," the man said. "Someone pulled the wires right out of the motor."

"Can you fix it?" Art asked.

Frustrated, the man cried out, "Can't you see what's been done? No, I can't fix it! The wires have been pulled out from the motor itself. It's not like they were cut and can be spliced. They're pulled right out of the housing. Now the entire motor has to be removed so that it can be repaired." The man realized how upset he was. He turned to Art and said, "I apologize. There was no reason for me to explode at you. I'm sorry."

Art replied, "No, I understand. I'd be really ticked if it was me. As it is, I'm ticked along with you because we were planning to accomplish some things today and now it looks like we're going to get delayed."

"I can't believe that it was either of the two people who were here to buy fuel. They were not what you'd expect for vandals. Both were older gentlemen and they operated fairly expensive boats. In fact, both of them have been here before. One is a longtime customer. As for the other fellow, I know he's done business here as well because there was something familiar about him, too. Then again, there were other people on the dock; some were getting ready to go out fishing as they rent slips from me. But I don't recall anyone by the gas pump. I just don't know."

"Do you have any suggestions as to what we can do now?" Art asked.

"I guess you'll have to wait until tomorrow unless you can find someone to get you out to where you want to go."

"Can't we just borrow one of your gas tanks and get fuel somewhere else? We can still rent this boat, can't we?" asked Lavina.

"Well, yes, you could do that, I guess. I'm just not thinking straight right now. Sure, take the tank from this boat and you can leave for the islands when you get back."

Art disconnected the fuel line from the tank and he and Lavina headed into town to get it filled. When they returned, Art reconnected the line, started the engine and set out for the large island with the lighthouse.

"Here I had hoped that we would have an early start," said Art. "Now it's coming up to noon and we haven't even reached the island."

"I'm getting hungry," Lavina declared as though the word noon registered a need for food, more than the fact that they had not stopped for any breakfast.

"I know, babe. I guess I was so eager to get going I just never gave any thought to eating. Let me pull up alongside that restaurant by the sponge docks and we'll grab something. We've lost this much time, what's another few minutes."

Art maneuvered the boat to the dock and tied the bow line to a wooden support post. "I'll be right back," he said as he climbed up onto the dock and ran into the little Greek restaurant that bordered the water. True to his word, he was out in minutes, his arms cradling two large Styrofoam containers. "I got us some shish kebab. It smelled so good, I couldn't resist."

"Hand them down. I'm starved," Lavina replied.

Not waiting another moment, they opened the boxes and feasted on the meal. Once finished, Art stowed the trash under one of the seats, threw a leftover piece of meat to a seagull, started the engine and resumed his course toward the island.

"Omigosh!" Art's wife called out suddenly. "Look at all the pelicans!"

"Wow! I didn't notice them before. There must be two dozen of them," Art commented.

"I never realized how big they are. This is the first time I've seen one this close."

"Me, too. They must know when the fishermen who went out early in the morning are coming in with their catch. See! There're two fishing trawlers heading in from the Gulf now."

The water was smooth even outside of the waterway and they made good time. As before, other boaters waved as they passed by. Nearing the island, they observed three fishermen on the side opposite the lighthouse.

"Oh great!" said Lavina. "We've got company."

"They look like they're pretty intent on their fishing. I don't think they'll pay any attention to us."

"Yes, but if we turn toward the lighthouse here, they'll know we're coming to the island."

"So?" Art queried.

"I just don't want anyone poking around while we're digging. What if they should be curious and come upon us with all that money?"

"Here's what I'll do. I'll go past them, turn left as though we're headed into the Gulf, go around the other side of the island where we'll be out of sight of them and then turn in toward the lighthouse from that side."

"I'd feel a little better about it if you did."

They followed Art's course and once out of view and sound of the fishermen, they worked their way toward shore. The tide was receding as they approached the familiar inlet leading to the lighthouse. There was just enough depth to allow them to glide onto the embankment. They quickly hauled their shovels out of the boat after tethering it to a bush.

They walked rapidly up the slight grade and toward the lighthouse. Art turned diagonally to the right as he remembered the approximate location of the willow tree. He passed through the thicket of marsh grass, vines and palm trees that had kept the willow hidden at ground level. Finally, he spotted the dwarf willow tree. He broke into a run but stopped suddenly in his tracks. He turned abruptly and looked at his wife who was closing in on him. His face registered a look of disbelief. His mouth hung open yet no words came out. It was as though he had gone into shock.

As his wife drew closer, she gave him a quizzical look as though to say, *What's the matter?* Silence hung in the air until Lavina finally asked, "What's wrong?"

"Look for yourself," was all Art could say.

As she looked beneath the willow tree into a five-foot wide hole, the only thing that came out of her mouth was a sound as if she were gagging. It was followed by, "What! Who knew! Who's been here?"

Something caught Art's eye as he walked around the edge of the hole. Reaching down beneath some of the wild grape vines, he picked up a book that had obviously been tossed aside as it was open to the middle and the pages were bent. His wife recognized it immediately.

"Is that our book of poems?" she asked incredulously.

"Not exactly," Art began. "It's the same book, but not ours. Look inside the front cover. PROPERTY OF THE NEW YORK STATE PRISON. It's the book I borrowed—the one we copied—the one I returned to the prison library."

"How could they have known?" she asked.

"I don't know . . . I just don't know," Art answered despondently.

Suddenly, without any warning, Art grabbed his wife by the arm and shouted, "C'mon! We've gotta get outta here! I've gotta check something at the marina. Someone broke that gas pump—someone who knew we'd be back and who didn't want us to get here first. One, or maybe both, of those guys that bought gas had to have damaged that pump."

There was no time to waste on greetings to other boaters as Art went full throttle toward the marina. Some people yelled at him as he created a powerful wake while cutting through the water where the posted speed limit read five miles per hour.

When he reached the dock, he ran inside and asked the owner if he could make a credit card call on the marina's phone.

"Sure, help yourself," the man replied.

Art dialed the prison administration number and asked for the warden without giving his real name to the secretary. To his dismay, the warden was there. He hung up without saying a word just as the warden answered the phone. He felt sure that there had to be some connection to this man. Now he was at a loss.

After hanging up the phone, Art was deep in thought when his wife interrupted his thinking.

"What's going on?" she asked.

"I just had this strong feeling that the warden was the person who had been out to the island. Don't ask me why—I really can't account for it other than who else would have access to that book of poems?"

"And . . . ?"

"And the warden is in his office, so it's not him."

"Hmmm . . . what about the men who fueled their boats?"

"That was my next question. Where did the marina guy go?"

"He's in his office," Lavina replied.

Art walked over to the office door. It was open so he knocked on the door frame to get the man's attention.

"Hi," the man said. "You done with the phone?"

"Yes, but I have something else to ask you."

"Okay. What is it?"

"You said you recognized those men this morning—the ones who bought gas. You said one was a good customer. Who was the other guy?

"I have no idea. I've been trying to remember why I know the other one, though. He's been here before. That I do know. But for what, I can't remember."

"So he's not a regular customer?" Art asked.

"Nope. And it's bothering me as to who he is. You ever see someone and it drives you nuts when you can't remember why? Well, that's been going through my head since this morning. At first, I thought I knew this guy—that's why I didn't believe he could have damaged my pump. But he was the last one to use it. I came in here to go over my records to see if something might click with one of these names." As he spoke these last words the marina operator tapped his log book.

"No luck so far?" Art asked.

"Nope. I've gone back only a couple of weeks, though. It may be before that. By the way, you didn't answer my question—why are you so interested?"

"Because I think this guy may know something about that dead guy on the island—remember?"

"Hah! Remember? How could I forget something like that?" The marina operator stopped short and a strange look appeared on his face. He furrowed his eyebrows and his eyes darted back and forth as though in deep concentration.

Art was about to say something when the operator blurted out, "That's it! That's it! That's the guy!"

"What guy?" Art asked.

"I knew if I thought on it long enough and hard enough it would come to me. What you said triggered it—the dead guy, that's what you said—then I knew."

"Who?" Art asked.

"Just a minute—let me look back in the book." The operator flipped through a dozen more pages before he said, "Here it is!"

Art walked around the desk and looked over the man's shoulder.

"You'll remember," the man said. "The guy from New York—George Weekly."

"Weekly! Of course! I'd almost forgotten about him. I've got to use your phone again!" Art exclaimed.

"You know where it is," the man replied without any hesitation.

Art placed a call to the Tarpon Springs Police, asking for Officer Harry Poulos. Luckily the cop was there in the station.

"Mr. Booker, how are y'all?" Poulos asked.

"Right now I'm not sure. But you can help me. Do you recall the name George Weekly?"

"Of course. In fact, I tried to do some research on him from his driver's license number and date of birth; the information I got from the log book at the marina. I ran his name through NCIC, NLETS and LEAPS, but he came up clean—no record, not even a traffic violation."

Art recognized the acronyms for the law enforcement criminal investigation information networks having used the same systems at the state prison.

"They even sent me his photo from the DMV records in New York," the officer continued. "He's nobody I'd recognize. Obviously, there was a connection between him and the dead man on the island as the motel room where I found y'all's books was registered to Weekly. Now, the real funny thing is we tried to get the state police in New York to find this guy, but his only address was a post office box and his residence turned out to be an apartment house and no one there ever heard of him. It's a real mystery, especially how he managed to get a driver's license."

"Officer Poulos, could I take a look at that photo?" Art asked.

"Sure y'all can. Anything that might help us would be welcome. After all, y'all have a big stake in this—y'all're still involved in a murder case."

"Ya know, ya didn't have to remind me of that," Art said.

"I'm sorry, Mr. Booker. I spoke before thinking."

"That's all right. I'm just giving you a hard time. Anyhow, I'll be right down," Art said and hung up the phone. He told the marina owner that he had a lead and he would be in touch.

"If you find this guy," the man said, "I'll be wantin' to talk to him about my gas pump."

Art nodded his head as he took hold of his wife's hand and headed out the door.

CHAPTER TWENTY-FOUR

It Begins to make Sense

"I don't believe it! I just don't believe it!" Art exclaimed as he looked at the photo. "That's Warden Weiss. He was in charge of the prison before the new warden came into power. I knew there had to be a connection between the two of them. Wow! Does all of this ever come together now."

"This was the prison warden?" Poulos asked in disbelief.

"It sure was. I'm getting framed by a guy whose supposed to uphold the law," Art said.

"I'll have to get my chief reinvolved now that we have some better direction. Chief Lecouris is well connected in the national police community. He'll want to get things into gear to investigate what y'all are alleging. In the meantime, I'll put out an alert for this fellow, Weiss. If he's in the area operating a boat, he's bound to pull into harbor somewhere. If y'all will excuse me, I'll be wanting to get a hold of the guy at the marina so I can show him this photo and, if it's the same one that ripped him off, I'll find out what kind of boat he's got and what the registered name is."

"Do you mind if we tag along? I mean after all, we are involved and maybe we can be of further help," Art said.

"Well . . . ," Poulos hesitated. "Ordinarily, we wouldn't allow anyone to do that, but where y'all're working in law enforcement, I guess it'd be okay. Y'all'll have to take y'all's own vehicle."

Art thanked Poulos as they walked out to the parking lot. Once inside their rental car both agreed not to say anything to Officer Poulos about the money that was now in Weiss's possession. Art followed the policeman back down to the marina. After parking their cars, Art and his wife accompanied the cop inside and walked up to the owner of the facility. There Poulos showed the photo of Weiss to the marina operator.

"That's him!" the man exclaimed. "That's Weekly! Is he in custody? I want him to pay for what he did to my gas pump."

"No, he's not in custody . . . yet," Poulos answered. "We're trying to find him now. Can y'all tell me what kind of a boat he had and if y'all can remember the name on the stern?"

"Yeah. It was a fairly new Bayliner—blue and white. The name . . . the name . . . ? I know there was something about the name. Give me a minute. I'll think of it; I'm sure."

Art, Lavina and Poulos remained quiet allowing the man some time to recollect.

"*Po-Boy II!*" the man shouted out suddenly startling everyone. "That was it. I remember because of the sandwiches with the same name."

Harry Poulos went to his cruiser and radioed to his station asking them to contact the Coast Guard for the listed owner of *Po-Boy II*. Within minutes he received a reply. The boat was owned by a marina in Clearwater. Officer Poulos requested the dispatcher make contact with that marina and see if any information was given by the person who obviously rented the craft as to his destination.

Again, within a short period of time the radio operator called back. The only information given was that the renter was going to be using the boat to go fishing for a week on some islands. The marina operator from Clearwater just assumed the man meant Anclote Key.

"He'll have to pull into dock somewhere to get fueled," Poulos said to the Bookers.

"Yeah, maybe," said Art quietly. However, his mind was now racing even if his voice did not show it.

"I'll make sure the Coast Guard and the police departments along the coast are aware of this. Then I'll have them contact all the dockside fueling stations as well," the officer stated.

"Uh. . . . okay," said Art. "I guess Lavina and I will go back to the motel until we hear from you."

"Where are you staying?" Poulos asked.

"Oh, sorry. The same place as last time," Art replied as he took a hold of his wife and began to walk quickly toward his rental car.

Lavina looked confused as she hustled to keep up with her husband. She got into the passenger side saying nothing until he got into the operator's side and both doors were shut.

"What's going on here?" she asked.

"Just something that cop on the radio said about fishing on the islands."

"Well, of course, and he obviously caught the prize when he dug up the treasure."

"No, not that," Art replied. "He knew it wouldn't take long to find the money once he knew where it was."

"Then what?" Lavina asked.

"Why would he rent the boat for a week if he knew he only needed it for one day?"

"Maybe to throw us off his . . . his . . . trail?"

"Now you sound like an actor from an old TV western," Art said.

"Well, I guess I don't *know* then," his wife said sarcastically.

"I think I do," Art responded.

"What do you mean?"

"I'll explain everything to you when we get back to the motel. Right now we've got to call the airport to see if either Clearwater or Tampa has flights to the Cayman Islands," Art said as he put the car in gear and headed to the motel.

8—8— —8 —8

"Why the Cayman Islands?" Art's wife asked when they were finally back in their motel room.

"I was trying to figure out why Weiss would want a boat for a week. Assuming he would find the money right away, now that he knew the final spot to look, he would need to hide it himself. He could not just haul it back to New York on an airplane with everything being scanned nowadays. Besides that, I am sure he would not want to share it with the present warden. I am positive that he would have told the warden that we had beat him to it and that the money was gone. So, the question became, where would Weiss hide the money? It was then that I remembered that Weiss was always traveling to the Cayman Islands for vacations. What better place to hide money? It's offshore, as they say, and several of these independent islands are known for having banks where rich people can deposit tax-free money."

"Of course. That just makes sense. But how is he going to pilot a boat to the Cayman Islands? He must have help. That's a long way to go."

"I don't know," Art replied. "There's a lot I don't know about Weiss. Maybe he does have help. If there is someone else on board with him, I pity that person when they get to where they're going. He had no problem killing Fowler and another one wouldn't make any difference to him now. And then again, maybe he does know what he's doing. Maybe he has had experience with operating a boat over open water. All I *do* know is that we had better get there before he does."

Cayman Air had space available on their early morning flight out of Tampa. The Bookers booked reservations using their credit card. They were advised that they would need a current passport in order to enter the Caymans.

"Passport?" Art said weakly over the phone.

"Yes, sir," said the man with the island accent. "Or, if you have an original birth certificate with an embossed seal. Either is acceptable."

"Birth certificate! Okay. We've got those. Like the American Express ad says, 'Never leave home without it'."

"We're set," Art exclaimed to his wife as he hung up the phone. "It's a good thing we started to keep our birth certificates with us after that fiasco to Bermuda."

"Well, how was I supposed to know that they needed some form of identification. I mean, the island's right off the coast of North Carolina. Who would have guessed?"

"They finally did say they'd accept your driver's license," Art replied.

"Well I never want to be in that position again."

"Maybe we'd better start carrying our passports as well," Art suggested.

"Yeah, right!"

CHAPTER TWENTY-FIVE

A Minute Possibility

They arrived at the airport two hours before flight time. The day was brilliant without a cloud in the sky. As near as they could determine, it would take two and a half days for Weiss's boat to reach Grand Cayman. Of course, that depended upon the condition of the sea. If everything went smoothly Art and his wife figured they would be on the island a day and a half before Weiss arrived. This would give them ample opportunity to become a bit familiar with the island in preparation for a confrontation with Weiss. Or better still, a means by which to beat him at his own game. In other words, to rip him off before he gets a chance to deposit the money into his bank account.

Before leaving, Art placed a phone call to the police station. Believing that Poulos would not be in at this hour, Art left a message stating that he and his wife would be out of town for a few days and would be in touch with him upon their return. He left him no clue that they were going to the Caymans nor their reason for leaving the area.

The flight was ten minutes late in taking off, but the pilot made up more than the lost time in the air. That was better than most of the large commercial air lines could do. As it was, they would now land eighteen minutes ahead of schedule. The plane had been fairly full for such an early morning flight. Had it been later in the day, they probably would not have had seats. This was the time of the year tourists flocked to the Caribbean. It was fortunate for the Bookers that most vacationers travel by the large commercial airlines. That was what gave Art and his wife a break; the smaller airlines are in demand only by people who are familiar with them. They had been told that only local Florida travel agencies would know to recommend their service because they are in a class considered below what many Americans would fly.

As they spotted Grand Cayman Island through the window, Art could not help but remark on the shape of the western end of the island. "It looks like a whale's tail."

"What?" she asked.

"The island . . . look at it. It looks like the tail of a whale."

"You're right. It does. The flight path shown in the seat pocket magazine is so small, I could not make out anything other than three dots below Cuba. I guess I should not be surprised—look, you can see from one side of the island to the other. It really is skinny."

"Yeah. It is that," Art replied as he refastened his seat belt in preparation for landing. The plane touched down so smoothly on the tarmac that the passengers commented on the landing and, when the flight attendant announced that they were on Grand Cayman, there was loud applause for to the captain. Soon they were at the terminal and ready to deplane.

As they walked down the stairs that had been rolled against the plane's exit door, they were hit by a blast of hot air. The heat was intense. The sun was about at its highest point in the sky. Fortunately, at this hour the humidity was low. It actually felt quite bearable.

Walking from the tarmac and falling in line with the people as they approached the terminal entrance, they were greeted by three men sitting outside the building in the shade of a large palm tree, singing and playing musical instruments in a medley of island songs. Lavina loved the sound of the steel drums that accompanied the other instruments and wished they could remain outside for a while in order to listen to this beautiful and friendly music. However, everyone was moving swiftly into the building. Suddenly the line stopped just inside the doors. Most of the passengers must have known the importance of getting inside—not because of the heat, but because of the delay they would encounter in getting through airport customs. No one seemed to move very fast. It was as though the island people proceeded in low gear. The fact that Art and his wife had a day-and-a-half leeway before Weiss's boat could arrive was definitely a good thing.

As they walked out of the airport after retrieving their luggage, Lavina turned to Art and asked, "By the way, where are we staying?"

Art stopped in his tracks and turned to her with a dumbfounded look. Both suddenly realized they had not made reservations for accommodations. Their minds had been so focused on getting to the island and getting Weiss that they completely forgot they would need a place to stay once they arrived. It would not be the same as in the States where one could just pull into any motel with a vacancy sign.

"I cannot believe I forgot to do that. I never gave it a thought. The only thing I was concerned with was getting here."

"Now what do we do? Sleep on the beach?" she asked half-seriously.

"Let's go back and see if there's someone who can help us."

Quickly they went back inside the terminal to the information booth and inquired about hotel rooms. The woman in the booth gave them an incredulous look, which told them, *You came to Grand Cayman without any arrangements for lodging?*

They said it was a spur of the moment decision and they were looking for an adventure. Whether they realized it or not, that was the truth.

The woman said their best bet would be in one of the hotels on Seven Mile Beach just outside of Georgetown, the central business district on the island. That was a good thing, the woman related, as the hotels there are almost all new and the quality is exceptional. Also, they usually had rooms available even in the busy season—although the prices would be steep. That is the advantage of reservations—there were better rates if one booked in advance. The woman made arrangements for them at the Westin.

Taking a taxi from the airport, they discovered two things: the Cayman dollar is worth more than the U.S. dollar by twenty percent, and all costs are significantly higher than in any other country including the United States. The taxi driver explained that this was because there were no taxes of any kind on the island. When Art asked him how municipal services were paid for, the driver said that that was the reason for the inflation rate of twenty percent on the dollar. The extra percentage is what covers the cost of the island's necessary services. The cost for the taxi ride to the Westin came as less of a shock now that Art realized how things were done on Grand Cayman.

"This place is a palace!" Art exclaimed as they walked into the hotel and viewed the grand lobby. Art finalized arrangements with the hotel clerk and was offered a room on the fifth floor, the uppermost level of the hotel. They were later to find out that no building on Grand Cayman can exceed five floors in height.

The bell man unlocked their hotel room door and briskly walked in, carrying their luggage, turning on the lights, adjusting the air conditioning and holding the door for Art and his wife all seemingly in one motion. When Art tipped the man, he displayed the widest smile Art had ever seen. As the bell man retreated from the room, he bowed to Art and said, "Thank you *very* much." Great emphasis was placed on the very.

"Hmmph. . . ." Art mumbled after the man closed the door behind him. "Maybe I gave him too much."

The room was exceptional. Art's wife scanned the amenities taking note of the large screen television, the convenient bar and refrigerator, the king-size bed, and the oversize closet with a built-in safe in which to store valuables.

Art went immediately to the window and looked out at the view of the magnificent lawn and gardens and beyond that at the sand and sea.

"Mmm . . . mmm . . . mmm . . . this is so fine," Art said, smiling with satisfaction.

"Perfect, just perfect," was Lavina's reply as she sidled up next to him and put her arm around his waist.

After getting settled in their room, they wanted to explore. They began with the Westin itself. They donned their bathing suits and went down through the lobby and outside the doors leading to the pool, where they found the most beautiful palm-treed patio surrounding dual swimming pools with semi-sunken bars.

"Whoa!" shouted Art. "I could get used to this. I think I'll dive in and work my way over to the bar for a piña colada."

"Before you do anything, you better read that sign," Lavina said. "It says NO DIVING. And don't you think it's a bit early to have a drink?"

"Yeah . . . maybe. But it's just so inviting."

"You think that's inviting? Have you even looked at the Caribbean? Look at that water! It's turquoise and absolutely crystal clear."

"Mm . . . mmm," said Art. "You're right, babe. Let's go sample some a that."

They ran toward the water like two young kids and jumped in, splashing themselves by the giant strides they were making. The water was magnificent—refreshing, but not cold. The beach was crowded but nothing like the crowds that indwelled Coney Island or Rye—the ones they had been most familiar with in the States.

As Art and Lavina walked back up onto beach, they moved two of the hotel's beach-lounge chairs under the shade of a large casuarina tree. Art's first inclination was about to be fulfilled as a beautiful young girl approached and asked, "Would you people like anything to drink?"

Art just looked at his wife and smiled, his teeth glistening in the sun like a Cheshire cat.

Three Cayman coladas later—the island drink similar to a piña colada but with the addition of a raspberry liqueur—Art found out that his waitress's name was Jill Palmer and that she had come from Fredericton, New Brunswick, in Canada. She had been working on the Caymans for two years. Her intent was to return to college in Canada and graduate with a business degree.

"Why are you working here if you want to go back to Canada?" Art's wife inquired.

"Strictly finances," Jill began. "You know the Canadian dollar is devalued against the American dollar. Just imagine the devaluation to the Caymanian dollar—it's about half. So, by working here I make good money and when I return to Canada the cost for my schooling will be half as much after I convert my currency."

"Pretty smart thinking," said Lavina, nodding approval. "No wonder you are going after a business degree."

Art then asked Jill, "You say you've been here two years? Then you must know something about the island."

"Well, yes—some."

"If a private yacht were to come to the Cayman's from Florida's west coast, can you tell me where it would most likely come in?"

"Hmmmm . . . that's not easy, ey. But, you've asked the right person. Of course, I can." She thought for a moment before speaking and then said, "Coming from the west it would probably go to the Island Yacht Club. That's where most private craft dock. You see, the big commercial ships enter by tender off of Georgetown. The water is deep but there are no docking facilities large enough on the island to accommodate them. A private boat would have no trouble, so that would be another port, but less convenient."

"What if," asked Art, "the boat was not privileged to use the private club's moorings?"

"Well, if it belongs to an island resident who was not a member of the yacht club or renting a slip there, they might pull in to Governor's Harbor. It's directly across from the governor's mansion on the West Bay Road. Those are all expensive private homes and each one is on a canal so that boats can be tied up right by the owner's home."

"No, that would not fit. This person I'm looking to find I don't believe is a property owner."

The Key

"You mean if the craft belonged to someone who was not an island resident, ey?"

"Exactly."

"The only other area where they might be able to come in would be at Morgan's Harbor Marina. It's actually the most northwestern location on the island for a boat to dock and, perhaps, the best protected inlet against storms."

"Can you tell us how we can find it?" Art asked.

"You asked the right person. Of course, I can. The best bet would be by asking one of the taxi drivers in front of the hotel, unless you have a rental car. It's at some distance from here so you could not easily walk it."

"Thank you, Jill. You've been a wealth of information. We'll stop back and see you later—for some more Cayman coladas."

Jill left them so that she could finish tending to her other customers as Art and his wife went back into the Westin to change into some shorts. Within a very few minutes they were outside the lobby accosting a bellhop named Robert Tiofilo in an effort to locate a cabbie, none of which seemed to be out front of the hotel. Robert emitted a sharp whistle and a wave of his hand, out of nowhere then appeared a Ford Econoline with the word TAXI on its hood.

The driver went by the name of Roy D. He was an island native—a handsome black man like Art, but with many more years, as attested by his white hair and mustache. When asked the same questions as those posed to Jill, he concurred. He continued on and talked incessantly. In no time at all, he had given them a history of Grand Cayman since it first experienced its major growth in the 1960s. Sometimes his Caymanian accent was a challenge to Art's wife, but usually he repeated and explained things so much that she caught on with little effort. It was interesting that every time he said Cayman, the word sounded like "K-mahn" with the emphasis on the "mahn."

They drove the length of Botabano Road to where it ended at the harbor named for the pirate John Morgan. If any place could be more perfect than this for Weiss to land, it did not exist. This was a remote spot, very small, with very few houses anywhere near by—and those were owned by local residents. There was a small restaurant/bar at the end of the road adjacent to the dock. It had recently completed renovations. It would be the only activity here.

Now the problem would be the waiting—how to know when Weiss would arrive and where to stay in watch for him.

"Okay, Roy, we've seen enough of this place," Art said to the driver. "How about taking us back to the hotel."

"Yes, suh. I can do dat," Roy responded. "Maybe yo would like me ta take yo aroun' an show yo da res' a da islan'."

"Why not?" said Lavina. "We've got some time."

"Okay, babe," Art replied. Then, turning to the driver he asked, "What can you show us, Roy?"

Roy drove them all through this section of the island, pointing out where the local folk live. He showed them the yacht club and drove them by some fantastic homes on the man-made canals that come in from the northern side of the island. He pointed out the home where the man who invented Styrofoam lives and explained that although he was an American, he moved here to get away from all the taxation in the States. He then took them to Georgetown where the streets were crowded with traffic and tourists and the going was slow. Roy did not mind, however, as the taxi meter worked not only on miles but on minutes as well.

As they drove, Art asked Roy some other questions. "Roy, what can you tell me about the banks here on the Caymans. I mean, I understand that there is no agreement with the Internal Revenue Service of the United States. So, this is a good place to hide money and not pay taxes, right?"

"Suh, dis is what I can tell yo. In da las' ten yeahs, de banks heah don't take cash. Dat's becuz a da money laundering from da drug dealahs. Dose what have accounts heah mus' use cashier's checks or electronic transfers to make deposits. No cash, no mo'."

"Well, what if someone was established at a bank?"

"What do yo' mean?"

"What if someone had been doing business for a long time with a bank, so that they were well known?"

"Oh . . . dat might be different. If da customer was a friend of da bank, den maybe he could do cash-money business."

"Are there a lot of banks on the island?"

"Ho, ho . . . mon, day'se mo' churches den bars and more banks den churches. De udda ting is dat if someone should ask about an account, dey not gonna get an ansah. So yo' tax people can question all dey want—dey findin' out nuttin'."

"Roy, you don't sound like the rest of the Caymanians I've heard speaking but you said you were born here."

"Dat's becuz at de age a sixteen, I was sent to Baltimore to work in da steel yards for Mistuh Ludwig. You know Mistuh Ludwig?"

"No, I'm afraid not."

"He a big millionaire in steel. He send mo' den a hundred of us from de islan' to Baltimore and Mobile. I been many places workin' da big machines. An' when I come back to de islan' I dredge all de lan' fo' de new homes. When I left heah, dey was no 'lectricity, no phones, no television. Now dey got everthin'. I travel so much I don' have de islan' voice now."

"Roy, if someone were to deal with a local bank for a long time, any idea which one it might be?"

"Oh no, suh, day'se so many from England and Switzerland and Canada, it be impossible to tell. De islan' even got its own bank but it's not dat old. Dat's de Cayman National Bank wit' a big office on North Church Street in Georgetown."

It was late afternoon when they arrived back at the Westin. They immediately headed to the beach to see Jill. She had just delivered some drinks to two of the guests and was starting to check with others to see if they wanted refreshments.

"Hi, you guys!" she called out as she spotted Art and his wife walking in her direction.

"Hey, Jill," Art responded. "We've got a question for you. We are starved. Can you suggest any places we can go to for some outstanding food?"

"You asked the right person. Of course, I can—definitely The Reef Grille. If you like sea bass, their's is the best. Also, the place has a nice atmosphere, right overlooking the water. And I can recommend it because I have eaten there a number of times."

"That's all we needed to know," said Lavina. "I'm famished and that sounds terrific."

"If you go there, let me know what you think of the place," Jill said before they parted. "Oh, and one more thing, it's a very popular place, be sure you call first for reservations."

The early evening was beginning to cool a bit so they decided to walk to The Reef Grille. The traffic heading out of Georgetown was extremely heavy as most of the island residents live in the western part of Grand Cayman beyond the luxury hotels.

On the way to the restaurant they passed a place called Galleria Plaza on West Bay Road. They noticed that there was a store called The Book

Nook. Wanting a precise map of the area where they were about to set up watch, they knew that a quality bookstore would carry the most detailed map. They spoke with the owner, Barbara Levey. A hint in her voice told them she was a native New Yorker like themselves. When she heard their familiar accent it was like old home week. She could not have been more pleasant. They spoke of places well-known to both of them and Barbara made them feel welcome on Grand Cayman. While they were in the store they picked up a map and some reading material about the island.

The Reef Grille was just as Jill had described it. They ate outside on the deck, which had a magnificent view of the Caribbean, a light balmy breeze enhancing their appetite, and wonderful service by a waitress, also from Canada, but from one of the western provinces. Art and Lavina took Jill's suggestion to try the sea bass and were pleasantly surprised at the awesome flavor. They could not wait to tell Jill just how much they enjoyed their meal. But that would have to go on hold. Right now they were eager to work out a plan of attack on Weiss.

They recalled passing a shop that rented motorbikes on the main road to Georgetown, not too far from the hotel or the restaurant. They stopped there on the way back to the Westin and rented one with an extra-long seat that would accomodate a passenger. Lavina had made it known that there was no way she was going to drive *anything* on the island. It was as they were making arrangements for the motorbike rental that they discovered they needed a Caymanian driver's license. Luckily, that was simply a matter of filling out a form and paying a ten-dollar fee—Caymanian ten dollars, of course—after showing that they possessed a valid New York driver's license.

Art assumed the position of operator, which was fine with his wife. After watching how the Caymanians drove, she almost hesitated even to be a passenger.

They returned to the hotel. They were tired after a long and busy day and they knew that tomorrow would be a challenge. As Art lay down on the bed, his mind filled with a number of questions. What if they were wrong about Morgan's Harbor? What if the timing was not as they had anticipated? What if it were not the Caymans at all? Art did not even want to think negatively. He would pass a fitful night leaving him somewhat drained by morning.

As the sun rose the next day, its brightness shone into the room where Lavina remained asleep as Art sat in the chair next to the king-size bed, having come fully awake at four o'clock from his restless night.

What is my plan? he kept thinking. *We're here and we have no plan. I can't just walk up and say, "Hey! Weiss! That's my money—give it to me. It was promised to me and I earned it." Weiss has killed once; he'd do it again. My God, what have we been thinking? This is not a game! Have I been so blind that I didn't even consider that this could be the consequence?* Throughout these past three hours he was plagued over and over by what he should do.

His wife stirred from her sleep, opened her eyes gradually from the brilliance of the sun, and then suddenly shot up as she saw her husband sitting in the chair.

"What's wrong?" she asked anxiously.

"Everything," he replied quietly.

"What does that mean?"

"It means that I must've been nuts to think I could just chase after Weiss to try to take the money away from him. I mean, the guy killed a man. Who knows what he'll do if he sees me. He doesn't care about taking a life—especially down here. He'll probably get away with it! I don't know what the laws are like here.

"And then it hit me. Even if we get the money, we can't hide it in any of the hundreds of international banks here. Isn't that ironic? Remember what the cabbie said? They don't take large amounts of cash from strangers!"

"Will you calm down?" Art's wife demanded. "You don't even know what we're facing for sure. And we won't know until we get a full picture of what Weiss is planning to do. Sure, it's an awful chance in a way, and if it gets to the point that we can't handle it, I'll be the first to say we'd better back off. I'm no fool and our lives are worth more than any amount of money. But, we've come this far. Let's, at least, see what he does next. Okay?"

Art slowly nodded his head and then said, "Okay, babe. That's cool. I'll chill."

"Let's get some breakfast and go back down to the harbor and find a spot where we can watch for Weiss," Lavina suggested.

With that, they made themselves ready for what would prove to be a long day.

CHAPTER TWENTY-SIX

The Loser

They arrived safely at Morgan's Wharf just before noon, having remembered to drive their rented motorbike on the left-hand side of the road per British regulation. There were several boats tethered to the long dock in front of the restaurant by the wharf. Others were tied up to shorter docks, which ran off a walkway parallel to the shore. The restaurant was doing a brisk business, mostly from the boat owners who had apparently pulled into the harbor sometime since the previous day. The few cars in the parking lot confirmed his belief that the patrons came from the boats.

Art drove the motorbike up near the restaurant's front door. Lavina hopped off first, giving Art plenty of room to swing his long leg over the seat and rear wheel. She had to adjust her shorts as she walked to the door because the bike's vibration had caused them to bunch way up on her legs. They took a table where they could look out at the dock as well as the front of the building, and ordered a light meal of fried conch and mango. As they waited for their food, they concentrated on the places they might check out as points of observation. Across from the restaurant's entrance, beyond the street which ends at the water's edge, was another parking area. This had been for a business of some sort, which was now defunct. To the right of that building, extending outward to the road, was an eight-foot-high, wooden fence decorated with modern artwork—the only thing recognizable being multicolored paintings of fish.

Lavina said, "That fence might make a good blind to hide us and the motorbike. There are trees in back of it, which would keep us out of sight. And, we get a great view of the harbor."

"I think you're right, babe," Art said thoughtfully as he focused on the area his wife spoke about.

"Let's walk down by the boats after we eat. That will give us an idea as to the lay of the land as they say."

"Good thinking," he responded.

When they finished their meal, they walked the length of the walkway and checked out each of the docking piers as they strode by. There were two empty slips. One was just beyond the restaurant and the other was at the far end of the walkway. Three boats, averaging thirty feet in length, were tied up at the other slips. A couple in their sixties sat on the deck of one of the boats that was backed in to the dock. They were sipping colorful drinks from tall glasses. They smiled at the Bookers as Art and Lavina walked past and waved. No one else appeared to be around.

Continuing down the walkway, they noticed that the rear of the restaurant had an employees' parking area. It was unpaved and went back as far as the trees that surrounded the restaurant at a short distance. Access to the lot was at the left side of the building as the right side bordered the walkway for the docks.

Art and Lavina came back and crossed the road so that the front of the restaurant was now behind them. They tried to walk along the water's edge, but this side offered no walkway. The water lapped against a natural, tree-lined embankment, which left no room for passing. A four-foot high fence separated this inaccessible section from the street.

They walked back and got onto the motorbike and drove around the area. When they became familiar with this part of the island, they returned to the harbor and pulled the motorbike up between the fence and the trees next to the closed business site at a spot out of view of the restaurant patrons.

They remained virtually out of sight for the next three hours. It was nearly six o'clock when Art nudged his wife and pointed toward the open water between the two tips of land that formed the entrance to the harbor. A small blue and white power boat was making its way toward the landing. The Bookers were suddenly nervous and excited at the prospect that this could be Weiss.

Art and Lavina moved behind the fence and peered out through a wide, broken slat. From the front of the fence the hole lined up with the eyes of one of the painted fish and, had anyone been looking from that vantage point, it would appear that the fish was watching as the Bookers' eyes moved as they kept track of their quarry.

The boat slowly motored up to the main dock and Weiss stepped out from behind the controls, after putting the engine into idle, and jumped from the boat to the dock carrying a length of nylon line. He secured the boat to the long dock at the end farthest out into the water and went back on board to shut down the motor. He returned to the dock and walked the length of it to shore, continuing into the restaurant where a number of customers were sitting down for supper.

"If only I knew for sure that he was alone on that boat and would be tied up for a while in the restaurant," Art said, "I'd take a chance on tossing his boat for the money."

"Let's not be stupid about this," his wife retorted anxiously. "That's how people get hurt—by doing dumb things."

"Okay. Okay. I didn't say I was *going* to do that. I just said. . . ."

"I *know* what you said. And I *know* how you think. If I'd have said, 'Why not?' or even nodded slightly, you would have been over there in a minute."

"No, I wouldn't," Art said defensively.

"Let's not argue over this."

"I can see him through the window. Look, he's sitting at the bar. For crying out loud, the bartender just served him a drink. I'll be right back."

"What are you doing?" Lavina asked nervously.

"Just taking a quick look to see if anyone else is there. Don't worry, will you. I'll only be a minute."

"Art! No!" she exclaimed, but he had already moved out from behind the fence and was walking with his head tilted down, collar up, in the direction of the main dock, all the time keeping his eyes on Weiss, whose back was toward the window.

Lavina panicked when she saw her husband go to the far end of the boat and climb on board. It was at an angle out of sight of Weiss, but not to her. She said to herself in a low voice, full of anger and fear, "What's the *matter* with him? I can't believe he'd be so stupid."

Now totally hidden from view from both his wife and Weiss, she began to shake as she watched Weiss suddenly come out from the front door of the restaurant with a second man. She did not know what to do. There was no way she could warn her husband. She tried to think of some way of intercepting Weiss but nothing came to mind short of running up to him and doing something brainless. By the time she considered this, Weiss and the other man were on the pier. It was too late. She began to cry quietly in fear and frustration.

She watched as the man from the restaurant pointed to the nearest open slip as Weiss got back on board the craft. The other man loosened the dock line and threw it onto the deck of the yacht. Weiss then started the engine, backed the boat away from the dock and nosed it in to the open slip. The two men secured the boat there and Weiss handed the man what looked like a credit card. The man then returned to the restaurant and Weiss went below deck.

Again, Art's wife began to shake—more so than before. Tears welled up as she feared for the life of her husband. All she could think was what Weiss would do when he found Art down in the cabin. Nerve-racked, she thought for sure her bladder would let loose and she would wet herself. As she stood there rocking from side to side because of her discomfort, she was torn as to whether to keep watching what would happen or to squat down and pee in the bushes. She could no longer take the pressure and ducked down in the thickest part of the brush, pulled down her shorts and relieved herself. To her horror, someone was coming through the trees directly behind her. She felt faint—her head was starting to get dizzy and she was becoming nauseous. She tried to remain perfectly still hoping the person would pass by without seeing her—especially in this exposed condition.

"What are you *doing*?" Art whispered loudly as he approached his wife.

"Omigod, where did you come from? I have been dying here. You've taken ten years off of my life. And look at you, you're soaking wet. What happened?"

"Look at *you*!" Art said. "Pull up your shorts and I'll explain everything."

Lavina pulled herself back together. She was so glad to see her husband and to know that he was all right that she hugged and kissed him even as wet as he was. She then asked him to tell her what went on at the boat.

He said, "I couldn't believe it. I had just climbed onto the deck after I looked through the windows and knew no one else was on the boat when I spotted Weiss coming back. There was no place for me to go except to slide down into the water. It's a good thing everyone was inside the restaurant eating their supper. No one even noticed me. I had to stay below the surface until I could get to the other side of the dock. I just made it when Weiss started the boat's engine; otherwise I might have been made into hamburger by his propeller."

"How did you get to where I was?"

"I managed to make my way to the far side of the wharf where it's so inaccessible without actually being in the water. Then I found an opening through the bushes and came up behind that building and over to you."

"Well, you about scared me to death. I told you it was stupid to try what you did but I'm not going to get into that again. I'm just thankful you are back and all right. By the way, was that the restaurant owner who came out with Weiss?"

"I don't know. I noticed that he was in the restaurant when we went in for lunch. He must work here."

"I figured that because he took that credit card from Weiss and went back inside."

"I wonder if he gave him George Weekly's card?" Art said.

"Nothing would surprise me with this guy."

"When it gets a bit darker, we should move to that other fence. It's too hard seeing what's going on from here," Art said. "And, hopefully, I should be dry by then."

"Okay," she said.

Weiss never left the boat after making the arrangements for the slip. The man from the restaurant came out only long enough to return Weiss's credit card and have him sign what looked to be a receipt. Art and his wife left the motorbike and worked their way over to the four-foot-high fence by the water. Again, they waited.

"What are we going to do?" Lavina asked.

"I don't know yet," Art replied. "It looks like he's on his own so maybe we'll have no trouble finding a way to get the money. I'm almost tempted to wait until the wee hours of the morning when everyone, including Weiss, should be sound asleep. . . ."

"And then what?" she asked.

"Maybe slide onto his boat," Art replied.

"Are you crazy? For all we know he's still got that gun!" she exclaimed.

"Yeah, but he doesn't have any idea that we're here or that we have even an inkling that the Caymans are where he's at. Besides that, if he's asleep. . . ." Art started to say.

"If! . . . If! . . . As long as there's an 'if' you are not going on board that boat!"

"Okay. Okay. I hear ya," Art responded. "We'll just wait and see what tomorrow brings. In the meantime, let's keep watch a bit longer and when all appears settled for the night, we'll return to the hotel, get some rest and come back early in the morning. Maybe he'll make some kind of move by then and we'll get an opportunity to get what should be ours."

By 11:30 there were only a few drinkers left in the restaurant bar. During the course of the evening, a couple of cars came and left and a motorbike, similar to the one Art rented, pulled into the employee's parking lot at the backside of the restaurant. It was now very dark except for the dim lights in the front parking lot and along the pathway to the pier.

Faint music could be heard coming from one of the boats. And flickering light made it obvious that people were watching television in another of the craft. Others were silent—a sign that people were sleeping.

Suddenly, Art's wife whispered loudly, "Look! There's some guy walking out from the back of the restaurant and onto the small dock toward Weiss's boat. That's not the same person who he dealt with earlier."

"No, you're right, babe. This guy's a lot shorter. I wonder who he is?"

Their eyes remained fixed on the little man as he stopped next to Weiss's boat and looked all around. In the faint light cast by the lamp on the pathway, they saw the man gently place his left foot on the rim of the boat's hull. He then pulled up his pant leg, removed something, and carefully climbed on board. There was only one light visible in the boat's cabin and it was not enough to cast any shadows so it was difficult to tell what was going on.

Within moments there was a loud popping sound accompanied by bright flashes of light, but it was nothing like Art or his wife had ever heard before. Things, again, went quiet. The boats in the adjoining slips turned on lights and a couple of people came out looking around for whatever it was that caused the unusual noise. Satisfied after a few minutes that all appeared normal, they returned to whatever they were previously doing.

It was not too long thereafter that the little man who had climbed on board the boat reappeared from below deck and climbed over onto the dock. This time he carried with him a fairly large suitcase. He walked quickly to the back of the restaurant and across to the employee's parking area at the left side of the building, out of sight of Art and Lavina.

"Art!" she exclaimed. "We've got to see what's going on. Something happened on that boat, I can just feel it. That popping noise . . . the guy walking out with that suitcase . . . something tells me that's the money."

"I know, babe. I know. You just stay here. I'll go look. If I don't come out, go get help."

Art's wife hesitated. She was once again torn between a decision—whether to go with Art or do as he said and stay where she was. In that instant, Art was moving quickly toward the boat, slowing only as he passed by the rear of the restaurant. The other man was nowhere to be seen.

It seemed as if Art just went on board when he was out again sprinting to where he left his wife.

"Weiss is dead. I just took a fast look. He's got three bullet holes in him and there's blood everywhere from what I could see by the light in the cabin. Where's that guy?"

"He hasn't come out from the back of the restaurant." Just as she said that, they heard the engine start on a motorbike.

"Quick!" Art shouted. "We've got to get to the bike before we lose him."

They ran to where their bike was parked as the man pulled out from the restaurant parking lot with the suitcase lashed to the back of the seat.

Art started the engine as his wife climbed on behind him and they took off after the man on the other bike. The man had a head start but Art was closing the gap. Art's headlight caught the man's attention as the man looked back in the rearview mirror. The man accelerated. The road was dark and empty. There were no houses visible on either side.

The little man must not have remembered to keep to the left while driving in territories that have been under British influence. Force of habit came into play as he headed down the right-hand lane. Without warning, a car pulled out of a hidden driveway to his right and was heading straight for him. The little man panicked. He quickly braked, turned left and, when he spotted a side street, accelerated in its direction to get out of the way of the oncoming car. As he turned the corner, the motorbike skidded on sand and slid sideways with enormous momentum into a utility pole. The man's back hit with an immense impact and the bike crumpled beneath him. His internal organs were ruptured from the crash and a pool of blood began to form under his body. He was conscious, but all feeling was gone from him.

Art drove up next to him. Lavina jumped off the back of the seat followed by Art. The top of the suitcase that had been strapped to the fleeing man's bike seat was ripped and all Art could see were fifty-dollar bills wrapped with paper binders. Art knew that he could walk away with the suitcase full of money but he still had some compassion toward the injured man. Art leaned down over the man and asked him if he could hear him. The man only moved his eyes before he replied, "I can hear you but I can't feel anything. And I can't move." Neither man realized that the injured man's neck was broken.

"How about pain?" Art asked.

"No, man, nothing. But I can hardly breathe," the man whispered hoarsely. The sudden realization that he was in great trouble caused the little man to start crying.

Art then asked him, "Who are you?"

The man began to choke on his own mucous as the crying caused his body fluids to fill his lungs and throat. He knew he was going to die and he became very afraid.

Once again Art asked him, "Who are you?"

"It doesn't matter now. Nothing matters now. All this for nothing."

Art looked around. The street, being in such a remote location, was deserted. The car that pulled out of the driveway was long gone. Art turned to his wife, "Go across the street and see if anyone is home at the house where that car came from. Tell them to get an ambulance down here and have them call the police as well."

"Okay, honey," she replied as she turned and dashed toward the driveway.

Art leaned down over the man and said, "My wife's gone to get help. You just hold on. Okay?"

"It's not gonna do any good, man. I know I'm done. You asked my name . . . you can call me 'loser.' That's what I am. Ever since the beginning, I've been a loser. The loser has become the lost."

"What are you talking about?" Art queried.

The man sucked in some air and took a moment to regain some strength. "You don't know me, but I know you," he finally said. "I've been following you for a long time . . . a very . . . long . . . time. You, and those before you. Ever since . . . ever since . . . " He stopped and again took in more air. "Ever since I caught Warden Weiss snooping around in the apartment belonging to Ed Fitzgerald's friend, Steve Cokkinias. . . ."

"Ed Fitzgerald! How do you know about Ed Fitzgerald?" Art interjected.

". . . I followed him . . . but he never even saw me," the man continued speaking about Weiss, not listening to Art or responding to his question. "I found out . . . where he worked . . . .It was after that that I took . . . I took . . . a job in the kitchen . . . at the prison. I saw you, but . . . you didn't . . . see me."

Who *are* you?!" Art demanded, now speaking loudly enough to get the man's attention.

"It doesn't matter any more, I suppose. My name is Carlos Dominguez." Again, he took in a deep breath. "The people who know me call me Chico. I used to work . . . I used to work in the armored car company with Ed Fitzgerald. The company that was . . . was responsible for . . . for . . . this . . . money," he said as his eyes looked up at the broken suitcase still strapped to the seat of the motorbike. "I lost. . . ." Again, he stopped for air and to rest. "I lost my job because of Ed. I know he . . . he was . . . mad at what happened . . . to him . . . his job with the police. . . ." Chico opened his mouth wide and gulped in more air.

"I . . . I didn't . . . think . . . he would . . . leave me . . . holding . . . the bag. My wife . . . left me . . . All I wanted . . . was another . . . chance . . . that's . . . why . . . I . . . came . . . came . . . after . . . money. I. . . . " He gasped for air again, but it was harder this time. "I . . . I . . . uhhhhh. . . ." There was a little whoosh of air and then he was gone.

Art's wife came running back to the accident scene as Art was removing the suitcase from the damaged bike.

"There was no one at home," she panted out of breath from running. "The door was locked. What about him?" Lavina asked pointing to Chico. "What do we do now?"

"He's gone. I'll tell you everything later. Hop onto the bike."

As she climbed onto the seat, Art set the damaged suitcase on her lap.

"You're going to have to hold onto this," he said. "This is gonna feel like it weighs a ton so hang onto it tightly."

Art then took the rope that had secured the case to Chico's bike and used it to hold together the suitcase so that it would not come apart.

"Right now," Art continued, "we've got to get back to the hotel and make a call from the lobby phone to the police and let them know about the accident."

"Are you going to tell them about the shooting?" his wife asked as Art put the motorbike in gear, gave it some gas and started down the road.

"Nope. Let them discover that when the dock owner goes to check on Weiss in the morning or whenever."

※ ※ ※ ※

"Jill," Art said, "I need some help." Again, Art and his wife were on the beach, the money was secured in the room safe, the police had received an anonymous call for the accident and the biggest problem was going to be getting home with the money.

"What can I do for you, ey?" Jill asked, a broad smile filling her beautiful face.

"Do you have any idea where we can charter a boat to go home rather than travel by air? This is such a beautiful place and we want to take advantage of a slow return."

"You asked the right person. Of course I can," said Jill as she set down their Cayman coladas.

Epilogue

The Caymanian Police linked the shooting on the boat to the dead man on the motorbike. First, by the fingerprints found inside the yacht and then by the fact that the .22-caliber bullets taken from the deceased Warden Weiss matched perfectly to the small handgun found strapped to the leg of the man on the motorbike. The handgun was a cheaply made, mostly plastic weapon. It passed through baggage security in the airport by being placed in Chico's shaving kit. The police could not determine any motive for the killing but later, after an investigation, reasoned it must have been something to do with the fact that both men had a connection to the same state prison in New York.

These particulars, in turn, were communicated to the U.S. Coast Guard who further relayed the information to the marina in Clearwater that owned the boat. With information gathered from the marina, the Coast Guard then contacted the Tarpon Springs Police. An inquiry was made by Officer Poulos as to whether a German Luger had been located on board the boat. Once the weapon was reported found, Art and his wife were off the hook as suspects in the shooting of Tom Fowler.

Art and Lavina chartered a boat from Grand Cayman Island through a person Jill knew in Georgetown. It took them four days to return to Florida. Upon their arrival in Tarpon Springs, after retrieving their rental car from the airport in Tampa, they stopped in at the police station to let Poulos know that they were back in town. He advised them of the news coming out of Grand Cayman and they reacted with surprise, as though this was the first they had heard of it.

Officer Poulos said nothing for a few minutes but regarded them with some skepticism as he asked them only one question, "Did you find the missing treasure?" Art only smiled.

In a meeting, which included Attorney Apostoles along with Art, Lavina, Officer Poulos, the plainclothes detective and the local district attorney, Chief Mark Lecouris reviewed all of the evidence and information that had been brought to light and made a recommendation to those involved in the investigation. Based upon that recommendation and the new evidence, the case was officially closed. The Luger was returned to Gabrielle.

Once receiving the good news of their release from suspicion and the details of the island incident, the Bookers booked passage on Am-Trak for their return to New York. This way, they avoided having their carry-on luggage go through X-ray machines such as those found in all airports.

Art did not return to work at the state prison. Hiring a lawyer in New York recommended by Apostoles, they made arrangements to sell their house and leave the area shortly after their arrival back home without letting anyone know where they were going. Art paid off the mortgage on his in-law's home and invited them to come to Florida to live. They said they could never leave New York City; it was what they were used to and could not imagine living anywhere else.

The prison warden was interviewed with reference to the deaths of the previous warden, a former inmate and of one of the prior kitchen employees. The warden was dumbfounded especially after hearing that unbeknown to him or anyone else, Weiss had gone to Grand Cayman Island and had sold off his house and all his furnishings in New York. True to what Art suspected, Weiss was going to take off with all the money and leave nothing for his partner back at the prison. The warden plead ignorance when questioned. He would have to be satisfied from now on with what he could make from the telephone and commissary funds. That scam was the only thing he would inherit from Weiss.

Art tried to make some kind of a settlement with Gabrielle for all the suffering she endured, without making it obvious to anyone that they found the money, but she refused any gift. So Art and his wife now make a practice of stopping and buying antiques for themselves, for her folks and for their friends for every holiday or celebration.

The biggest challenge to the Bookers would be the long and gradual transfer of cash into money market accounts in a manner that would not arouse curiosity by the Internal Revenue Service. In time, Art discovered that by putting no more than nine thousand dollars every two weeks into different bank accounts in the area and then by electronically transferring that money to an account on Grand Cayman, he could meet this challenge. So, Art and his wife returned to Grand Cayman to visit with Jill and to open up a small bank account in Georgetown.

Eventually, Art and Lavina would retire to Tarpon Springs where they built a new home with enough room for his in-laws to visit and where Art and his wife became best friends with Officer Poulos and his wife.

About the Author

Peter Mars is a native of Brookline, Massachusetts. His undergraduate studies in criminal justice and police science were accomplished at Northeastern University. He has a master's degree in public administration from Columbia and is currently completing his doctorate in sociology on incarceration and recidivism at that same institution.

He was a Boston area policeman for twelve years, serving several years with the Yarmouth Police Department on Cape Cod before moving to Maine where he continued in police work as chief of administrative services for the Kennebec County Sheriff's Office.

In 1997, he took an early retirement in order to write of his experiences in law enforcement some of which have culminated in the most unusual results in recent times.

He is working on the true story of a Catholic priest who was for years one of the police chaplains for the Boston Police Department. Father Michael Hennessey had been a good guy who got caught up in an unexpected love triangle involving himself, his church and a young woman who had been violently abused by her husband. *The Chaplain* is due to be released in the summer of 2001.

Mars lives with his wife, Margery, in a small town in south central Maine.